DESPERATELY SEEKING Suzanna

ELIZABETH MICHELS

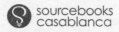

sourcebooks
casablanca

Published by Sourcebooks Casablanca, an imprint of
Sourcebooks, Inc.
P.O. Box 4410, Naperville, Illinois 60567–4410
(630) 961-3900
Fax: (630) 961-2168
www.sourcebooks.com

Printed and bound in The United States of America.
VP 10 9 8 7 6 5 4 3 2 1

For Sylvia—who knits, but not in an evil way. You're the best mother-in-law ever! I love you bunches!

One

"WHO ARE YOU SUPPOSED TO BE?" HOLDEN ASKED, adjusting the animal skin draped over his shoulder as he attempted to settle further into the chair.

"I'm Helen of Troy, of course," his cousin April stated as she adjusted the folds of her skirts around her legs. "I simply adore dressing for dinner, don't you?" As she straightened, her gaze turned serious and her eyes narrowed on him. "Who are you, anyway?"

"Attila the Hun, although I'm regretting the decision at the moment."

Only the Rutledge family would concoct such a plan for the evening of his homecoming—a historical dinner involving costumes, no less. He finally pushed aside the fur with a shrug of his shoulders. He'd worn the damned thing through dinner; surely he could remove it now without issue. "I suppose it would be outlandish to dress as ourselves and talk of the damp English weather."

"It would indeed." April drew back in mock

dismay, bumping into one of her sisters on the settee beside her in the process and causing a clatter of tea-cups and squeals.

Holden chuckled as he glanced toward Aunt Penelope and Uncle Joseph, who were sitting and chatting in the corner of the drawing room, seemingly unaware of the din of girlish voices around them.

It was nice to be back. He liked the familiar sights and sounds of Torrent Hall, even if he had to dress sometimes in a ridiculous costume. It was a price he was willing to pay, for this was the closest thing to home and family he'd ever known. He grinned and took another sip of his drink.

Piles of books lined the walls of the drawing room, stacked so high the room almost appeared to be made of a patchwork of leather. Abandoned embroidery, paints, and stationery covered the side tables, leaving only small spaces where polished wood was visible.

As it often did, the room rang with laughter as April attempted a dramatic fling of her arm indicating the tea tray. It would have been a convincing Helen of Troy imitation had one of her bracelets not flown from her arm and hit Uncle Joseph on the head.

"Sorry, Papa!" April scurried across the thick rug to retrieve her lost jewelry, her bright pink dress swirling around her as she moved.

"No damage done, dear," Joseph replied, rubbing his balding head and shifting Caesar's wreath of leaves askew in the process.

Holden couldn't contain a chuckle over April's ensemble now that he truly looked at her. She had taken the excuse of her historical persona to wear every piece of jewelry in the family's possession. Her arms were laden with jewels. Pearls were layered on top of diamonds surrounded by sapphires, all shimmering in silver and stacked up to her elbows. No wonder she was losing them with every shift of her arms.

What gentleman would she tie herself to this season? So far she had been more interested in the ball gown she wore than the gentleman with whom she twirled the floor. That would change soon. With the Rutledge dark hair and exotic eyes, she was too lovely to remain unwed for long. He would have to keep an eye on her while in London—all of his cousins, really. Not that he minded surrounding himself with his lovely cousins. After all, Holden Ellis, Viscount Steelings, was always surrounded by beauty. Beautiful ladies, beautiful clothing, a beautifully appointed town home. He was known for it.

There was always a lady longing to be on his arm and have her name linked to his for a time, a short time anyway. His thoughts were pulled back to the present with the barking of the puppy Jan played with on the floor, the curl of her dark ringlets shining in the light of the fire. At least he wouldn't need to worry about her presence in society for a few years yet. He would have his hands full with only three Rutledge ladies in London.

"May, you're not in character. Joan of Arc would never say that." June pushed her spectacles higher on her nose to level a proper glare at her sister.

"I only asked for more tea. Have you ever worn armor? It's terribly heavy. I'm positively parched from the effort." May shifted her breastplate to the side and sank further into the chair.

June's eyes darted over her sister's attire before giving her a shrug of her shoulders. "I simply don't see Joan of Arc as a tea drinker. And you need to at least speak with a French accent if you aren't going to attempt the true language."

"You aren't in character either, June," May returned, finally tossing the armor to the floor and reaching for the pot of tea on the table. "You may be wearing bed linens, but you've yet to say anything profound or insightful."

"I'm Socrates!" June countered. "I'm quite certain he was opinionated."

"Yes, and he spoke his opinions in Latin," May returned with a grin.

"That's a dead language."

"Precisely." May smiled and turned her dark head away from her sister.

Holden's attention drifted to April as she asked, "Mama, is all planned for the ball?"

Aunt Penelope's eyes filled with happiness at the possibility of her daughter's involvement. "There's always much to do, if you're volunteering."

"No," April replied a bit too quickly before offering her mother a smile. "I was only asking so that I might begin selecting my gown. I want to coordinate with the décor but not match it."

He heard May mutter into her cup of tea. "Why does it matter? It will look just as all your other gowns do—pink."

Aunt Penelope frowned in response before turning back to April. "You will look lovely, my sweet. Don't forget your mask, though." She beamed and clasped her hands together. "I already have Sara preparing mine for the event."

"It's to be a masquerade ball this year then?" Holden asked, unaware of the change in plans as he'd only arrived at Torrent Hall that morning.

"Yes, did I forget to mention that fact? I do hope you have a mask with you. If not, we can find one for you to wear."

"As it happens I brought one." He'd discovered long ago that it paid to be prepared for all wardrobe eventualities when staying with the Rutledges.

"Oh, perfect!" Aunt Penelope exclaimed with a jump, making her Cleopatra costume catch the lamplight and cast green sparkles around the room. She grew still as she watched Holden, making him tense about what might be to come. "I feel as if I've forgotten to tell you something..."

Aunt Penelope did this often. She was a bright lady, although her mind frequently traveled in two directions at once. Down one path lay glittery masquerade masks and down the other lay her opinion on how Holden should be living his life. He didn't mind. It was actually nice to be worried over. He waited, returning her gaze. What would it be this time? His blond hair had grown too long for fashion? He needed to eat properly or drink less?

"Lady Rightworth came for tea yesterday while you were out."

"Rightworth," he repeated, trying to remember the name. "Is she the one with the hook nose?"

"No! She's quite handsome, but that's neither here nor there." Aunt Penelope waved away the comment with the back of her hand. "She asked after you, wanted to know if you would be making the rounds in London this year, since you're back in the country. I assured her you would."

"Why would she want to know my schedule? I'm not even entirely sure of whom we're speaking."

"I believe she has her eye set on you for her daughter. She's introducing her to society this year. Evangeline, I believe."

May gasped. "That's horribly unfair of her. She should be focusing her efforts on Sue who is almost on the shelf as it is. Now, with Evangeline coming out, Sue won't stand a chance."

April rounded on her sister with a superior "I'm far older and wiser than you" voice. "May, you can't force gentlemen to dance with such an obvious wall-flower as Sue. Some ladies are perfectly content with spinsterhood, you know. Lady Rightworth cannot make her elder daughter a diamond of the first water any more than I can make flour into a cake."

"When have you ever gone to the kitchen and tried to make a cake? Which proves my point perfectly, just so you know." May crossed her arms with a frown.

Aunt Penelope intervened before anyone came to blows, which she did so often as to not be upset by it. "Girls, it is not our place to interfere with the goings-on inside the Green household. Lady Rightworth can see to her family as she chooses. I only brought this up to let Holden know he was spoken of over tea yesterday."

Holden leaned forward to regain his aunt's attention. "Why would she be interested in me? I've never met either of her daughters."

"Holden, you are getting to be of an age…"

"Nine and twenty is an age, all right. Thirty, forty, and fifty are ages as well, and I plan to see them all without a leg shackle, thank you."

Uncle Joseph leaned into the conversation, his toga draping over the arm of his chair. "Don't be defensive, Holden. Your aunt is only trying to help. Perhaps this would be a good time to peruse the available ladies."

"Uncle, I peruse ladies every chance I get. I just have more interest in young widows with no interest in marriage."

Aunt Penelope gasped and shot him a look of disapproval. "Holden! Don't speak of such things in front of the family."

"My apologies, Aunt Penelope. At this point I'm not even certain how long I'll be in England. This trip was rather sudden."

"Speak of what in front of the family?" Jan asked from her seat on the floor before the fireplace. "What did Holden say? Was it clever? What did I miss?"

Holden needed to change the subject to something far from the topic of his marriage prospects. He glanced at his youngest cousin where she sat curled on the floor in a Leonardo da Vinci costume playing with her new dog. "Da Vinci killed puppies for sport."

"He did not!" Jan pulled the puppy in her lap closer into her arms to protect him from harm.

"You're right. It was only the brown ones with white paws he favored for puppy murder." Holden laughed in response as he'd just described the ball of fur Jan was holding.

"Holden," his uncle murmured when the conversation around them turned to Jan's newest pet.

Holden turned to face him.

"I understand your reservations in regards to marriage. Every man experiences a young man's love of freedom, but what of an old man's loneliness? Look at all I have." He smiled at his family scattered around the room. "I want the same happiness for you. I only ask that you consider it."

Holden gave his uncle a tight-lipped nod before returning his attention to Jan and her puppy. It wouldn't take him long to consider the issue of marriage. There. He'd considered it. And it was never going to happen. It couldn't.

⁂

Sue raked her eyes across the garden, searching for movement. All remained still. Only a slight breeze rustled the trees beyond the stone walls. They were safe.

Straightening, she started to push the sash of the window closed. *Squeak!* She cringed at the sound, although the herd of cats at her back in the darkened hallway was making far more noise than any window was able to produce. That's what she called them, for that was the way they acted—always preening, strutting about, and demanding attention as they drifted through life on a smile and a coy rejoinder. They were also known as her sister and twin cousins. Sue rolled her eyes and slammed the window shut with one swift motion.

She turned, shooting identical glares at her identical cousins through the holes in her dark masquerade mask. "Shhh…we'll all get caught if you two don't stop arguing. Does it really matter why she stepped on your toe, Victoria?"

"It matters to my toe," Victoria huffed as she adjusted the bright green, bejeweled mask higher on her cheekbones, shook out her matching gown, and took a dramatic step away from her sister.

"For goodness' sake! Isabelle didn't mean to injure your toe." Sue lengthened her stride to catch up with her sister, pulling Isabelle along with her as she hissed over her shoulder at her other cousin, "It's dark and she was crawling through a window."

"She did it on purpose," Victoria stated with a raised chin, looking like the exotic peacock she was dressed to resemble, the feathers woven into her hair trembling with indignant hauteur.

"I did not," Isabelle argued from Sue's side, her yellow mask shifting as she scrunched her nose.

They were halfway down the hall now. The farther they drew away from the window, the more Sue relaxed—which was very little. This was a terrible idea. At least she was of age, but her sister and twin cousins hadn't even been presented at court or had any sort of introduction to society yet. It was only a matter of a week, since they would leave for London in a few days, but if they were caught at a masquerade ball, Sue knew exactly who would take the blame.

She'd said no when the girls first approached her about attending tonight. Yet, with Evangeline and Victoria involved, Sue knew they would have come anyway. It always fell to her to be the sensible voice of reason. Sensible, simple Sue Green. She rolled her eyes. No wonder she was still in the market for a husband after four failed seasons. Who would want to marry someone like her?

She glanced to the side, watching one of Isabelle's blond ringlets fall over her cheek in perfect bounces with every step. She would be betrothed within the month. And, of course, Evangeline would have no troubles. Renowned beauties rarely had issues capturing a gentleman's attention.

Evangeline threw her hand out to stop their journey down the shadowed hallway. Sue bumped into her sister, her nose squashing into the back of Evangeline's deep blue gown.

Sue ran her fingers over her mask, checking for dents as she peered around her sister to see what had stopped their progress. "What? Did you hear something? Is someone coming?"

"*EEEEE!*" Evangeline squealed as she turned around to face them. "I hear music from the ballroom!"

Sue gave Evangeline a shove in the shoulder for causing her heart to stop, if only for a brief moment. "Of course you hear music from the ballroom! We're sneaking into a ball."

Victoria drifted up to them now and peered over their shoulders to see why they'd stopped. "I need to find a mirror to pull myself together. I can't be seen with leaves all over my skirts."

Isabelle tensed at Sue's side. "I said I was sorry. I thought I saw a servant approaching."

"I fail to see how pushing *me* into a bush would have saved *your* skin, even if there had been a footman patrolling the gardens," Victoria returned.

"I swear I saw it move, though." Isabelle's eyes were wide beneath her mask as she gave a tiny shake of her head.

"Isabelle, it was a statue, a replica of *David*. Was he going to throw down the pebble in his hand and banish us from the grounds? Really," Sue snapped.

She'd had enough. Why hadn't she stayed well away from the herd's antics this evening? She could be back at her cousin's home painting, sleeping— anything but listening to this incessant bickering. "Stop arguing! Victoria, we will find a place to repair your dress. Isabelle, stop jumping at every squeak of a floorboard. And Evie, if you squeal again, so help me, I'll kill you. We are ladies, and we need to blend in or we'll be thrown out on our ears."

"Sue, calm down," Evangeline replied with a light laugh. "We're wearing masks. Of course we'll blend in. How could we not? Come along."

Evangeline led the way down the hallway, trying two doors before finding one unlocked and slipping inside. She laughed and spun around, throwing the door open for Sue and her cousins to enter. It looked to be a private parlor. The lamps were turned down to a flickering glow, which Victoria quickly brightened as she muttered, "I hope the owner of this parlor likes pink roses because if not she would run in horror."

Bright pink. Every surface in sight was washed in it, draped in it, or otherwise covered in it. Sue blinked in surprise. Pink draperies, pink chairs, even a rug depicting blush roses adorned the floor. "It must belong to April Rutledge. No one else would abide such a wealth of one color."

"Do you know her?" Isabelle asked.

"Only by the sight of her pink ensembles," Sue returned. "It's her color. I believe she owns it."

Isabelle moved to a side table draped in pale pink fabric. "Look! There are even two bottles of champagne set out."

Victoria joined her sister, lifting one bottle in investigation. "How thoughtful of our gracious host to provide us with champagne while we make ourselves presentable."

"I don't think we should…" Sue's words were drowned out by the pop of the cork and three squeals. What had she been thinking when she'd agreed to come this evening? They were sure to be caught. If not by the missing champagne, then the squeals of delight were sure to give them away. Was there any use in attempting to halt their actions? Her family was an unstoppable force. She flopped down into a pink chair, feeling like a rancid remnant from a bakery sale in her dark rose gown and thin pelisse.

"Oh, I'm such a mess," Evangeline exclaimed, gazing in the gilded mirror that stood in the corner of the room. She pinched her rosy cheeks and pushed her pale blue mask into place with the nudge of a finger.

Sue snorted. "I don't believe I've ever been so close to perfection that a pinch of my cheeks would do anything other than increase my blotchiness." Her head tilted to the side as she watched her younger sister primp. At times it was hard to believe they were related.

Victoria patted the ringlets on her head and touched a finger to her lips before declaring herself ready and reaching for the bottle of champagne Isabelle was holding. Passing the bottle to her twin sister, Isabelle smoothed her skirts for a moment before gazing at Sue with a combination of pity and determination. *Oh dear.* "The last time you had that look in your eye, I ended up with a fringe of hair around my face that took over a year to grow back."

Isabelle huffed in response, her eyes still locked on Sue. She meant well; it simply never seemed to work in Sue's favor to be on the receiving end of her cousin's agenda.

Sue looked away, sinking further into the chair. Perhaps if she didn't look directly at Isabelle, her cousin would become distracted. She could hope.

"Sue." Isabelle's version of a pert declaration of war sounded in her ear just as a bottle of champagne was pressed into her hand.

"Yes, Isabelle?" Innocence dripped from her voice like hot wax.

"Drink a bit of that. You need it."

Sue sighed. "I suppose if we're going to get caught trespassing we may as well enjoy the champagne before we're led away in chains." With that said, she took a large gulp, allowing the bubbles to slide down her throat. She could feel some of the tension leave her body, replaced by the warm effervescence of the champagne.

"Is my mask straight?" Evangeline asked.

"Yes. You look perfect," Sue offered without looking. "You all look lovely. Shall we go now?"

"Sue, what about your looks?" Isabelle's voice was small and coated in a sweetness her forceful sister could never achieve.

"What of my looks?" Sue lifted her feet off the floor and held them out to properly see the entirety of her gown. She appeared fine. She always appeared fine. Fine wasn't bad. There was nothing wrong with fine.

"Well, you look a little... Evangeline, can I have the brooch you removed?"

"Certainly. It did nothing for this ensemble anyway." She dug into her reticule to retrieve the brooch and hand it to Isabelle.

Isabelle beckoned Sue to stand up. She wasn't likely to be distracted from her evident plan to make Sue into an exotic beauty. Seeing no escape, Sue set the champagne down and stood—at which point Isabelle reached her hand straight into Sue's bosom.

"What are you doing?" Sue gasped.

"Take another sip of champagne and trust me," Isabelle commanded, gathering the fabric between her cousin's breasts and securing it with the brooch.

Sue had never in her life exposed so much skin. Her eyes widened, but before she could speak, Victoria shoved the bottle back into her hand. Sue took another drink.

"Here. Take these feathers and fix them into her hair. I'm not going to use them after all. Essence of feathers is all I require this evening." Victoria lifted her chin and tossed her head to show off the feathers that remained on her head.

"Oh, you don't have to..." Sue's words were drowned under a sea of commands to drink.

"Victoria, did you bring that rouge you got in town last week?" Isabelle asked as she inserted feathers into Sue's hair.

"Rouge? Oh no!" Sue tried to step away, but Isabelle pulled her back within reach.

"You need a bit of color on your cheeks, Sue. And something on your lips wouldn't hurt."

"I don't want to look like a light skirt, Isabelle."

"You'll look alluring and lovely. Just *shh* and drink."

"Too bad we don't have any ribbon. This dress could use some ribbon here, there, and perhaps some here." Isabelle grabbed at the fabric of her gown, gathering it into folds and revealing triangles of a darker underskirt in the process.

"I have some black ribbon."

Sue was starting to feel off balance as three sets of hands set to work making her presentable. Every time she complained, they told her to take another sip of champagne, which was most likely contributing to the off feeling surrounding her.

She couldn't stop laughing at Victoria and Isabelle as they worked. They were twins. Twins were funny. She didn't know why. Then Evangeline put something on her lips and told her to press them together. Why were her lips numb? "Numb." That was a funny word. Numb lips and twins, numb twins. She snorted to herself. After a few minutes, Isabelle stepped back.

"Sue, I believe you're ready for the ball."

"I'm almost afraid to look." Sue pushed through her family to approach the mirror in the corner. She studied her image for a moment, not recognizing the sight before her. Never before had she appeared as scandalous as she did now. In fact, she didn't believe it possible. Even her nondescript shade of light brown hair appeared to sparkle in the flickering candlelight. She touched her lips, amazed at how dramatic the red looked against her pale skin. This must be what beauty felt like.

Her plain rose gown had been gathered in places around the skirts and on the shoulders with black ribbon tied into neat little bows. A wide ribbon now made a sash at the high waist of the gown, which only drew attention to the scandalous amount of exposed skin at her neckline.

"I don't look like Sue a'tol. No, ladies." She turned with a smile. "Tonight, I'm Suzanna!"

"Suzanna?" Evangeline arched a brow in her direction.

Sue twirled toward the door, the black ribbons that tacked her dress together flying around her like wisps of smoke in the night. "Yes, she is wild and irresistible to all gentlemen who lay eyes upon her."

Isabelle giggled. "Ah. She's your evil twin then."

"Why is it always an *evil* twin?" Victoria scoffed. "I, for one, resent the implication. I'm not evil, Isabelle. I'm just more entertaining than you."

Evangeline stepped between the two with a smile aimed at Sue. "I think it's time we go downstairs and make our grand entrance."

Perhaps tonight wouldn't be so disastrous after all. The sound of the music floated on the air around her, lulling her with its spell. Pulled down the hallway as if in a dream, she could feel the pulse of the melody in her veins. Was it the champagne or the drugging effect of feeling truly lovely? Sue didn't want to know the answer. She only knew tonight was special.

Tonight anything could happen. Tonight she had joined the ranks of her feline family at last.

"Tonight the world is ours! Bring the champagne

on silver platters! Bring the handsome gentlemen—also on silver platters!" She giggled, not even minding the chatter of her family. Nothing could touch this magical feeling as they drew near the top of the stairs.

Torrent Hall was a grand estate built into the side of a hill that rolled down to a series of lakes visible from the terrace and south lawn. The house had remained in the same family for some generations now and had been added onto in various styles over the years. The result was a rambling estate with turning hallways and multiple stairs joining the collection of rooms that made up the home.

They'd entered through a window off the upper gardens nearest the border of Sue's cousins' new estate. The ballroom was tucked away at the rear of the home and one level down in a very unconventional style—much like the occupants of the house, if rumors could be believed. She knew the eldest two girls in the family by sight, but no more. They looked normal, yet there was always talk about the family.

Evangeline smoothed her skirts and glanced at her cousin beside her. "Isabelle, tug your dress down a bit and you'll be sure to catch a gentleman's eye with that neckline."

"How is my neckline?" Victoria gazed down into the deep, lace-lined scoop of her gown.

"Victoria, if you pull your dress down any farther, it will be around your knees."

"Evangeline, I'm not showing anything that ought not to be shown at a masked ball. You make me sound so tawdry! Meanwhile, you're showing more skin than all of us put together."

Sue turned, leveling a glare at her family that stopped their movement down the hallway. "Ladies, if it's skin you wish to show, Suzanna will show you how it's done." She turned, tossing what she imagined to be a sultry smile over her shoulder as she stepped to the top of the darkened staircase leading to the ballroom on the first floor.

Wrapping her hand around the railing, she hitched up her skirts and lifted one pointed toe to her knee before flicking her foot out in a kick that exposed her stocking-clad leg to the thigh. Taking a step down, she gave the empty stairway a shimmy of her breasts and kicked her other leg out. Turning with her gown gathered in her hands at her waist, she kissed the air in front of her sister. Enjoying the laughter swirling around her, as well as the effects of the champagne, she took a few more steps down the stairs.

"Do the kick again!" Isabelle said between giggles.

"Yes, you must!" Evangeline encouraged, dabbing at what must be tears of laughter before they fell on her mask.

Sue smiled, hurried to the landing where the stairs turned to the left, and spun to face her family. She held the banister rail behind her back and allowed her arms to slip to the sides as she arched her back and shot a seductive look over her shoulder into the darkness. The girls laughed as Victoria called out, "Suzanna, you light skirt!"

Gathering the hem of her gown once more, Sue dipped one foot down to the next step as one might test cool water in a pond. Then she ran her foot up her other leg and began kicking with each step down the stairs. She paused her descent every few steps to shimmy her bosom for the enjoyment of her family. They were still laughing as she neared the bottom of the steps. She raised her skirts to the point of indecency and kicked as high as her leg would allow, attempting to finish her dance with flair.

It wasn't until the toe of her beaded slipper met something hard that she stopped and immediately fell back onto the step behind her with a thud.

Her eyes grew wide beneath her mask as she looked up at the figure wearing black at the base of the stairs. His golden blond hair was the only bit of color shining in the dim lamplight cast from a single wall sconce. His head was bent away from her so she couldn't see his face. Who had she injured? Had he seen her dance? She wasn't even supposed to be here. Oh, what had she done?

Two

"YOU BROKE MY NOSE!" HIS DEEP VOICE WAS MUFFLED behind his hand.

"Oh...I...I didn't...well." She attempted to gather her wits while her heart beat a rapid *oh dear, oh dear, oh dear.* "If you hadn't been hiding in the shadows watching me dance, you lecherous man, it wouldn't have happened!"

"This is my fault, is it?" He snarled the question as he ripped a handkerchief from his pocket and covered his face with it.

At his raised voice, her family pushed past her with Evangeline in the lead, scurrying away from danger and leaving her to clean up the...blood? Was he bleeding? This could not be happening. At the last swish of Isabelle's dress around the corner leading to the ballroom, Sue sank further onto the wooden step at her back. If she wished hard enough, could she seep through the grain of the wood and land in a puddle under the house—alone? She closed her eyes but when she opened them, she was still there on the stairs with the bleeding man. She sighed.

She must make some excuse for injuring him. Yet, for the first time in her life she struggled to force words to come to her lips. She'd never fought to find words before. Loquaciousness was one of her finer qualities, although her mother would have said quite the opposite. She opened her mouth and finally stammered, "I wasn't aware I had an audience, you know. I only…" She waved one hand toward the stairs at her back. "And then you appeared from nowhere."

His head was now tilted back as he tried to stem the bleeding. "I was on the way to *my* bedchamber in *my* family's home. What are *you* doing here?"

She stiffened. "Breaking into your home" was the first thought that came to mind, but perhaps it was best to keep that information quiet. The memory of her scandalous arrival did, however, serve to strengthen her resolve. After all, if she'd survived breaking into his home and her family's antics this evening, she would surely survive this man. "I was…descending the stairs, as you could clearly see."

"I've witnessed plenty of descents over quite a few stairs, and I've never seen anything like that." He pointed with his head toward the staircase behind her, his blond hair catching the dim light with the movement.

"I suppose I'll take that as a compliment." She watched the strands settle back into perfect array around dark green eyes. The handkerchief covered the remainder of his face, but those eyes more than made up for the loss. Sparkling with some untold inner warmth, his gaze dipped to assess her. She took a shallow breath and lifted her chin.

A slight vee appeared at his brow, which only

served to draw his eyes down into an intense stare. "Who are you?"

She twitched under his examination as time seemed to stretch out in one never-ending second. Then he blinked. Long lashes covered the hardened green for a moment, like looking through tall grass on the edge of an enchanted wood. Blast it all, he was gorgeous.

Of all the gentlemen she could have injured and spent time with in a darkened hallway, why did it have to be this god-like creature with the perfect shiny hair and the captivating eyes? Oh, no. Not with her luck. With some average-looking gentleman, she would at least stand a chance of using the situation to her advantage by furthering her chances at marriage. But this man would no doubt stop bleeding and then leave her sitting on the step while he went with extreme haste to ask for a dance with a lady like Evangeline.

Someone like him would never look in the direction of someone like her.

Her eyes dipped to her skirts pooled around her feet. She was reaching to fluff them out in preparation to stand and leave him when her hand grazed over a piece of ribbon. "I'm Suzanna," she whispered into the still air of the stairway. It was more a reminder of how she was dressed and what she had done than a pronouncement of her identity, but he heard her all the same.

"Suzanna," he repeated. "I would say it's a pleasure to meet you, but I must admit I had more pleasure in mind a few minutes ago than I do now since you've kicked me in the face." He gave her a bow with as much flourish as possible with one hand clasped to his nose. "I'm Holden Ellis, Lord Steelings."

She'd heard a few ladies sigh the name "Steelings" over the years but had never met the gentleman in question. He was said to be living surrounded by the theatrical sort in Paris—which she was fairly certain was a nice way of saying French ladies of the night. He must have returned for the season. And now she'd broken his nose.

"May I do something? About your nose, I mean?"

"You haven't done enough?" He quirked a brow in her direction.

"You must allow me to make amends somehow."

He ignored her as he adjusted the handkerchief at his nose.

She sat forward on the step, arching her neck to gain his attention once more as she added, "I want to help you. Please."

His gaze snapped back to hers as if he was struck. Why would her offer of help have affected him so? Her eyes narrowed on him beneath her mask, trying to comprehend his actions.

"Very well," he replied, extending his hand to help her to her feet. Was he smiling beneath that hand-kerchief? What did he now find so amusing? He was injured, for goodness' sake.

She considered him for a second before placing her fingers within his grasp. His grip was solid as his long fingers curled around hers. He moved to pull her to her feet, which clearly didn't take the strength he'd allotted for the motion because she slammed into his broad chest. Her hand came up to keep her from traveling forward and landed on his stomach. His muscles tensed beneath her fingers.

She heard his intake of breath. "Damn, you're small." His voice rumbled through her, setting all her nerves on edge.

She tried to step away from him. However, the edge of the bottom step was just behind her. Needing to put space between them, she pulled her hand away from his body and stood as straight as possible. But with his hand still wrapped around hers and no place to move, she found she was now staring directly into his chest, her breasts grazing the fabric of his coat with every ragged breath.

Why was his warm hand still engulfing hers? And why wouldn't he take a step away from her? This was the closest she'd ever stood to a gentleman. Was this what it felt like to dance a waltz with a man? Four seasons and she'd never had the experience.

"How did someone so small inflict so much damage upon me?" His words danced with warmth across the top of her head, tickling strands of her hair as he spoke.

"I do endeavor to live larger than my size. Perhaps in this case I overdid it a bit." Her voice came out in a nervous squeak. He was so close, so handsome, so tall, and obviously so upset with her.

Then he began laughing. It was a well-used laugh and shook the tension from her shoulders. She looked up into his eyes and smiled. He was still close, still handsome, and still ever so much taller than her, but now with laughter softening his eyes, he didn't frighten her anymore. Of course, that opened the door for other, more dangerous emotions she chose not to name while in a darkened hallway with the man in question. Her palm began to sweat beneath his grasp and she wiggled it free before he noticed.

"My vision is a bit blurred. Would you mind accompanying me up the stairs so I can clean this up?"

"Certainly, my lord."

"It's Holden. I believe we moved past formalities when you flashed your nether regions at me and broke my nose."

She laughed as she turned and put a foot on the first step. "I suppose you're right. I apologize. This is all rather new for me."

"Ah, so you don't roam the countryside in search of noses to bludgeon."

"No, only yours."

"I feel so special."

She held her arm out for him to steady himself on the journey upstairs; however that clearly wasn't what he had in mind as the weight of his arm fell across her shoulders. He wrapped his hand around the exposed skin at her neck. The warmth of him surrounded her, making her shudder. *Don't be silly, Sue. You're only assisting a gentleman you injured.*

"Would you mind placing your arm around my back? Stairways are treacherous things." There was a teasing note to his voice that she didn't understand.

Stairways were dangerous. Many people were injured on stairways. She didn't see the humor in the situation, but he didn't explain his amusement further. She slipped her hand behind his back, tucking her body closer to his in the process. "Of course. Is that better?" she asked, glancing up at him as they took another step together.

"Yes, quite." His grin was growing beneath the handkerchief. She could see it reflected in his eyes. He shifted his hand on her neck as they took another step. His thumb grazed the side of her neck in a gentle caress.

Her breath caught in her throat. It had been a clear attempt to tighten his grasp on her to keep from falling. Yet, even knowing this, she fought to keep from leaning into his touch. What was wrong with her addled mind?

They took another step. The abrasion of his coat against her skin and the weight of his arm began to wear on her ability to speak. Only instead of making her weary, they were creating an energy inside her that begged for freedom. Her mouth turned dry. Licking her lips and tasting the lip color with her tongue, she asked, "Where am I leading you?"

"To my bedchamber."

She almost missed the next step and had to tighten her grip on his waist to keep from stumbling. "To your...oh."

"Not to worry. I have no sordid intentions at the moment." However, the sentiment didn't quite ring true by the look in his eyes. There was something there, something she'd never seen before.

What was happening? She knew his motivations couldn't be sordid—not with her anyway. She forced her mind to work, to make sense of her situation. "I didn't assume your intentions were less than honorable. I'm only concerned over how it might look to others."

"You mean the friends who abandoned you when you injured me? They'll think you're caring for the poor gentleman you wounded." He paused at the top of the staircase and looked down at her. His fingers traced thoughtless circles on her shoulder as he spoke. "Who else will know?"

No one would know. It was only the two of them and she had already come this far unscathed. "Yes, I suppose you're right. Who else will know?" She relaxed and smiled up at him. "Which door is yours?"

"Just there on the left." Although they were up the stairs, he didn't release her. He held her close until they crossed the threshold into his suite. The door closed behind them. He closed the door? This wasn't proper in the least.

She took a shallow breath. His hand dropped from her only to turn up the lamp he'd left burning on the table just inside the door. As he moved across the room to light another, she turned to assess his bedchamber. Much could be told about someone by their bedchamber, and she was more than curious about Holden.

The room was dripping in opulent greens over tan brocade wall coverings. Heavy furnishings carved with intricate swirls and leaves filled the floor space on top of a thick rug. Her eyes drifted up to the fireplace on the far wall.

Her gaze, however, halted on the painting above his fireplace.

"It's lovely, isn't it? I found it in a shop while in London on a visit a few years ago and had it brought here. There is something about this artist. The way in which he captures the light... His identity is a mystery, you know. I wished to have more work commissioned, but the shop owner wouldn't pass on his information. SAG is all anyone knows."

She swallowed. Holden Ellis, Lord Steelings, had purchased her landscape of the countryside near her home? She shook her head in wonder as her mouth fell open. A few years ago, she'd begun selling some of her paintings to a shop owner she'd befriended in London. She knew her paintings sold, but to see one here, now, in his bedchamber, was beyond unexpected.

"Yes. I'm familiar with this artist's work," she hedged.

"Are you? A lover of art?"

"You could say that." She swallowed, lacing her fingers together before her to have something to do with her hands.

"I have a few more by this artist at my home in London."

"Do you?" She pulled her gaze from the painting to look at him. He had more of her paintings?

"Perhaps you can come and see them sometime." He watched her as he began pulling at the knot of his cravat.

"Perhaps." She had to look away from him. This was dangerous. She knew it, but she couldn't make her feet move to leave, nor could she look away from him. He held her there, captive under his beautiful spell.

Finally, he broke the connection when he ducked behind the leather screen set up in the corner to repair the damage she'd inflicted to his face. His coat came flying out to land on a chair a moment later. He was undressing—with Sue in the room.

She blushed and searched for something to say so as not to think about it any further. "This isn't your only home then?" She paused before adding, "You mentioned a home in London."

The shirt he'd been wearing was flung over the screen to land beside his coat. "This is my uncle's home, actually. But he allows me room here and has for many years."

"Oh. It's quite nice." She turned, trying to focus her attention anywhere but on the half-naked man behind the screen in the corner. Her eyes landed on a wardrobe beside her. "I especially like the, um, carving on the furniture."

"Thank you. It's French. I found it while I was away and had it shipped here. I'm rather fond of it." The sound of water splashing in a basin punctuated the end of his statement.

Lovely. Now she was envisioning the body she'd accidentally touched earlier covered in droplets of water.

Spotting a decanter of some liquid across the room, she moved to pour a drink. Her nerves were in shreds from the events of this evening, and the effects of the champagne were beginning to wear off. She didn't care at the moment what was in that bottle; she only knew she needed it to strengthen her spine if she was to make it out of this to safety. Pouring a glass full of the liquor, she tossed it in her mouth, the heat of it burning its way down her throat. She set the glass down. Perhaps the drink had been a mistake. Her insides felt as if they were on fire.

Her eyes raked the room in search of water as she tried to stifle a cough. Finding a bowl of candies on the table beside the massive poster bed, she popped one in her mouth and sat on the edge of the bed. As the flavor of strawberries filled her mouth, the warmth of the liquor began to seep through her limbs. She ran her hand across the emerald-colored bedding. Holden's bed was quite soft. She slipped another piece of candy into her mouth and lay back on the bed. He seemed the type to take an hour tying a cravat, so she might as well enjoy her wait in comfort.

"I've never been to France," she called out, so he might hear her from behind the screen across the room. "It seems like a lovely place. I've certainly seen enough of their fashion plates to last a lifetime, and I've heard they have fine food as well. I imagine sweet shops on every corner...chocolatiers lining the streets." She waved a hand above her head at an invisible Parisian road. "Please don't tell me I'm wrong or I'll be terribly disappointed."

There was movement at the edge of her vision. "I wouldn't want to disappoint you." His voice was close, too close.

Her head whipped to the side at the same moment she tried to sit up from his bed, landing her propped on one elbow in a sprawled position across the thick quilts. And there he was, shirtless at the foot of the bed.

Lean muscles wound around long limbs in the most dazzling arrangement. Never had she seen such a sight or even imagined this was what lay hidden under all those shirts and coats in town. His waist narrowed where a trail of blond hair disappeared into the waistband of black breeches slung low on his hips. She blinked at him, not-sure what to say in this situation. "I...I thought you were putting yourself to rights."

"I am. I keep my shirts in the wardrobe." He made a halfhearted gesture toward a piece of furniture in the corner. "I thought you were admiring my furnishings."

"I am. You are...I mean you *have* a beautiful... ceiling...above your bed." She pulled her gaze away from him, training her eyes straight above her head. She swallowed and shifted the candy in her mouth with her tongue. The heat of a deep pink blush crept up her neck as she continued with a thick voice, "I was just admiring..."

"My candies?"

She took a breath to think. The candy from the dish. He must have seen her take the sweets. "Well, yes. I see candies set out and I feel it's my responsibility to try one. What if they're horrid candies? Positively inedible? I wouldn't want to inflict that upon you." Her head turned back toward him, her gaze instantly falling to his bare chest.

"Thank you for your service. Do you find it horrid?"

"No. It's fascinating. I've never seen anything so..."

"The candy?"

"What?" She ripped her gaze from his chest up across strong shoulders to rest on his face. His face. The only mark on it was a small dark line beneath one eye. At least she hadn't done permanent damage to such a beautiful specimen of mankind. She watched as his lips, set in a strong jaw, turned up, revealing a bright smile. Was she supposed to be talking? Who could keep track when he was standing there looking like a half-clad god tossed from the heavens for bad behavior?

"We're discussing the candy."

"Oh, yes. I mean, no, they're quite nice actually. Would you like one?"

"Perhaps in a moment." His eyes slid over her as amusement warred with curiosity in his gaze. "Suzanna, who are you?"

She tensed for a fraction of a second before her lips curved into what she imagined to be a sensual smile. "Don't you think it a bit unsporting to ask a masked lady her identity?"

"I suppose it is." He leaned one hand on the post at the foot of the bed as he watched her with a wry grin. "How about a game of sport, then?"

"What kind of game?" Her eyes narrowed beneath her mask. This could be more dangerous still. What had she gotten herself into? But then, this situation would never happen again. Without a mask and her family's influence, he would never look her way. Evenings like this didn't exist in her life. Some small voice inside her was screaming to run—a voice she steadily ignored.

"I get to ask two questions of you, and you can ask the same of me." He eyed her with a casual, inconsequential look in his eye that she was sure couldn't be further from the truth.

At her pause, he added, "My nose is already bent out of shape so don't further wound me, Suzanna."

"I can ask you anything?"

"Certainly."

"I accept your challenge." She smiled. How dangerous could questions be anyway? And she could find out more about him in the process. "Are you wed to anyone?"

"Never. Your question is too simple, Suzanna. Now it's my turn." He rounded the corner of the bed and sat on the corner facing her. "I've never seen you here before. Who did you come with to this ball?"

"The Fairlyns, your new neighbors. You, too, ask a question that's too simple, and now you only have one left."

"Ah, that was shameful, wasn't it?" He leaned back to lie across the bed beside her, his hands laced behind his head.

"Terribly so. This is your game after all." She chuckled as she looked across at him. "And now it's my turn." She put a hand to her mask to ensure it was still present.

There were plenty of questions she could ask him. She could ask his thoughts on her paintings, what he enjoyed most in life, or even his goals for where he wanted his life to go. Yet the only question that came to her lips was, "May I touch you?" Blast it all, had she said that aloud? She clamped her lips shut, afraid of what would come out next.

He said nothing but his eyes became alert as he looked at her. With slow motions, as if he was afraid he would frighten her, he rolled to his side and propped himself up on one forearm above her. She was shaking. This had been the worst and best idea she'd ever had. She released her arm from behind her head and fell to her back, the soft bed cradling her as she looked up into his heated green eyes. She had asked to touch him, yet her mouth seemed to be more brazen than her hands. She didn't know what to say or do. The silence seemed to stretch between them.

"It *is* my game. And you asked so sweetly. Go on, then."

When she waited another moment, he moved his hand across her stomach and lifted her hand, guiding it to his chest. His skin was warm. She stretched her fingers across his tense muscles, feeling them jump beneath her touch. His heart was beating at a rapid pace deep within his chest.

His hand fell away to land on her hip as she danced her fingers down to his stomach. He sat completely still except for the hand at her hip. Every time she moved her hand lower on his stomach, his grip tightened on her before loosening again. Until she did what she longed to do and ran the backs of her fingers across the hair where it disappeared into his breeches. His hand grasped for more of her side as he let out a choked breath.

Had she done something wrong?

She looked up into his face to see his eyes had grown dark. His lips were close. What would he taste like? What would his lips feel like against hers? Neither one of them dared to move for a second. Should she say something? Her mind raced for a subject; however, the only thing on her mind was Holden. His lips just beyond her reach. The warmth of his body close to hers. His hand resting low on her hip.

"I suppose it's my turn."

"Yes."

His mouth descended on hers in a gentle kiss—the kind she'd dreamed about. Soft and seeking, yet not overpowering. But as he pulled back a fraction she felt a sense of loss, even disappointment. Was this all there

was between ladies and gentlemen? What was the fuss
about? Then he shifted closer. His lips covered hers
once more, but this time was different. This time he
seemed to be demanding a response from her.

Her hand slipped around his side to his back, pulling him closer still. She was distracted for a moment
by the hardness now pressed into her thigh, but was
pulled back into the kiss as his tongue slipped past her
teeth to tangle with her tongue. The taste of strawberries that still filled her mouth melted with the warm
male spice of him to create a delicious concoction that
she could not get enough of. She mimicked his actions
and tasted him. A guttural, almost animal-like sound
came from deep in his throat as he moved over her.

He thrust one muscular thigh between hers, causing
her to whimper and grasp at his back. The kiss deep-
ened between them still. His hand came up to cup
her breast, and she arched into his grasp. She wanted
more. She didn't care if she appeared to be a wanton
trollop. This was most likely her only chance to
experience passion, and she didn't want it to end. He
bit at her bottom lip in teasing motions before letting
his mouth slide across her jaw to her neck. He trailed
kisses down to her collarbone, pausing to capture her
raging pulse between his lips.

She buried her hand in the soft blond hair on the
back of his head to hold him close. *Don't leave*, she
thought, not sure if she said it out loud or only in her
mind. But his head only dipped as low as her breast,
which had become bared at some point. When had
he pulled down her dress? The thought disappeared as
he traced his tongue around the tight, pink center of

her breast. Catching it with his teeth, he drew a gasp from her mouth.

He looked up at her and smiled a devilish grin. He knew precisely what he was about. How many times had he done this? It was without a doubt a high number, for he understood precisely where to touch her, when, and how. With torturous slow motions, his mouth traveled back up her neck. It wasn't until she felt his fingers trace a line up the inside of her leg that she realized he'd pulled her gown up as he moved over her. She should be running from him, but instead she found her leg falling open to grant him more access to her skin as her eyes locked with his deep green gaze.

He kissed her again with increased urgency, claiming her mouth as conquered territory. She was so focused on the feel of his lips as they slashed across hers and the soft curl of his hair as she wound her fingers around the back of his head that she jumped at the nudge of his fingers as they grazed over her private parts. She shouldn't allow him to, but how could she not? The backs of his fingers rubbed gently at the apex of her thighs, soothing her reaction and heating her blood. With every graze of his fingertips she fought the urge to squirm under his attention.

His hand shouldn't be *there*, and yet she wanted his touch *there* more than ever now. She didn't understand what he was doing to her, but she also didn't care. A need for him, more of him, dimmed all thought from her mind. She flattened her hand across his shoulder blades in an effort to pull him closer and fulfill this desire she couldn't explain. But it wasn't contact with his skin her body screamed for; it was contact with his devilish hand.

He drew small circles with his knuckles that made her cry out in a muffled yell captured by his mouth. She arched her hips into his touch as he slipped a finger into her damp heat. It felt as if he were pulling her apart with every twitch, every flick of his fingers. Something was building within her. She didn't know where it led, only that she wanted it more than air. He broke their kiss to look down into her face with an all-too-innocent grin. "I'll stop if you want me to."

"No!" The word was wrenched from her throat on a scratchy yell. "Don't stop. Don't ever stop."

By the satisfied grin on his face, she knew that was the answer he'd planned on hearing. He was playing her like an instrument he'd practiced all his life, and she didn't care. He thrust his fingers into her again. "You're so beautiful, Suzanna."

The room tipped sideways as she lost the last of her control over her body. The tightness and urgency within her released in a sudden crescendo and turned her into a shaking mass in Holden's arms.

"Beautiful, simply beautiful." He kissed her forehead as he pulled his hand away from her with one last caress.

She swiped her fingers across the beads of sweat gathered on his brow. No one had ever told her she was beautiful, until now. This man, this gorgeous man, was interested in her. He thought she was beautiful. In that instant she knew she would do anything he asked of her.

Slipping her hands down his stomach, she pulled

at the waist of his breeches. One golden brow shot upward as he quickly unbuttoned the placket to assist her. When the hard length of him sprang free, she blinked. She wanted to show him the same pleasure he'd shown her. But how? She touched his smooth skin with a tentative slide of her fingers. He allowed only a moment of this before he pulled her hand away and moved over her, poised between her legs. She could almost feel the brush of him against her. Yes. He could have her. She was beautiful and his.

"Devil take it! Damned bloody nose!" He snarled as he crawled off her, pulled up his breeches, and stalked across the room uttering a string of profanities—with one hand covering his face. She wiped away the single droplet of blood he'd left on her bare shoulder. All she could do was watch him go as she sat up and tugged her gown back down over her knees—alone and beautiful.

❧

The sore nose and blackened eye had been worth it. He'd put himself to rights and retrieved the mask he'd gone in search of in the first place, while Suzanna repaired her hair and shook the wrinkles from her dress. Her burnished gold hair had been twisted into an elaborate knot on the top of her head and pinned with feathers when he'd first spied her on the stairs. Now wisps of hair fell around her masked face, reminding him of how she'd looked sprawled across his bed.

Holden smiled down into Suzanna's upturned face as he spun her around the dance floor. She fit perfectly in his arms, even if she did have to take an extra step every now and then to keep up with his long stride as they danced. She was small in stature, yet her body was lush with all the right curves. The way she kissed him with those full red lips and encouraged his attention had been his undoing. He shouldn't have let things go so far, but what sane man would have stopped with a willing masked lady in his bed?

They hadn't been able to complete what they started tonight, but he was sure there would be time for that later. She wasn't going anywhere. His hand slid lower on her back, pulling her past what would have been the point of decency if they'd been waltzing in any typical London ballroom. But they were in the country and wore masks, which somehow made it acceptable behavior.

God bless the invention of the masquerade ball. Holden had always been amused at the liberties a proper lady would allow simply by covering her cheekbones. Suzanna had yet to remove her lace-trimmed black mask but it suited her somehow. Her eyes, the color of falling autumn leaves, seemed to glow within the shadows of the mask.

"What do you find so amusing?" she asked.

"You."

"Really?"

"You sound surprised."

"I am—a bit."

"You shouldn't be. This is certainly the most memorable masquerade ball I've ever attended."

"I imagine most masked balls don't include being kicked in the nose by a lady's grand entrance." She laughed, the sound reminding him of raindrops falling on metal. Where had this delightful woman come from? She was part lady, part angel, part bawdy temptress, as far as he could tell. He wasn't aware that the combination had ever been attempted on English soil before.

"No, I believe you are unique in that respect, Suzanna." He laughed and spun her to the side of the room with a flourish just as the music ended.

She stopped spinning and looked up at him with a laugh lingering on her lips. She was intoxicating. Her small fingers were still curled within his from their dance. He wasn't inclined to release her and she didn't seem to mind. No one seemed to notice their connection because of the rather large crush in the ballroom. Aunt Penelope would be pleased, and with Suzanna in his grasp, he was rather pleased as well.

"Would you like a drink? The unmasking will occur soon and then the champagne will be in short supply." A drink and then he would slip her away—to the gardens or back to his bed? He would have to wait and see how she responded to the champagne. He smiled and squeezed her hand. This was an entertaining evening indeed. And it would only improve from here.

"A drink would be lovely."

"Very well, then. Wait here by this…"—he quirked a brow at the sculpture they were standing beside before turning back to her—"truly hideous Grecian man. I'll return in a moment."

❧

Holden had only been gone a few minutes. And yet the country dance playing in the ballroom seemed to stretch on forever in his absence. Sue wound her fingers together and feigned interest in the dance before her. In her heart, however, she was back upstairs under the weight of him, with his hands on her and his mouth—she blushed.

Glimpses of Evangeline and Victoria passed by as they moved around the floor with gentlemen hanging on every swish of their skirts. Isabelle was on the opposite side of the ballroom laughing at some remark the gentleman beside her made. It seemed like a lifetime ago when Sue had descended the stairs with her family. So much had happened. The very air around her was new and alive. She would never be the same now and she was happy for it.

A hand wrapped around her shoulder, spinning her toward the back terrace doors. Although the grip was a little tight and lacked the warmth of Holden's earlier touch, she turned with a smile for him.

"Back so soon?" The smile slipped from her face.

"Back? Who were you expecting, Sue? Dressed as you are, I'm not sure I wish to know." Her mother's thin lips were drawn into a straight line of disapproval as her eyes swept over Sue's hair and down her face to land on the gathered neck of her gown.

"Mother."

"Yes, I am. Who, however, are you? No daughter of mine should be here disguised as some disgusting creature of the demimonde."

"That's not how I'm dressed at all. I only came here because…"

"I will not hear your excuses," her mother hissed. "You will come with me."

Her long thin fingers wrapped around Sue's wrist, propelling her toward the nearby terrace doors. Sue only dared to throw one glance over her shoulder, searching for Holden, but he was still in the next room acquiring drinks. He wouldn't know where she'd gone. How could she inform him? The question was pushed from her thoughts as her mother pulled her into darkness. The crisp night air hit Sue's face as she left the ballroom, washing away all the warmth and happiness she'd found there.

Her attention returned to her mother as the mask was stripped from her face and thrown on the stone floor. Sue blinked at the rush of cool against her skin.

"Shameful." Her mother pulled a handkerchief from the edge of her glove and trapped Sue's face between the two fingers clamped on her chin. Dragging her into a rectangle of light falling from a window, her mother began rubbing at the rouge on her cheeks. The rough linen scrubbed across her skin, leaving her cheeks raw in its wake.

"Mother, that hurts."

"As it should. It pains me to have our family represented in such a fashion at a friend's ball."

Once Sue's cheeks were raw and her mother satisfied with her work, she began cleaning the color from Sue's lips. It was as if the entire evening was being wiped away. Scrub. Holden's kisses. Scrub. Her smiles. Scrub. Their laughter. She blinked away the moisture gathering in her eyes.

"Now to be rid of these feathers. Really, Sue. Such

excess. Evangeline may be able to wear such adornment, but not you. You don't have her lean grace, nor her face." With that explanation, her mother ripped the feathers from Sue's hair and tossed them into a nearby bush.

Next came the ribbons. The artful bows were stripped from her gown, releasing the folds of fabric around her. This must be what it felt like to be the wrapping on a parcel. She was the plain paper that had once wrapped an exquisite gift and was now left behind for the maids to dispose of. When the last ribbons were released and her gown relaxed around her shoulders in a stretched mess of fabric, Sue looked down at the brooch clasped at her bosom. Running her finger over the dark stone in the center, she savored its solid existence. Her mouth quirked up at the corner. The last piece of Suzanna and of this magical evening was still clinging to her heart.

"That brooch doesn't belong to you. Did you take it?"

"No, I didn't." Any other words she would have said were stripped from her along with the brooch.

"Sue Green, you will return straight away to your cousin's home. Your father and I will be along shortly. If I find you anywhere but in your bed when I arrive there, you will be sent back home while the rest of the family travels to London. It is what wisdom tells me to do already. Yet I am a forgiving mother, even under such…"—she looked down her superior nose at Sue as if something foul surrounded her on the air—"circumstances. I will have to think on what to do with you. We shall discuss this tomorrow."

"Yes, ma'am." Sue glanced down at her rumpled, plain rose gown and turned to leave. Inside the ballroom, the unmasking had begun. Squeals of laughter rang out as she made her way through the crowd. She pushed past a group of ladies as she tried not to be stepped on in her haste to leave. On her way to the door that led to the carriages outside, she neared the statue where she was to meet Holden. He wasn't there.

She paused for a moment, partly to catch a glimpse of him one last time, partly to recapture the joy that had been present in her heart only moments before her mother's arrival. If she stood in this same place, would her joy find her again as if she'd left it on the polished wood floor?

"Pardon me, miss." There was a nudge against her arm and she turned, looking into Holden's green eyes.

"Ah, you found champagne." She smiled up into his unmasked face. She began to raise a hand to accept her glass, but her hand only made it halfway to him. She held her hand there in midair for a heartbeat waiting for him to look at her—really look at her.

He lifted the glasses higher and well beyond her reach. "Yes, I found a footman with a bottle in the next room. If you'll excuse me, I can't chat at the moment. I'm meeting someone here."

"Oh." The word was more of a sound ripped from her heart than a coherent response. He didn't recognize her. Her hand dropped to her side with her fist clenched to keep it from trembling. She searched his face but his eyes didn't stay on her. He was now scanning the room, looking for Suzanna. Was she so different? She'd been beautiful in his arms.

But now...

She looked away as the room began to swim through her unshed tears. She was only Sue. That was all she would ever be. She needed to leave. She didn't belong here among the beauty of the masquerade ball. She turned away from Holden, not that he noticed her departure.

"Sue, what's happened?" Evangeline asked, her hand snaking around Sue's elbow.

"Mother is here. You should leave." With her warning stated, she threw off Evangeline's grasp and fled for the main hall. Tears were beginning to burn the backs of her eyes, and in another moment there would be no blinking them away. He hadn't recognized her. His gaze had been cold as he dismissed her. Taking a breath, she pushed away from the railing of the main stairs and back into the crush of people at the masquerade.

Her feet were moving toward the door without any thought to who she bumped into or how she now appeared with tears beginning to roll down her raw cheeks to land on her horribly wrinkled gown. They couldn't see her anyway. After all, Sue Green was invisible.

Three

Against his better judgment, Holden raised his hand and knocked on the front door of the Fairlyns' neighboring manor house. It rankled to no end that Suzanna had managed to slip away last evening. He left for one damned minute and the chit was gone. And now he was here, chasing after her like some foolish schoolboy.

Calling on the day following their meeting? He'd never stooped so low in his life. Ladies chased *him*, not the other way around! He ran a hand through his hair and looked across the lawn in the direction he'd come. He should leave. Taking one step backward, he was about to turn and abandon this ill-fated idea when the door opened.

"Yes, m'lord?" the butler's voice rang out.

Realizing it was too late to run, Holden turned and faced the man. "Ah, I'm Viscount Steelings. I'm here to call upon…" His words were drowned out by the bright voice of a young lady inside the home.

"Cardwell, do we have a guest? Do invite our caller in, won't you?"

"Yes, Miss Fairlyn." The door was opened wide to reveal a large, echoing hall—a surprisingly empty hall.

Holden stepped inside, glancing around the large room devoid of any furnishings. The smell of fresh paint hung thick in the closed-off air. Didn't they know how to open a window? *It's for Suzanna. You're enduring this for Suzanna.* He sighed and offered the butler a pleasant smile as he passed.

Aunt Penelope had mentioned the new neighbors, but he hadn't realized how new until now. The last time he'd set foot within these walls, he'd been no more than eleven. The rooms had been stuffed to overflowing with foreign artifacts—much like his friend Thornwood's home, only here it was to the point of excess. He could remember being worried a sarcophagus might fall on him, squashing him flat. The new neighbors appeared to agree with his views on décor for every shred of the former home's furnishings had been stripped away, leaving behind a hollow shell.

His eyes fell on the lady standing by the doorway that led to a parlor, if he recalled correctly. She couldn't be more than eighteen, he would wager. She was lovely in the traditional English way—with blond ringlets surrounding pale skin and blue eyes. Yesterday, he would have thought her beautiful, but that was before a tiny lady with all the right curves had kicked her way into his life.

"Welcome, Lord…"

"Steelings," he supplied, taking a step toward her and the parlor door at her back. Could Suzanna be inside the parlor? His heart sped up at the thought. Perhaps this would be easier than he'd anticipated. He would find her in the parlor, and they would be finishing what they'd begun by nightfall tonight. Splendid!

"I'm Isabelle Fairlyn." She dipped into a well-rehearsed curtsy. Her dimpled, rosy cheek winked at him as she smiled. "I believe we're neighbors, aren't we? I've heard your name mentioned, at any rate."

On any other day he would find her charming company if he were to be honest, but not today. Today she was slowing his path to Suzanna. He ground his teeth within his smile. He'd never been unkind to a lady, and he wasn't going to begin now. This was Suzanna's friend after all. "It's a pleasure to make your acquaintance, Miss Fairlyn. I spend a good amount of time with my cousins at Torrent Hall, so, on their behalf, allow me to welcome you to the area."

"Torrent Hall seems a lovely estate. Your cousins must enjoy living there." She glanced around him toward the butler before adding in a whisper, "The ball last night was enchanting."

"Yes, the masquerade was a fine evening's entertainment. My aunt will be pleased to hear of your enjoyment. I'll be sure to pass on your appreciation."

"No!" She lurched forward with the vehemence of the command, her fingers clasping the fabric of his coat. Then, seeming to collect herself, she released her grasp, straightened with a sheepish smile, and clasped her hands before her. "I mean, that's not necessary, Lord Steelings. Why don't we go into the parlor where it isn't so terribly…loud? Would you like some tea?"

"I can only stay for a minute, I'm afraid. I don't wish to take up too much of your time." That was the truth. What had that bit regarding the masquerade been about? Something was off with Miss Isabelle Fairlyn, and he didn't particularly care to lounge about over tea to find out what that something might be. If not for the prospect of Suzanna behind the parlor door, he would flee. "Actually, I'm here to call on your friend Suzanna. I believe she's a guest of yours?"

"Suzanna? Oh, Suzanna." She laughed with a forced titter, and her genuine smile was instantly replaced by a smile that looked as if it had been left to dry on a wire and bake in the sun too long. She swept around him, nudging him in the back as he entered the parlor. "Of course. You must come into the parlor. I insist."

This was a strange interview, to say the least. His eyes scanned the room in search of burnished gold hair and lush curves, but she was nowhere in sight. And there wasn't much of anything in sight, for that matter. He moved into the sparsely furnished room, circling one of the two chairs before the fireplace but not pausing to sit. Instead he stood with an elbow resting on the back of one chair, making for a fast exit once he found Suzanna. After a moment's silence, he narrowed his gaze on Miss Fairlyn. His patience was growing thin.

He watched as she settled into the opposite chair, fluffing her skirts where they fell around her ankles. Finally she looked up, catching his gaze with a bland smile. Was she going to speak? Ever? He'd asked her a question! He took a breath and tried again. "Would you be so kind as to inform Suzanna I am here?"

"Oh, that. Well, I can't."

Can't? Why the hell not? He smiled. "Is she unwell?"

"No, she…left the estate."

"Left…the estate."

"Yes." She took a deep breath that seemed to be one of relief. "She left early this morning. So she's not here. No, no one here who would answer to the name 'Suzanna.' That much is certain."

"Do you mind informing me where she might have gone?" His hand had formed a tight fist on the back of the armchair at some point. Whether he longed to hit something, grab Suzanna, or strangle someone was uncertain. He forced his fingers to relax as he studied the woman opposite him. Something was afoot. She wasn't being honest; that much he could guess. The truth of the situation and why she was hiding Suzanna remained a mystery. The parlor door banged open, disrupting his thoughts. And good God, there were two of them now. He was doomed.

"Isabelle? Oh, there you are," the other Miss Fairlyn stated as she hurried into the room. As her eyes landed on Holden, her pace slowed to a stop. "And you're with a guest."

"Victoria, this is Lord Steelings. Lord Steelings, my sister, Miss Victoria Fairlyn."

"Miss Fairlyn," Holden offered with a slight nod of his head.

Victoria glided farther into the room with her chin raised to resemble a swan crossing a pond. She landed a smile on him that would make most gentlemen weak in the knees yet only served to make Holden wary. "Lord Steelings, it's a pleasure to have you call on us today. Won't you sit?"

Isabelle cleared her throat to gather her twin's attention. "Lord Steelings is here asking after Suzanna."

"Ah, I see." There was a look between sisters. What did that mean? It was as if they had their own language, all spoken in raised eyebrows and pursed lips.

Isabelle continued, "I've just told him she is…"

"Indisposed." Victoria interrupted with a smile back in Holden's direction. "She's in bed ill as can be, the poor dear."

"Away," Isabelle said with a pointed look at her sister.

"Away?" Victoria spun away from Holden.

"Yes, you remember, Sister? She packed her things and left this very morning."

"Oh. Which is why she's away. Away, yes. Far, far away."

"Traveling and ill. Suzanna does seem quite busy today," Holden threw in, knowing they were both lying for their friend. Why did she not want to see him? Had he taken things too far with her on their first night together? Had he overwhelmed her? If so, it was no reason to avoid him. He could slow things a bit. He could give her one more evening to become accustomed to his presence before he allowed things to progress further between them. But he couldn't even offer her that courtesy if she wouldn't see him.

"Traveling ill? Oh no, she must be feeling much better." Isabelle shot a look at Victoria that insisted on her agreement.

"I'm happy to hear it." Holden needed answers. Facts! Truth! "Do you know her destination this morning? I would like to offer my appreciation for the dance last evening."

Isabelle opened her mouth to speak but clamped it shut again with a barely audible whimper.

Holden waited. His gaze turned to Victoria.

She pondered him for a moment before moving to shut the parlor door. Turning back to their conversation, she held the look of a man of business settling into a large stack of papers. "I'm sure Suzanna will be pleased to know you called upon her." Her voice was smooth as she spoke. This was no doubt the oiled tone she used to lure helpless men into some trap. "You know, Lord Steelings, our Suzanna can be a bit shy at times. I have no doubt it was nervousness that drove her away today. However, my sister and I would like to assist you."

"We would?" Isabelle asked.

"Yes, Isabelle, of course we would," Victoria admonished with a false laugh.

"Oh. Yes, we would," Isabelle agreed with a nod of her head, causing her ringlets to bounce all around her.

"I'm sure I don't require your assistance." In no way did he want to be entangled with these two identical terrors. He could find Suzanna on his own. It would be difficult, yet dealing with these ladies was proving to be arduous as well. He would take his chances.

"We know Suzanna's schedule for the season." She raised a hand and began ticking off fingers. "Which balls she will attend, the parties and gatherings where she can be found, even what color gown she will be wearing. Are you sure you don't require our assistance?"

Damn. He did need their assistance. "Why would you offer this?"

"For Suzanna. You see, Suzanna has left…a string of gentlemen behind her. She's ever so desirable—as you well know—but alas, she runs when things turn serious."

"This is not serious!" Did they think this would involve marriage? Because that would not happen!

"I didn't mean to imply that it was, my lord, only that we wish to see her happy. And with her scampering away when any kind and well-respected gentleman, like you, becomes interested…" She shook her head in despair while artfully pursing her lips. "I'm sure you can see the issue. What Suzanna needs is to be…made to stay put, chased down when she tries to flee…trapped, if you will."

"Trapped? But Victoria…" Isabelle shot a shocked look at her sister, which Victoria quickly dismissed.

His reaction was much the same as Isabelle's. Why would Suzanna's friend wish such a thing on her? However, if Suzanna had a history of running from gentlemen, he could see the issue with that, assuming these girls wanted to see their friend married. But still, trapped?

He shook his head. "I don't wish to *trap* her."

Perhaps that wasn't the most honest statement he'd ever made. Right now, with the memory of her still on his skin, he did wish to trap her—only not in the sense these ladies envisioned. Ladies' ideas of trapping usually involved a leg shackle of some kind, which wasn't nearly as much fun as what he had in mind.

"Capture, then? Find?" Victoria waved an impatient hand through the air. "Whatever the terminology you wish to use, my lord, we can help you achieve that end."

He should say no, damn it all. He didn't trust these ladies, especially Victoria with her sly grin and man-eater eyes. However, they knew how to find Suzanna. And he didn't even know her surname. "Very well."

Victoria clasped her hands together. "Perfect! She will be in our company at the Dillsworth ball next week in London. I do hope you'll be in attendance."

"Certainly. I should be leaving now." Deals with the devil always made him want to leave with haste—not that he'd made many deals of that nature. Or did that depend on one's view of what constitutes a deal with said devil? At any rate, he wanted out of this parlor—now. He offered the Fairlyn ladies a smile. "I would hate to take up any more of your time on this lovely afternoon."

Victoria laughed. "Oh, you're no burden on our time. I've enjoyed our little chat immensely."

"Yes, it's been very enlightening. I will see both of you in London. Until then." He offered the ladies a slight bow and headed for the door. As he rounded the corner into the hall, he could hear their voices echoing in the nearly empty room behind him.

"What was that about?"

"I'm simply making our season in London a bit more interesting."

An "interesting" season was precisely what had Holden concerned. He grimaced and walked out the front door. By anyone's definition, this qualified as a deal with the devil.

⁂

The tea grew cold while Mother instructed one of the maids in the pinning of Evangeline's dress. Sue sighed and set her cup down on the small table at her side, which already teetered with piles of fashion plates. Every surface of the small drawing room they'd been given during their stay with the Fairlyns was covered in samples of fabric and ribbons and sketches of gowns for Evangeline's come-out season.

Sue shuddered to think what any man would think if he walked into such an eruption of femininity. But that was hardly a problem since the only men around were footmen, who were forced to endure such chaos; her uncle, who was out hunting something on his new lands; and Father, who remained perpetually locked inside the library.

Normally, she would have stayed locked away in her suite painting during teatime instead of suffering through yet another one of Evangeline's fittings—but not today. She'd been instructed to stay at Evangeline's side until further notice. Sue assumed her mother wanted a bit of her sister to rub off on her like the green of wet grass on her knees when she sketched outdoors—only Evangeline would somehow make her clean and perfect. Ha! She snorted and covered the sound with a cough. Her sister and cousins had presumably slipped away from the ball last night without notice, lucky felines that they were.

Sue wouldn't know. She'd gone straight to bed last night although she hadn't slept at all once there. Her eyes burned from the tears even now. She closed her eyes for a long blink, savoring the darkness. But when Holden's face swam through her thoughts, she snapped her eyes open. Tired eyes were better than seeing his face again. She refused to think about him for another second today. It was over. Done.

Taking a large bite of the bread in her hand, she allowed the warmth to melt on her tongue and slide down her throat. It was the first morsel of food she'd ever been allowed to eat without listening to a lecture in return. She licked a crumb from her lips and settled further into the cushions of the armchair, curling her feet underneath her. She'd spent years starving for half of the food Evangeline was allowed to eat.

Only a few months ago, her mother had berated Sue, grabbing a cake from her hand and giving it to Evangeline. "Evangeline is a head taller than you, Sue. She needs more sustenance. Besides, you could stand to lose a bit around the middle if you ever want to catch someone's eye."

Sue remembered looking down and smoothing her hands over her waist as she uttered, "Yes, Mother." She hadn't been able to bear watching Evangeline eat that last tea cake with her stomach so empty.

"It is a shame you aren't fortunate enough to have your sister's figure. She takes after me in that way." Her mother had lifted Evangeline's chin with one long finger, smiling down into her upturned face. "I knew when you were but a child that you would be special."

Apparently, "special" meant possessing flawless beauty and doing as one was told. Sue shook off the memory with a roll of her eyes and looked out the window, watching the breeze blow through the trees beyond the Fairlyns' well-kept lawn and smiling as she licked a crumb from her finger.

The sad truth was that every bite that passed Sue's lips could equal a feast for her long-limbed sister. She'd been cursing her lack of height and curvy body for years. If she looked like Evangeline, then perhaps things would be different—perhaps last night would have ended under happier circumstances. Her throat tightened and she set her jaw against the emotion.

Alas, she took after her father's side of the family who navigated the world on cunning and family titles, not like her mother and sister who could acquire anything they wanted with a smile. There was no sense in being upset over the long-known fact; Sue was plain.

She ignored the voice in her head calling her beautiful—a voice that rang out in Holden's deep tones. She sniffed to keep from crying again. He hadn't found her beautiful without a mask. He hadn't even recognized her. The hurt of it had receded from a sharp slice to a dull ache, tearing at her heart every time she thought of it. So, she wouldn't be thinking about it anymore.

So far, her efforts had been quite unsuccessful, but she was endeavoring to try harder. The masquerade ball did have its purposes after all, for now she was allowed to eat for the first time in her life. Her new-found freedom came at the price of Mother finally giving up on her. Although there was a fraction of sadness over this occurrence, there was also relief.

She reached for another piece of bread, watching her mother instruct Mary to place more pins in Evangeline's gown. Supervising the maid as she drew the fabric up between her fingers, her mother then tugged on the gown until it draped in pristine folds from Evangeline's thin shoulders. Then she batted Mary's hands away, dropping the fabric as she made another attempt at perfection.

"No, no, no! This will not do! That modiste may claim French blood, but her fitting skills are abhorrent."

"It looks perfect to me," Sue offered, never understanding why her mother was so upset. Sue's gowns fit *fine* and had been put away out of sight weeks ago. "And perhaps after the nine hours we spent in her shop trying on gown after gown, she'd grown a bit weary by the time she reached that particular ensemble." Who could blame the poor woman? Sue grew bored of it after a few minutes.

This afternoon it seemed she should have kept her opinions to herself, for her mother shot her a dark look from across the room. Turning back to her work, she tossed out, "You only think it perfect because you have no eye for fashion, darling."

Evangeline gave one silent shake of laughter, because ladies do not snort aloud. With a whispered "the poor dear," she put a hand to her mouth to contain her smile.

Sue listened to them giggle with a pang of annoyance. She popped the last of the bread in her mouth, seeking comfort in its softness.

Mother dismissed the maid and backed away from Evangeline, assessing her work as she spoke in a carrying voice. "Of course, with the ensemble I found Sue wearing last night, she would be a welcome addition to any brothel."

Evangeline went still. Her eyes flashed in Sue's direction in the mirror. Evangeline knew it had been her idea to attend, yet she would never utter a word of support for Sue in front of their mother. Sue had known she would regret attending that ball. For a time while there, she'd thought otherwise. How wrong she'd been. Holden Ellis, Lord Steelings, was a lecherous rake, and she'd fallen for every line of his prose. *Idiot!* She blamed it on the champagne…and her sister. It appeared now she must pay for her crimes. She returned her mother's gaze as if staring down a wild animal on the attack.

"Sue, we do need to discuss your activities of last night. Your father and I have conversed on the matter and made some decisions on your behalf."

"Yes, ma'am." Sue braced herself for the verbal lashing that was to come. Surely that's all this was. That's all it ever was. A few minutes of how disappointing she was as a daughter and it would be over. Only…"decisions on her behalf" did sound rather ominous. Her fingers curled into balls as she drew her arms around herself, waiting.

Her mother moved closer, taking slow steps while her eyes never swerved from Sue. The swirl of her mother's deep blue gown moved in like storm clouds as she descended on Sue with a downpour of disapproval. "I've been thinking about your prospects this season."

Sue didn't know she had prospects. She sat up a little straighter in her seat. Perhaps this wouldn't be so horrible.

"Let us speak openly, darling. You are not likely to find a husband this year."

Sue sank back down into the chair. "That's a bit too open, if I can speak openly on that subject as well."

"I had long hoped we could find you a match this year. An old gentleman more in need of a caretaker than a wife or a gentleman with some abnormality… perhaps even someone's destitute fourth son by the season's end." She sighed. "However, after seeing you dressed as you were last night…"

"Can't we move beyond this? I thought we were to discuss my prospects." Sue tried to entice her mother to cut short her ranting with the discussion of the season that lay ahead. It was a sound plan if she could control her tongue—which she couldn't. "And it was a masquerade. I was dressed appropriately for the occasion. Mask, ball gown, dancing slippers…"

"Rooo-oouge?"

How did she manage to turn one syllable into four? This ability had always impressed Sue.

Sue sighed. "Even still, Mother. There were many others there dressed in similar attire. I was particularly fond of the ribbon embellishments. One would think you would be glad of my newfound interest in fashion."

Her mother drew back in consternation, her dark eyes turning round as saucers. "The women there dressed in a similar fashion were of the demimonde. Light skirts. Paramours."

"That doesn't mean I'm light of skirt." Sue ignored the heat of a blush creeping up her neck, for that was exactly what she had been in Holden's arms.

"You were certainly dressed for the role, Sue Green." Her mother placed her hands on her waist, rapping her nails against her corseted middle as she spoke. "At a ball when you were to be at home. Disgracing your cousins' family name when they are new to the neighborhood. I will not have a daughter of mine seem to be sinking into a life of ill repute."

"That's very well since I have no desire to join the

ranks of the demimonde. I want to be wed, Mother."
Surely there was some gentleman out there for her,
even if he was old with eyesight so dim he couldn't see
her beyond his large belly. Find her that gentleman.
He would do.

"It matters not what you want in life, Sue. We must
play the hand of cards we are dealt. Unfortunately,
this crumb-covered, woefully mediocre facade is
your hand."

Sue tried not to be hurt by her mother's words.
Something tightened within her. Was it her broken
heart or her resolve? Either way it caused her fists to
clamp, leaving crescent-shaped indentations in her
palms. "It *does* matter what I want. It matters to me."

"A gentleman's wishes are all that matter in this
life, darling." Her mother's lips pinched down to a
wrinkled blotch of disgust. "A sentiment you appeared
to be quite familiar with last evening. Which is why
your father has made the decision to send you to
Aunt Mildred's at the end of this season. She requires
a companion and you won't be able to destroy the
respectability of the family name while living in the
wilds of Scotland."

Silence fell in the room; even the rustling of
Evangeline's gown ceased.

Sue pulled back as if she'd been hit, and truthfully
it felt as if she had. Mother wanted her to give up
on the dream of marriage to become Great-Aunt
Mildred's companion? She blinked up into her
mother's hardened face, searching for understanding
in the thin lines at the corners of her eyes. When Sue
finally spoke, her voice was as small and insignificant

as she'd always been in her mother's eyes. "You want to send me away to Scotland for dressing inappropriately one evening?"

"I believe we both know this isn't the result of one evening. Last night's little stunt simply advanced the issue we have with you. The truth is that this family can't shelter, feed, and clothe you forever, and Auntie was so kind to make this offer some time ago." She shook her head and gazed down at Sue. "Your father had held out hope that you would find a match, but we can't afford to have you bring shame upon the family. I'm sure you understand."

Sue's head ached from attempting to understand any of this. "Is that the life you want for me?"

"Heavens no, Sue. I want you to be married," her mother said breezily with a casual wave of her hand.

Sue almost relaxed, but she knew better when it came to matters involving her mother. Instead she sat and waited for the inevitable contradiction proving why she couldn't have the life she so desired. And today, she didn't have long to wait.

"But since that doesn't seem likely at this point, we must make difficult decisions."

There it was: the truth of her situation according to her mother. She tried to breathe. *Remain calm, Sue.* "Decisions to send me away to live with Great-Aunt Mildred. She's the one who can't abide sweets, isn't she?"

"She has an intolerant constitution, it's true."

"The Scottish Highlands with only an old lady who has an intolerant constitution for company?"

"Yes, but do try not to talk her ear off." Her

mother's eyes narrowed on Sue. "I know how grating that can be."

A lifetime without decent conversation or sweets? Sue could only blink in response.

"It's only something to think over…an eventuality to become accustomed to, should you not succeed this season."

The room swam before her eyes. Was this happening? She blinked up into her mother's face. "I can't believe this."

"Neither can I, darling. But until last night, I couldn't imagine you gaining enough attention to dishonor our family. I suppose we were both wrong."

"That's not precisely what I meant. Mother, you can't mean this. Great-Aunt Mildred is awful. I attribute her disagreeable temperament to the distinct lack of chocolate in her daily routine. Enduring her for only an afternoon is enough."

"Oh, my darling Sue." Her mother looked down on Sue as if she were a half-starved dog in the streets, wet and pitiful. "Perhaps you can ply her with the sweets you so adore once you are her companion, and the two of you will be quite happy together."

"You're truly sending me away?" Sue's voice cracked as the words were ripped from her throat. She tried to swallow, finally finishing in a whisper, "This can't be."

"Not until the end of the season, dear, so there's no reason to fret."

"No reason to fret," Sue repeated with her mouth, although no sound accompanied the movement. Her gaze dropped to the floor. Oh, no fretting at all; there was only the small inconvenience of being tossed from her home. She swallowed and lifted her eyes to her mother, who was apparently still talking.

"You will have to leave behind the niceties you've become accustomed to, like the drawings and such. I'm quite certain Auntie wouldn't permit such excesses. And you'll have no need of your ball gowns. Of course your ball gowns never suited you to begin with, based on the way you decorated yourself last night. That ensemble was more suited to someone else..." She smiled, her thin lips curling up into sharp points. "...Someone like Suzanna?"

How did she know? Sue's eyes flew to Evangeline. She watched as a blush crept up her sister's face, her eyes averted in the mirror as she fumbled with a fold on her gown. "Mama, these pins are sticking me."

"Oh, yes, my precious. I didn't mean to become so preoccupied with your sister. Let's get you out of that gown."

Sue gaped at her mother's retreating form. After four failed seasons, she would either find a suitor this year or be shipped away from everything she knew to keep Great-Aunt Mildred company...for the remainder of her life?

She looked down at the crumbs covering her faded muslin day dress. It was true she had no marriage prospects. There didn't seem to be many options open to her, other than what her mother suggested. She certainly couldn't stay unwed and with her mother forever—compared to that future, one spent with her great-aunt was looking quite lovely.

Was being a paid relation to a bitter old woman the best she could hope for in life?

She flicked a stray crumb from her knee with a finger, watching it fall onto an abandoned drawing of a ball gown lying on the floor. Her family certainly thought her worthy of the occupation. Or perhaps some charming gentleman would choose her this year, but she knew that wouldn't happen—not to her. One corner of her mouth turned up in a wry smile. Her last season. She would attempt to enjoy this last summer knowing that in the end she would leave. Forever.

Four

THE COOL BREEZE WHIPPED THROUGH HER LOOSE HAIR and pinned the thin dress to her body as she slipped around the corner into the alley. Henrietta had lost count of the years she'd been locked within those walls. She laid a hand on the bricks at her side to steady herself. The wall was warm. She turned, squinting up into the afternoon sun. She'd been inside so long, she'd forgotten what the heat of the sun felt like on her skin.

"Warmth," she whispered. Most of her life was a blur, as if seeing years through a thick fog, but she did know one thing: she would never return to Brooke House Asylum.

The front door of the asylum creaked open and footsteps shuffled onto the stone steps. Someone must have noticed she was missing. Henrietta flattened herself to the bricks at her back, her breath catching in her throat as she held herself tight to the wall.

"Henrietta Ellis is not accounted for within the

building." Doctor Monro's sharp tones crept down her spine, making the hair rise on the back of her neck.

"She didn't get past me, Doc. You have my word," the guard's voice rumbled through the street.

"If she didn't pass you, where do you suppose she's hiding?"

"Last time she was in the kitchen. Could have gone there again, I suppose. Or there was the time with the broom cupboard, or the gate behind the mews."

"Insolent…" The rest of Doctor Monro's insult was drowned out by the sound of carriage wheels rolling down the street.

The sound of horse hooves grew louder as the conveyance neared the mouth of the alley. If she could reach the carriage, she could be away from this place for good. Could she get to the back of the vehicle before the guard or the doctor reached her? She took a breath and glanced down at her slippered feet. There was no hope of making it on foot. Perhaps she could have run for freedom in her youth, but not now. Her nostrils flared as she tested her legs, rocking to the side for a moment before taking off down the alley.

She moved at a slow lumber at best as she tried to catch the carriage before it passed. Wheels turned before her as she paused beside it, preparing to jump for the boot on the rear of the conveyance and her only hope at life.

"There she is, Doc!"

"Seize her!"

She lifted her arms toward the carriage in preparation to pull herself to the perch on the back as she'd seen young grooms do in her youth.

"No, Henrietta! You can't leave."

She reached for the rear of the vehicle, slipping on the mud in the street but straining to hold on to the freedom so close to her grasp. Her age-worn fingers wrapped around the spring iron as she braced her upper body on the boot. A grin covered her face as she lifted her feet and clung to the carriage. She was free.

"You're sick! You endanger yourself with this!"

Henrietta glanced back at the doctor and guard, now standing in the middle of the street and shrinking smaller and smaller into the distance. She'd done it. After all these years, she was leaving. She didn't know where this coach was traveling, but wherever it was it had to be closer to her son than she'd been while residing within the walls of the asylum.

The memory of her son's face was imprinted on her heart. He was her first thought every morning and her last thought every night. And now she could be with him forever, just the two of them…as things were meant to be. Holden would be so pleased.

Five

SUE'S MOTHER CLIMBED INTO THE COACH OPPOSITE SUE and Evangeline and sat down with a huff that shook the whole conveyance. Her eyes were fixed on Evangeline as she spoke. "Can you imagine? Packing your peach silk gown in with Sue's things? The nerve of that maid!" She thumped the ornamental cane in her hand on the floor one time for emphasis. "You would have been a wrinkled mess if I hadn't stopped her. Mark my words, she'll think twice before laying a finger on your finery again, Evangeline. You can rest assured of that fact."

Poor Mary. The Fairlyns had done their best in offering the Greens the use of one of their upstairs maids for their stay. However, that wasn't enough for Mother. She'd insulted the poor woman throughout their entire visit. Mary was most likely breathing a large sigh of relief now that they were rolling down the drive toward London. Still, Sue felt she should at least try to put things right for the maid. She didn't want anyone losing their employment because of her mother's ridiculous demands.

"Mother, my trunk was mostly empty. I was the

one who offered the space to Mary. She was upset that all of Evangeline's gowns wouldn't fit in the trunks for us to travel. I hope you weren't too hard on her. She was only trying to help."

"I don't want Evangeline's gowns packed with yours." Her mother recoiled, the feathers on her hat twitching with her outrage. "Your things are always covered in paint and dirt from some field. This is your sister's come-out season. All must be perfect. Doesn't that mean anything to you?"

"Of course it does. I want Evangeline to find happiness in life."

"Thank you, Sue," Evangeline offered while studying her gloved hands folded in her lap.

"Neatly pressed, clean gowns will bring Evangeline happiness. Isn't that right, darling?"

"Yes, Mother." But the sentiment didn't quite ring true in Evangeline's eyes. Sadness rimmed the pools of crystal blue. Evangeline had avoided Sue ever since her betrayal last week. Sue took hope for her sister's future that somewhere deep inside, Evangeline seemed to feel some nagging sense of regret over telling their mother about Suzanna and sealing Sue's doom for the remainder of her life.

Mother didn't seem to notice the change in Evangeline, though. She was too focused on ball gowns and planning what lord she could lure into the family. "Once we arrive in town, our schedules will be quite full. Sue, there will be no time for your silliness with those drawings of yours. I can't have you seen about town with smudges of this and that on your arms. That's what drove away…"

"Lord Amberstall. I'm aware, Mother."

"Well, it bears repeating. Evangeline, I've made a list of available gentlemen who would suit well for you."

"Did you make me a list as well, Mother?"

"I simply didn't have the time for that, Sue. There were so many preparations to make, you know."

"I see." Sue focused on the passing scenery, trying to tune out the discussion of Evangeline's marriage prospects.

"Evangeline, look over this list and remember the names." Mother handed Evangeline a piece of parchment and settled back into her seat. "When introductions are made, I want you to already know their rank in society, ancestral lineage, and interests. We have plenty of time on the ride to London, so let us begin with my first choice for you."

"Yes, Mother. First on the list is…Lord Steelings."

Sue choked. Clearing her throat, she turned to see the panic-stricken look on her sister's face. She must know he was the man at the base of the stairs. She had to know they'd danced together. Now, he would be involved with Evangeline?

"Ah, yes. He is the perfect choice for you, Evangeline. He's but a viscount now—courtesy title, you know." Mother wrinkled her nose in distaste. She had no use for anyone less than an earl like Father. "However, when his father passes, he will be a marquess! His cousins are the Fairlyns' new neighbors. So, of course, just for you, dear, I called on his aunt and mentioned you while we were visiting. I wouldn't doubt that his attentions will be turned on you these next few weeks."

She smiled, smoothing the folds of her skirt, clearly

pleased with her preparations. "I know a viscount title is not the highest in the land, but his father is quite well positioned. And I've heard his estate is quite fine indeed. It's said to have a nature walk and a lake. Just the place for my darling daughter to throw parties one day. Can you imagine?"

"Mother, I…um…wouldn't want to spend the remainder of my days on an estate such as that. I…I don't like the water." Evangeline's words rushed out, betraying the small lie in her reasoning.

"Don't stutter, Evangeline. You know how I despise that. But as for your objection, I hear Lord Steelings hardly ever visits his father. And once you do move there, the grandness will more than make up for any hesitation over water being about. You will do well, my girl."

"Oh. I'm pleased you think so." Evangeline's hands tightened into fists in her lap.

"Let us move on to Lord Steelings' interests."

Sue didn't want to hear any more. She turned to look out the window. What a lovely…field. It was ever so…green. And look, there's a stone wall. And another…field. Ah, a tree—how nice.

Despite her efforts, her mother's voice still penetrated her thoughts. "From what I gather, he is quite interested in travel and…"

"French trollops," Sue supplied under her breath as she kept her focus on the passing scenery.

"Sue Green! We do not speak of such things! He may have spent time abroad but he is home now, and we will not speak of the background of a gentleman who could very well be your brother-in-law soon."

Sue turned, leveling a glare at her mother. "They've yet to even meet, Mother."

"Sue, I will not hear one more word from you, or the end of your season will begin rather soon." Her mother's thin eyebrows had climbed all the way to her hairline, making her eyes bulge from her face.

"Yes, ma'am," Sue ground out through a clenched jaw.

"Now, where was I? Ah yes, Lord Steelings' interests. According to his aunt, he is quite interested in antiquities and has a sizable art collection."

"Wouldn't he be more appropriate for Sue, then? With the interest in art and all," Evangeline offered in a small voice, causing Sue's head to whip around to regard her sister.

"Heavens no. Sue could never catch his attention. He's quite handsome, you know. I met him some years ago and have had my eye on him for you ever since."

"I see." Evangeline swallowed, the muscles in her slender neck tightening—her only sign of emotion.

"And he will see as well, my beautiful girl. If he likes art, he will adore you. Your beauty outshines any swirl of paint."

Sue released the breath she'd been holding and attempted to unclench the knot in her stomach. Holden didn't collect just any swirls of paint. He owned *her* swirls of paint. She glanced again at her sister sitting at her side with the morning sun twinkling in her dark hair. She did outshine Sue—in every way imaginable.

"Thank you, Mother," Evangeline said with natural grace. She looked down at her knees as she continued, "Might I ask when I will meet Lord Steelings?"

"I'm sure he's invited to the Dillsworth ball. It's quite the crush every year, you know. Sue is certainly aware of that. After four failed seasons, she should be, anyway."

Sue didn't answer. There was no retort to give. It was true. She'd come to London and failed to find a husband four years in a row. Now it seemed she would be forced to not only see Holden again but to also watch him court her sister. Her last season in London was shaping up to be a rather dreary experience. Perhaps this was life's way of preparing her for what was to come. She blinked into the weak morning sun.

Or perhaps this was her last chance to enjoy herself in society before that life began. She tried to smile, but her lips refused to move. One thing was certain: she would be staying as far away as possible from Holden Ellis, Lord Steelings.

❧

Holden didn't know many things about life in general at this point, but he knew this: he needed a drink.

Had he truly changed his travel plans to return to London in time for the Dillsworth ball? Yes, he had. Had he, with a sane mind, canceled his arrangements with the well-endowed redhead in the tavern near Torrent? Yes, he had. Had he traveled all the way back to town on the word of a chit barely out of the schoolroom that Suzanna would be at the ball tonight? He ran a hand through his hair with a small groan. Yes, indeed he had.

He threw open the door to White's gentlemen's club

and breathed in the sweet smell of smoke and liquor. It smelled like freedom—freedom from ladies with their lies, taunts, and disappearing acts. A grin spread across his face as he made his way toward the bar.

"Steelings!"

Holden turned at the familiar deep rumble of his friend's voice. Devon Grey, Duke of Thornwood, was the only one who could have kept him from the soothing burn of a drink for a single second. He offered a wide smile in greeting as he moved past a cluster of gentlemen to join his friend.

They'd become fast friends in their school days beginning the night he'd slipped out to meet those local girls in the village and Devon had followed him. Chuckling at the old memory, he rounded a table and offered a nod to a passing gentleman. Since that night, he'd spent holidays at Thornwood Manor and managed to stay in touch with his old friend even in recent years when Thornwood had left the country for his explorations and Holden had remained in France—or so everyone believed.

"I thought you were set to be in the country for a few weeks. Back so soon?"

"My trip was cut short. It's a rather long tale as to why." He truly didn't want to explain that he was chasing one female on the advice of two others. That was ribbing ammunition that shouldn't be given to a friend unless it was unavoidable. "I will just say I've returned. It's good to see you, Thornwood. Care to have a drink?"

"Certainly," Thornwood returned as he clapped Holden on the back. "I'm looking for any excuse to avoid my home at the moment."

"Her Grace is in town?" Holden asked, pulling out a chair from a nearby table to sit.

"And wreaking havoc on my sanity. She has it in her head that this is the year she will convince me to bend to her will and marry. She believes my being settled will be to Roselyn's benefit next season. I keep telling her it won't happen, but does she listen?" Thornwood shook his dark head and settled into the chair opposite Holden, his large size at odds with the small table.

"Does anyone of the female persuasion listen when we proclaim what is truth?" Thornwood's mother equaled a large storm at sea in both effects on the small boats in her path and social bearing in the *ton*. On her, even the family's signature sharp, gray eyes looked as if they could snap a man in two—but Holden knew better. She was a caring mother beneath it all, which was something that had earned Holden's respect over the years. He'd always been fond of her.

They paused in their conversation to signal for drinks to be brought to their table. Finally, something to dull the humiliation of being pulled back to town by the cunning of a group of ladies. Holden stretched his long legs out before him and smiled in anticipation of a nice chat with an old friend, and the night ahead of him in which he would find Suzanna at long last.

"What are your evening plans?" Thornwood asked idly as he leaned back in his chair.

"I'm escorting my cousins to the Dillsworth ball." Then he would escort Suzanna to some remote corner and find some release from the torment she'd begun in him. He couldn't stop a smile from tugging the corners of his mouth upward. "Will you be there as well?"

"Hell no." Thornwood recoiled, his brows drawing together in concern. "That's the same ball my mother is harping on me to attend. Cry off from your cousins, and we'll drink ourselves senseless."

"Not a chance," Holden stated, his mind focused on his pending conquest.

His friend made an inarticulate sound and watched him in that way he'd always done when he was curious about something.

Damn, had Holden been so obvious about having other reasons for attending the ball? He attempted an innocent shrug, but it clearly failed to hit the mark, judging by Thornwood's narrow-eyed glare.

After a long moment of pointed stares, Holden sighed and leaned his elbow on the table. He wasn't going to escape this conversation without recounting his shameful jaunt across the countryside—that much was certain. Dropping his voice so as not to be overheard, he began, "You see, there is this extremely vexing female."

"There always is."

"Yes, well, this particular vexing female is said to be attending the ball this evening." He tried to leave it at that, but Thornwood was as bloody perceptive as usual.

After another round of glares, Holden gritted his teeth and admitted, "She's actually the reason I'm back in town so soon."

"Why am I thinking I'm about to hear the long tale you neglected to tell me of your precipitate arrival?"

"I wouldn't dare bore you with the details. I'll keep it to this: there was a masquerade at my uncle's estate not a week ago. I, of course, was forced to attend. I was having a typically dull time of it when this vision in dark rose…appeared." He stopped himself from telling everything, even though the vision of Suzanna on the stairs and then on his bed was now at the forefront of his mind. No need to go into specifics. His blackened eye had healed, and he wasn't about to share that dance down the steps with anyone. That was his and his alone.

He cleared his throat and took a swallow of bourbon to soothe his heated thoughts. "Anyway, we shared a few dances, a few laughs, among other things, and then the chit vanished. Gone, just like that." He snapped his fingers in the air for emphasis.

"I tracked down a friend of hers from the masquerade who informed me of her presence in London and the balls she is set on attending. Tonight I will find her." He grinned, imagining the scene already. He would spot her. She would inadvertently back herself into a darkened corner. He would steal her away into the night. They would finish what they'd begun. Simple. Her pale skin would be in his hands, her full red lips under his, her burnished gold hair would fall around them as they…

"My God, you're smitten!" Thornwood's eyes narrowed on him. "I can hardly believe it! Who is this temptress who's lured you in?"

"Her name is Suzanna. Lovely, isn't it?" Holden sighed on a smile and took another sip of his drink.

"And this is all you know of her?"

"Well, yes. She disappeared, you see. You have no idea how infuriating it is to have a chit vanish in such a manner. I only want to see her once more. Perhaps it's only a proper ending to things that I am looking for tonight." Or a proper beginning... He drank again, thankful for the distraction from his friend's interrogation.

"Disappearing ladies are annoying, to say the least." Thornwood ran a hand through his hair, and the grim expression surrounding his gray eyes seemed to indicate how he deeply meant his words. "She disappeared on you. She could be running from any sort of thing. She could be a thief. Did you check your pockets after that dance?"

"A thief? Why the devil would you think that?"

All of society called his friend the Mad Duke of Thornwood, and he was acting in accordance with his name at the moment. Holden had never believed his friend to be mad, though. It was said that the old duke had been mad and passed the sickness on to his son—an idea that Holden was quite certain was rubbish. But since his return to the country last year, Thornwood had become a recluse from society, absorbed in his shipping interests and little else. For months he'd hidden away in his library, surrounded by his maps, trade routes, and exotic plants. Tonight was different. Something beyond Suzanna's identity was troubling his friend. A thief, indeed. Holden narrowed his gaze on the man across the table in an attempt to read his thoughts or simply get him to stop accusing his Suzanna of thievery.

"It's a possibility to be considered. I'm sure it

happens occasionally." Thornwood leaned forward from his previous casual stance, his wide shoulders looming over Holden, which wasn't an easy feat considering Holden's height. At the moment he was quite thankful for the small table between them. Why was Thornwood so upset? This was Suzanna they were discussing after all. He didn't even know her.

"I hardly think a lady would steal from me at my uncle's home." Holden watched Thornwood as a look of wild fury crossed his eyes, almost hidden by the dark hair falling into his face. He certainly looked mad in this light. Unfortunately, Thornwood would never divulge what was truly on his mind. Holden knew that much of his friend. Yet he asked anyway, "What's gotten into you?"

The lines of concern etched on Thornwood's face relaxed into an easy smile as he leaned back again in his chair. "It's nothing. And I've changed my mind. I believe I will attend the Dillsworth event this evening. I must meet this mystery lady that has you chasing her all about the countryside."

"Spectacular!" Holden was surprised by this change, to say the least, but pleased at any rate. "I really wasn't looking forward to keeping the company of my cousins for the whole evening. They tend to squeal. It's quite annoying, really. But with you there, I can slip away easily." Holden relaxed in his seat, looking forward to the evening more and more by the minute.

"I suppose if it keeps you free of unwanted relations, you can use my notorious nature for good this evening."

"It should go to some good use. You certainly haven't used it recently, staying holed up in your

library working, with no time for any ladies or entertainment. Indeed, this will work perfectly. My cousins
are terrified of you as it is. I'll have the whole evening
free of them to find Suzanna. And you will finally
leave your home to socialize with me. Who knows,
perhaps you'll even dance." Holden grinned, knowing
his socially ill-tempered, brooding friend would never
set foot on a dance floor.

"Ah, but now you will have me taunting you as
you make a fool of yourself for a lady. Yes, this evening's entertainment is sounding more enticing by the
second. But there will be no dancing." Thornwood
rose with a grim smile and offered Holden a nod as
he rounded the table. "I'll see you there. I have a few
things to attend to first." With that, he threw open
the door and was gone, leaving Holden with an empty
table, an empty glass, and a mind full of anticipation
for the night ahead.

"I'm going to need another drink," he mumbled
to the tabletop as he checked the time. Four hours. It
would be worth every second's wait, for tonight he
would find Suzanna.

❧

Holden leaned over his cousin with a sigh to continue
the conversation they'd begun on the front steps of the
Dillsworth home. "We could have been here an hour
ago. You're aware there are colors other than pink
available for gowns."

"I am." April lifted her chin, displaying a smile for
two ladies passing them in the hallway.

Holden offered a nod in their direction before

continuing, "And you can purchase fabrics in blue, green, yellow…"

"Dreadfully dull colors, all of them." She stopped her progress down the hall, looking up at him to ask, "Why would I want to be dull, Holden?"

"I suppose you wouldn't." He shook his head at April's stubborn nature. Some gentleman would have a challenge ahead of him. He smiled down at her, watching as she twitched the fan in her fingers from closed to half open to fully open while watching herself in a nearby mirror. "For clarity's sake, you believe my blue waistcoat is…"

"Dull," she offered with a toss of her head, inciting laughter from her sisters.

With his cousins and aunt and uncle, they were creating quite the crowd in the hall. Other partygoers craned their necks to see around them, while a few pushed past on their way to the ballroom. Holden was already scanning the area for Suzanna, but there was no sign of her here. He needed to slip away. And this corridor was too crowded for comfort. Resisting the urge to loosen his cravat from around his neck, he stepped closer to the wall at his back in an attempt to pull his family from the walkway.

Aunt Penelope moved into their conversation, her elaborate gown filling the space in the corridor Holden had just created. "April, it's not proper to insult a gentleman's attire—even if the gentleman in question is your cousin." Aunt Penelope's eyes fell on Holden with a fond gleam. "I think you look quite nice, Holden."

"You're looking lovely this evening as well, Aunt.

And I'm glad someone around here appreciates my fine looks," he said with a teasing tone in his voice that caused April to roll her eyes.

"Always, dear." She pulled June closer so two gentlemen could move past, before turning back to Holden. "You could have joined us in the carriage, you know. We had room for you. I don't know why you always insist…"

"Thank you, Aunt Pen. However, as you know, I prefer to have my own transportation." He glanced around again. No sight of her. He needed to move along. What if she left early with a headache? What if her dance card filled? He sighed and turned his attention back to his aunt, who was still harping about his arrival on horseback.

"I know you say that, but…"

"Everywhere in this country worth going can be reached by horse."

"To a ball, though? Really, Holden."

June stepped closer and pushed her glasses higher on her nose. "I agree with Mama. It's quite unseemly, Cousin."

"My apologies for being *unseemly*."

May gave her sister a shove on the arm and smiled up at Holden as she interjected, "I think it's dashing and romantic to travel by horse."

"You would," April admonished.

"I suppose I could have walked." Holden threw the statement into the conversation mostly to eliminate the risk of a sibling argument in the middle of the Dillsworths' main hall.

Aunt Penelope gasped. "Walked? You can't arrive at a ball on foot."

"You see? My horse is looking better by the second." He grinned and nodded to a gentleman who passed by on his way toward the card room. Holden needed to be on his way as well. Only, his course would not take him in the direction of the card games and gentlemen. Not tonight.

When his cousins were distracted by the arrival of another family, his aunt tugged on his arm and added, "You do need to occasionally follow society's rules, Holden, or people might begin to talk."

She wasn't going to let this topic go, was she? "Are you saying you're in favor of propriety at all times? You? One of the infamous Rutledges?" He chuckled as he watched his uncle move closer through the crowd, finally catching up with them from his conversation with the party host. Perhaps he could make his excuses and leave now that his uncle would be around to take control of the group of females.

"I'm aware of our family's stance on normalcy. Yet, we shouldn't encourage talk when we can avoid it, Holden."

"I'll keep that in mind. I wouldn't want to incite chatter at a ball. Now, if you'll excuse me, I need to go and meet Thornwood."

"The Mad Duke? Do you truly not care for your good name?"

"Of course not. I associate with the lot of you, don't I?"

Uncle Joseph joined his wife, placing her hand on his arm and offering Holden a smile. "Will I see you in the card room later this evening?"

"Joseph! Your daughters' dance cards could very

well be full tonight. Don't you wish to oversee things to make sure no undesirable gentlemen pay them undue attention?"

"They survive Holden. Surely they can hold their own on a crowded dance floor." He shot Holden a teasing grin.

"I'm sure they can, but won't you stay anyway?" Aunt Penelope pleaded. "We could dance. Don't you want to keep me company?"

"Holden, explain to your aunt that a gentleman needs time in the company of other gentlemen."

"Oh, no. I wouldn't dare get involved in such a dangerous subject as dancing versus cards. Have a nice evening. I'm off to find Thornwood."

"Thornwood, eh? Ask after his ships for me, won't you?"

"Certainly, Uncle. I didn't know you had an interest in explorations beyond reading about them."

He shot a sly grin over at Aunt Penelope. "I feel if I don't spend time with gentlemen discussing mannish topics, soon I may start embroidering pillows and arranging flowers. Months abroad on a ship might be just what I need...or I could simply go play a hand or two of cards."

"Very well. Go and smoke those filthy cheroots you think I'm unaware of and gamble away the money you slipped into your pocket when you thought I wasn't looking. *I* will be in the ballroom seeing to *our* daughters."

"Perfect!" Uncle Joseph replied with a grin.

"Humph." The swat of his aunt's fan was swift and final on the sleeve of his uncle's coat.

"I'll leave you two to…settle or discuss…yes. Well, I'll see you later." Holden turned with a smile and left the disorganized group lingering in the hallway.

Making a straight path for the refreshment table, he pushed through the crowded hallway. Sustenance was needed if he was to conduct a proper search for Suzanna. Rounding a corner into a less crowded parlor, he spotted it—a table laden with cakes, fruits, and cheeses. His stomach grumbled in response. Just as he was closing the gap of floor between his mouth and the delicious-looking tea cakes on the towering display at the end of the table, he heard his name.

"Steelings, there you are. I was afraid I would have to find someone else to torment for the evening," Thornwood said, clapping Holden on the back in greeting.

"I'd hate to disappoint you, Thornwood. I was delayed by some devastating emergency involving my cousin's gown. You would have thought the world was coming to an end, all for a missing bead of some sort. There were tears and wailing." He shuddered. April could be so emotional at times, especially when it came to her gowns and the possibility of having to wear her sister's perfectly lovely blue gown instead. He shook off the memory.

"That does sound like quite the dramatic beginning to the evening. I do hate it when they wail, though. How are we to deal with that? Where did you leave them?" Thornwood cast his eyes behind Holden but there was no one there except for a few gentlemen deep in conversation.

"I made my excuses in the hallway. Now that

you're here, I must begin my search for Suzanna." He rubbed his hands together in anticipation.

"Ah yes, the mysterious Suzanna. What does this vixen look like?"

Holden exhaled a deep breath, the memory of Suzanna swirling around him for a moment. "It was at a masquerade, yet I would know her anywhere. She was just over five feet, hair the color of burnished gold..."

"*Burnished gold?*" Thornwood laughed, almost spitting out the liquor he'd just poured into his mouth.

A small part of Holden wished his friend would choke on his liquor. Her hair *was* the color of burnished gold. If Thornwood had seen her, he wouldn't be in such a teasing frame of mind. He should have kept quiet about his interest in this lady, for now he was paying the price. When it came to gentlemen, this was the price of friendship. He sighed. "Very well, blondish-brown if that's more to your liking."

"No, I believe I prefer 'burnished gold.'" Thornwood chuckled again. "Although I don't see that color in this side parlor. Perhaps we should look in the main ballroom?"

"Yes." Holden gave one final fleeting look at the refreshment table before turning back to his friend. Food would have to wait. "Isn't there a door that adjoins the rooms over there behind that potted palm?"

"Indeed. I recall making use of it once when Miss Rashings had me in her sights years ago. It made for a timely retreat."

"The face of a horse, that one, and the hindquarters to match," Holden mused as they made their way to the door.

"That's actually a bit kind where that particular lady is concerned." Thornwood's chuckle was lost in the sounds of the ballroom. The chatter from all corners of the room, the orchestra striking up a country dance from the balcony, and the tittering laughter of dozens of young girls learning to flirt echoed off the cream-colored walls.

Holden followed Thornwood through the small side door. Glancing up, he took note of the glass ceiling over the center of the ballroom. It was clearly meant to impress, and Holden had to admit the Dillsworth family knew how to throw a ball. From the abundance of roses to the ample number of footmen with trays of champagne, this ball was what the *ton* would consider a successful crush.

The crowd was thick, and somewhere in this mass of society's elite stood Suzanna. His eyes drifted over the dance floor, searching for a smallish lady. The phrase "needle in a haystack" came to mind. But he'd come here to find her—and find her he would.

"There are well over a hundred ladies here, and most of them are moving around. This could take all evening," Thornwood complained as a group of ladies passed by, none of whom were Suzanna.

"You act as if a moment spent in a ballroom will poison you for life," Holden returned, not taking his eyes from the dance floor. "This will be simple. I'll find her within a matter of minutes. Before you know it, you'll be back drinking in one of those lovely hovels you so enjoy." He pulled his eyes from their task for a moment to shoot a grin at his friend.

"Very well. Just over five feet, you said? You

couldn't be searching for a tall chit. No, it would have to be a tiny, hard-to-find one."

Holden determined she was not on the dance floor after only a few minutes. He would have to search the area under the balcony. Thankful for his height, he peered over the ocean of heads surrounding him. There, just inside the main doors leading to the hall beyond, stood the Fairlyns. Troublesome chits. They'd better be correct about Suzanna's whereabouts, for he didn't see Suzanna anywhere around them.

He turned, a sneer still lingering on his face. "I've spotted her friends by the first column near the main door. She must be nearby. Let's make our way in that direction."

"By the first column, you say?" Thornwood abandoned his drink on a pedestal holding a large vase of roses and moved to follow. Personally, Holden was of the opposite mindset. He grabbed a glass of champagne from a passing footman and drained it in one swallow. Handing the empty glass to another footman, he rounded the corner of the dance floor.

Lady Popensford stepped into his path with a coy smile and a toss of her jewel-encrusted head. "Good evening," he offered, attempting to move past her.

"Lord Steelings, it's wonderful to see you this season. I'm out of mourning now, you know."

"I can see that. Blue is certainly your color, my lady. The late Lord Popensford is without a doubt jealous of my eyes this evening, God rest his soul."

"Oh my lord, you do know how to flatter a lady." She batted her eyes in his direction, clearly wanting their conversation to continue.

He did not. Not tonight. Not with Suzanna some-where in the room. With a nod of his head he moved on, chuckling at the barely audible humph of femi-nine disapproval at his back. Progress, however, was slow in such a crowd. After slipping past a group of young ladies without pause, he spotted Lady Mosley. He was about to dive to the side to avoid being seen, and avoid spending the next hour in a conversation he couldn't escape, when she saw him. He dipped his head in a bow, hiding his grimace of exasperation within the motion.

By the time his eyes once again met hers, a pleasant look of greeting covered his face. "My lady, you're looking well."

"Lord Steeee-lings, I'm so very pleeee-ased to see you this evening." How did the woman draw one sentence out to last a lifetime? His quarry this evening could be dancing with someone else right now. Or she could leave early and he would lose her once again.

"Likewise, my lady." He glanced around to see if Thornwood was still following him through the crowd and saw he'd paused in conversation as well. Holden sighed and offered Lady Mosley a charming smile.

"I loooooked for you when I was in Paris last year. It was odd; nooone of my company could plaaaace you."

"You must keep good company."

"Of cooooourse I do."

"I don't. Paris is much more interesting in the shadows."

"You rooooogue." She hit his arm with her fan with a chuckle. "My loooord, are you acquainted with Lady Tottings?" She indicated the lady at her side with a wave of the fan.

Libby—he'd recognize those lips anywhere. Had it been four years already? Too bad the Sarah and Emily situation had brought that to an end. Although he would have ended things soon anyway. She'd aged well. He bowed over her hand. "Of course. We became acquainted some time ago. Lady Tottings, ravishing as usual."

"Lord Steelings, it flatters me greatly that you remember our…" She paused to clear her throat. "Friendship. It was some years ago. So long ago that I can barely remember it." The blush on her cheeks said otherwise.

"Truly? I remember it quite vividly." Holden grinned at her discomfort.

When she only made a small sound of alarm in response and Lady Mosley was distracted by her blushing, thinking her overheated, Holden saw his opportunity to slip away. "If you will excuse me, ladies. There is someone I must go speak with."

Lady Mosley glanced up from her vigorous fanning of her friend's face to offer a nod of farewell. "Very well. Dooooo come around for tea soon, my lord."

"I shall." He was already moving toward the promise of Suzanna, if he could only get to her. Another lady was trying to catch his eye as he passed. "Lovely ball, yet not as lovely as you this evening," he tossed out without a second's pause to hear her response. He was almost there.

When yet another woman saw him coming and tried to block his path, he swore under his breath. How many ladies were in this damned ballroom? Were there not any men left in the city of London?

With a quick motion, he stepped around her, calling over his shoulder, "Lady Channings, it's been years. We must become reacquainted soon." *Soon but not now*, he finished to himself as he turned back to his mission.

Pushing past gathered groups of chatting society matrons, he made his way toward the Fairlyns. What would he say once he reached them? He supposed he could demand to see her, in a nice manner of course. But then what would he say to Suzanna once he saw her? He almost turned back to think it over, yet he'd come this far.

Just then the crowd shifted enough that he could see the people gathered at the base of the column with the Fairlyns. It looked to be an army of young ladies. The twins he knew. Then there were a tall blonde, a tall brunette, and a small lady who he vaguely recognized from the masquerade unmasking.

"Bloody hell," he heard Thornwood say at his side.

He would have asked what had his friend cursing in the middle of a ballroom, but he was too busy looking around for Suzanna. Where was she? Not bloody well here, to take his friend's sentiments and extrapolate on them. Then his eyes landed on the small lady in the pale rose gown, the lady who had turned white as a sheet upon seeing him. The same lady who was now staring at him and looking terribly guilty. He would begin with her. She would lead him to Suzanna. He knew it.

With a smile at what certainly lay ahead this evening, he bowed in greeting to the lady in rose.

Six

"MOTHER, I'LL BE IN THE BALLROOM WITH VICTORIA and Isabelle if you have need of me." Sue didn't wait for her mother to respond before she was gone. The door to the retiring room slammed shut behind her. The paintings and doorways of the Dillsworth home slid by in a blur of rich colors as she put as much space between her mother and herself as possible.

If she had to listen to any more intense discussions about which necklace Evangeline should wear this evening, whether it was the best choice of necklaces, or thoughts on whether the one chosen sparkled enough, she was quite likely to choke her mother with said necklace.

Sue rounded the corner into the ballroom, slowing her pace to a ladylike stroll. Attempting a calming breath, she inhaled a large amount of rose-scented air. Calming breaths were supposed to settle one, weren't they? She should have known she wouldn't be calm this evening. Not here. Calm and the first large ball of her last season didn't mix. Candlelight from a thousand candles reflected off the glass-paneled ceiling, raining down like tiny stars on all of London's social elite below.

Pushing past a group of elderly gentlemen debating politics, she skirted two groups of ladies before she found a free space of floor near a column. Where were Isabelle and Victoria? Rising to her toes, she peered around the room. She'd never find them in this crush, never mind trying to find a gentleman to save her from her disappointing future. She didn't see any likely candidates on this side of the ballroom.

Glancing back over at the elderly gentlemen, she eyed them for husband potential. Only one wore a monocle. He was her best bet because of the poor vision. Her mother had always said she should find a husband who didn't mind plain looks, so what better choice than a half-blind man? Just then a lady sauntered up to him in a dark crimson gown and wrapped her hand around his arm. She tossed her head in laughter, showing off the gleam of diamonds at her neck. Just Sue's luck—even the old, doddering ones were taken. She was doomed.

She supposed this would be the last time she would attend this event. By next season, she would be packed off to spend an eternity with Great-Aunt Mildred. Turning her attention to the dance floor, she watched the swirl of colors sweep past, not really seeing anything. Perhaps somewhere on that dance floor was a marriageable man. Of course, if he was on the dance floor, he was dancing with another lady. That lady most likely had beauty and a large dowry. Sue had neither. But surely there had to be some titled yet penniless or untitled yet wealthy gentleman here who would marry her simply because…

He would overlook her appearance, excessive

chatter, and small dowry because... Because... "Blast it all." He wouldn't.

Had she just cursed aloud? Had anyone heard that?

She glanced around to see which matron she'd now offended and saw a tall, willowy figure hovering beside the nearby column. The woman clearly hadn't heard, for she didn't turn around or even flinch. Of course, she may not have been capable of flinching with a spine that straight. Her blond hair was secured in too tight a knot at the back of her neck. Truly, her hairpins must be painful. Could she blink, or were her eyes permanently open?

Sue craned her neck to see the lady's face. That's when she realized she knew this lady. "Lillian?"

Sue took a step closer, waiting for her friend to turn in her direction. "Lillian! I knew that must be you! It's been ages!"

"Sue!" Lillian exclaimed, bright blue eyes twinkling in the light of the ballroom. "You have no idea how happy I am to see a friendly face here tonight. It's been ages, has it not? We must catch up!"

"Yes, we certainly must! Isn't this ball exquisite?" Sue smiled, trying not to think about the prospect of finding a suitor here or her impending doom come the end of the season. "I always love attending the Dillsworth affairs. Have you tried the cakes in the parlor yet? They never last very long, especially the ones filled with strawberry jam."

That would certainly be Sue's next stop, for she hadn't eaten all evening and a cake sounded divine at the moment. She would move in that direction in a few minutes when she was done chatting with her old friend. "You would think from year to year they would realize the popularity of the cakes and prepare more. But alas, we are forced to clamor over a single table of sweets as soon as we arrive to get one. Who are you here with?"

"Two of my brothers are here as my chaperones. One is getting me a drink and the other I choose not to think about." Lillian's eyes narrowed at the mention of her brother. "Who is with you this evening?"

"My family. You remember my sister, Evangeline. It's her come-out this year. She is preening in the upstairs ladies' retiring room at the moment. You probably remember how she is, unable to take more than two steps away from a mirror to this day. It's rather annoying, if I can be honest," Sue finished with a laugh.

It felt nice to laugh and to be honest. Something inside her relaxed. Perhaps she wouldn't find a husband here. Perhaps she would be forced to move to Scotland and live without chocolate for the remainder of her days. But tonight she would enjoy visiting with Lillian. Tonight she would watch couples dance around the floor while she ate cakes. Tonight she would live life. Lillian's voice pulled her back to the present.

"I believe Evangeline must have been ten years old when last I saw her. I don't want to think about how young we were. Does this mean you're not yet married?"

Sue's reverie about her moment of freedom ended with that reminder. "This is my fifth season, if you can believe that. If I have to return home with my mother at the end of yet another year, I may die." She couldn't tell Lillian the truth—not when the truth was so horrible. "And with all of the focus on Evangeline's come-out, it's very likely I'll meet that doom in a few months' time." Sue made a slicing motion across her throat and pulled a face of pure horror. Surely that had added the necessary playful note to her tale to prevent unwanted questions.

"You mustn't end it all when we've only just met up again after all these years. If it eases your mind, consider that this is my first season and I'm a year older than you." Lillian offered a thin smile as she twisted her pearl necklace around one finger before releasing the strand and doing it again. She looked worried—and not about Sue's threat of throat slicing.

"What happened to keep you away so long? I've thought to see you in London for years now. Every year I've kept my eye out for you, as well as some of the other girls from school, but I'd lost hope that I would see you again."

As Lillian told Sue of her recent life, she looked down at her hands, her face falling with some deep thought, presumably about her brothers, who sounded rather vile.

Lillian seemed to need as much cheering this evening as Sue did. Perhaps this was fate's method of tossing her a small favor in life as she drew ever closer to the season's end—a friend for the remainder of her time in society. She grinned. "Whitby's loss is my gain this evening, Lillian. I'm thrilled to have someone to converse with other than Evangeline and my twin cousins. Oh, here they all are now."

The crowd of people by the door parted to allow Evangeline to enter the ballroom with Isabelle and

Victoria trailing just behind her. Heads turned, and how could they not when the three most beautiful ladies among the *ton* were breezing in the door of the first ball of the season? "Lillian, you remember Evangeline. And here are Isabelle and Victoria, my cousins."

"Lillian, how nice that you're here. I look forward to catching up with you," Evangeline offered in a well-rehearsed voice.

"I look forward to that as well," Lillian returned with a genuine smile.

Sue glanced up as a tall gentleman carrying two wineglasses joined them. "Here's your champagne, darling," he said to Lillian, handing her a glass. "It seems you have found friends already. That's splendid."

This must be one of Lillian's brothers. He was handsome in his well-tailored suit. Why had she never seen him around a ballroom before?

"We're just becoming reacquainted. My brother, Mr. Phillips, this is Miss Green; her sister, Miss Evangeline Green; and her cousins, the Misses Fairlyn."

"Good evening," Mr. Phillips offered with a slight bow in their direction before turning his attention back to Lillian. "Since you've found friends, do you mind if I find a few of my mates?"

Lillian spoke in hushed tones for a moment. Soon her brother left and she turned back to the group. She was taking a tiny sip of her champagne just as Evangeline disappeared into the growing crowd on the dance floor with a young dark-haired man. Victoria and Isabelle were next to leave on someone's arm, leaving Sue and Lillian behind. The group around them had now thinned as couples entered the floor for

a country dance. That was when she saw him. Holden
Ellis, Lord Steelings, was walking straight toward her.

"Sue? Are you well?" Lillian asked.

"Oh, yes. Quite," she stammered. She'd known he
would be here. Why did it come as such a shock to
see him now? She swallowed.

"You look as if you've seen a ghost."

"In a manner, I believe I have." He was still walking toward her. What should she say? Would he know
her now? Or would Suzanna forever be her secret to
bear alone? Her heart was pounding, yet no blood was
reaching her brain. Perhaps she should go…where?
Where could she go? Why was he looking at her with
that piercing gaze?

"Clearly something has you distressed," Lillian stated.

Distressed wasn't quite the right emotion, but Sue
preferred not to think of the proper word for now as
she feared it would be more along the lines of "panic."

"Is there something I can do? Do you need a drink?
The champagne has helped my nerves considerably."
Lillian took another sip as if to prove her point.

"No, thank you. Although perhaps I could use
some air." Her voice sounded a bit too casual. Her
eyes were focused on Holden. She needed to look
away. Why wasn't she looking away? She needed to
leave. Now. "Will you excuse me?"

"Certainly," Lillian replied.

Yet Sue had only taken one step away when she
halted. He was too close now. She couldn't go. She
would simply have to…

"Good evening, ladies," Holden offered, his eyes
never leaving Sue.

She darted a glance away for a moment to see there was a large dark-haired man at his side who seemed to be glowering in Lillian's direction.

"I don't believe we've been formally introduced. I'm Lord Steelings, and this is the Duke of Thornwood."

At Lillian's extended silence, Sue cleared her throat and said, "I'm Miss Green."

Another moment ticked by in silence before the duke offered a strained, "Pleasure to make your acquaintance, my ladies."

Sue slid a glance beside her to Lillian. Her mouth was clamped shut and her eyes wide on the duke. Clearly she was awestruck by such an infamous man of high rank. She was new to town after all. Sue felt she needed to say something to fill the dreadful silence. "Your Grace, my lord, may I introduce my childhood friend, Miss Phillips. She's from Whitby and only arrived in town recently for the first time. Isn't that right, Miss Phillips?"

"Miss Phillips from Whitby," the Duke of Thornwood returned with curiosity, his eyes studying every detail of her face. "This is your first time in our fair city?"

Lillian cleared her throat before stammering a quiet, "Yes, yes it is."

Sue turned her attention back to Holden as he observed, "Your family seems to have abandoned you here with Miss Phillips."

"That appears to be the case. I suppose the lure of the country dance is simply too great."

"So everyone accompanying you this evening is on the dance floor right now?"

"Well, no. My mother left to find a friend and my father is playing cards."

"Ah, but all of your female company are on the dance floor?" He was already craning his neck to see across the room.

"Yes, they are," she returned with more than a little bitterness in her tone. Why was he here talking to her when he clearly was only interested in her sister? Here he was, standing before her again and he still didn't know her. Or had he already lost interest in their night together? So soon? Her heart clenched but she refused to fall apart. She had more important things to attend to this evening, like finding a husband.

Holden turned his attention back to her to ask, "Miss Green, would you care to dance? If you're available, that is. I'm interested to hear about your family's well-being since I saw them last in the country."

She muttered a tight, "Certainly." He would want to know about Evangeline, of course. Mother had arranged and predicted it; Sue simply didn't want to believe it. She then turned to Lily with a tight smile. "I trust you will survive the duke's company for a few minutes."

"I'm sure I'll be fine," Lily said confidently, although her eyes told a different story as she fiddled with her pearl necklace.

"Yes, I have a feeling she can fend for herself quite well," the Duke of Thornwood said with something between charm and a snarl.

Sue wasn't quite so confident in her friend's abilities, but she could do nothing to assist her at the moment. Not when Holden was smiling at her and extending his arm for her to hold. With a feather-light touch, Sue wrapped her hand around the wool of his coat. She didn't want to feel the muscles under his sleeve, didn't want to have him under her fingers again.

She was staring straight ahead as if walking to an untimely death. She'd vowed they wouldn't touch one another again. Of course she'd also vowed she wouldn't speak to him ever again, and she'd already broken that promise. Sighing, she glanced up at him as they walked. He appeared to be unaffected by her presence, based on the bored expression that crossed his face for a moment before he noticed she was looking and smiled.

Her fingers twitched on his arm. She longed to step away from him, put distance between them, but she couldn't. She needed to simply act as if nothing was wrong. The dance would be over soon. He hadn't recognized her without a mask at the last ball, and he wouldn't know her now either. However, spending an entire dance with their hands grasping and his body close to hers was a bit distressing. Not to mention that he might know her by the manner of her dance. She took a ragged breath. The risk was too great. "I'd rather get some refreshments than dance, if you don't mind," she blurted out without preamble.

"I believe I would prefer that as well. Country dances aren't the best way to visit with someone anyway—all that twirling and changing of partners." He smiled down at her, and she almost melted into the wooden floorboard under her satin slippers.

"I wouldn't know. I've never danced one."

"Truly? Are you sure you don't want to now, then?"

"No. If I can be completely honest, I'm famished."

"Might I be honest as well?" He leaned down to add in a soft rumble, "I'm starving."

"Have you tried the tea cakes here?"

"No, but I saw them a few minutes ago."

"Come with me. You have to try one." Before she was aware of her own actions, she was pulling him through the crowd toward the refreshment parlor, away from the dance floor and the possibility of having his hands on her body.

"Perhaps it's the manner in which you drag gentlemen across a room that has your dance card so empty." Holden teased.

"I've never done this before either."

"Miss Green, have you lived at all before this evening?"

"Perhaps once." The night they'd spent together seemed full of life, in her memory anyway. It was surely an average Thursday for him, but not for her. For her it had been… She shook her head. It wasn't wise to think about such things now.

"Once in a lifetime," he reprimanded. "That isn't enough living, if you ask me."

"I'm sure not, from what I've heard of you." She pulled him through the door into the side parlor, smiling at the sight of the tower of cakes.

"What precisely have you heard?" he asked as they neared the refreshment table.

"Oh, just things here and there." She picked up two small cakes from the table and turned back to him. "Try this."

She held one cake out between two fingers for

him to take. He took it, just not in the way she had imagined. In one smooth motion he lifted her hand by the wrist and took the cake from her with his teeth. She gasped. His fingers covered her pulse at her wrist for only a moment, but he had to have felt her heart racing there. She couldn't move, couldn't breathe.

"Mmmm." The sound rumbled from deep within his chest. She watched as he licked a bit of icing from his lip.

She needed to look away. Her eyes, however, were not cooperating at the moment. Did he have any idea how devastatingly handsome he looked in evening attire? Most likely he did. And now with his lips sweet from the cake he'd eaten, she could think of nothing else but kissing him. *Sue, get hold of yourself. He doesn't even see you.*

She blinked and turned away a fraction, feigning interest in a portrait of an elderly gentleman across the room. "The food at this ball is delicious. Don't you think so? So often at these affairs all that is provided is watered-down lemonade and meat left sitting out too long." She popped the other cake into her mouth, letting the sweet taste of strawberries overtake her.

"I believe I'll have another. I was happy to see your family this evening."

"Oh?" Her family. This was why he'd wanted to dance with her, to find out if Evangeline was available, what her interests might be, and how she took her tea. She braced herself for a long discussion of all things Evangeline.

"Yes, you're of relation to the Fairlyn family, aren't you?" he asked as he lifted another cake to his mouth.

"I am. They are my cousins." So it wasn't her sister he was interested in; no, it was her cousins. This was an unexpected change. However, she didn't wish to discuss her cousins either at this point, not with him.

"Their property borders my uncle's property. I met them only recently."

"And you've captured me to quiz me on Isabelle and Victoria," she retorted, picking up another cake from the table. "My mother will be quite disappointed, you know."

"No, that's not… Why would your mother be disappointed?"

"Because of my sister."

"Who is your sister?" His eyes sharpened on her. Everything about him looked as if he was about to pounce on some prey he'd captured. "Is she your same height? Hair of…"

"No. Evangeline is tall and perfectly formed." Sue resisted the urge to roll her eyes.

"Evangeline." He seemed to deflate at the sound of the name. He exhaled on a deep sigh as he grabbed another cake from the table. "My aunt spoke of her recently. It seems our families desire a match there."

"Well, then. I do hope it all works out for everyone involved." Sue stuffed the cake she'd been holding into her mouth to avoid talking any further.

"What works out? A match?" He chuckled and shook his golden head. "I'm asking after your cousins' friend Suzanna."

She choked on the cake, finally forcing it down her throat with a series of coughs. He was asking about Suzanna. Fear warred with excitement inside her chest. Why had she ever thought that night would be a quickly forgotten adventure?

"Your cousins indicated she would be in attendance this evening. I know it's beyond poor taste to ask after another lady while eating cakes with you. However, I thought…"

"Suzanna," she repeated, her lips parting on some unknown question as she searched his eyes for answers. "You're asking after Suzanna. Then you aren't interested in courting Evangeline."

"Have I even met Evangeline?"

"I'm sure if you had, you wouldn't readily forget *her*." She couldn't stop the quick tilt of her chin and flair of her nostrils in accusation, nor did she particularly desire to.

"Miss Green," he led in with slow words, clearly recognizing he was no longer on stable footing in the conversation. "I only want to know where Suzanna can be found this evening. I will leave you be once I've seen her."

"Suzanna isn't in attendance."

"She isn't in attendance." He sighed and took a step away, running a hand through his hair. Turning back, he asked, "Where is she?"

"Not here, my lord."

"I'm aware of that. I'm asking if she had some prior engagement this evening. Or is she unwell?"

"She's at home."

"Your cousins told me of Suzanna's dilemma. It's all right to be honest with me."

She froze. How did her cousins know of her parents' decision about her future? Evangeline must have told them. And they had told Holden behind her back? Her heart sank at the betrayal. "Her dilemma?" Sue's voice was shaking. "What dilemma would that be?"

"The problem she has in reference to gentlemen…"

"I wasn't aware you knew of her situation. In fact, I didn't even think my cousins knew." They weren't present for the discussion of Great-Aunt Mildred. Did Victoria and Isabelle know this was to be her last chance to find a husband? Her eyes narrowed on him.

"How could they not know? They've been around Suzanna enough to know the truth of the matter."

"So you agree with them? Perhaps you should marry her, then." She spat the words out, then inhaled in an attempt to pull them back in.

"That would certainly keep her in one place for once, but I'm not suggesting that."

"Is that what you would do? Keep her in her place, locked away, not to be seen?" She sighed and looked away. She would be as good as locked away in Scotland for the remainder of her life. "Perhaps that is what she deserves. And it appears she doesn't have much choice in the matter anyway."

"Are we both speaking of her propensity to run when a gentleman gets near her?"

"Her…yes, of course we are." Sue tried to laugh but it sounded hollow to her ears. "That silly Suzanna. Always on the run."

"Then you'll assist me in finding her?"

"Of course." She smiled through her panic. How was she to assist him in finding…well…herself? This was a disaster.

"Where is she staying?"

Sue panicked. She couldn't tell him that! What was she to say? She could give him false information or... "I'm not going to tell you her personal information. You could be a murderer or a thief."

He shook his head. "How odd. Earlier this evening someone accused *her* of being a thief."

"Suzanna is not a thief! She is a kind person. Perhaps she has troubles with gentlemen, but that's neither here nor there. One thing is for certain—she would never steal, my lord."

"I meant no offense to your friend."

"You have a fine way of showing it."

"Listen, I..." He looked away and ran a hand through his hair. "Do you argue with all gentlemen?"

"No, only with you."

"I feel so special." He flinched as if surprised by some thought, then shook it off.

Her eyes narrowed on him. What was he thinking?

"This evening hasn't gone the way I'd intended. I'm usually charming."

"Really? I couldn't tell."

"May we begin again? I will swear on this most delicious tea cake that I am here in a friendly capacity."

"All right then. I swear on the very same delicious tea cake that I am here in a friendly capacity as well."

She watched as he tore the small cake into two pieces and ate half of it. He held out the other half for her to take, his fingers hovering a breath away from her lips. She froze, gazing up into his face. She couldn't eat from his hand, could she?

"You have to eat the cake, or the vow of friend-ship is null and void. It's written in the great law of swears on sweets." He smiled and shot her an "I dare you" look.

After another moment's hesitation and a glance around the room to ensure they were indeed alone, she leaned forward to take the cake from his out-stretched fingers. Only he moved his hand, causing her to stumble forward. She glared at him as he lifted the cake out of her reach.

"Oh, my mistake." He held the cake out again and waited for her to take it. Then once again he pulled his hand away with a chuckle.

"All right, I'll play fair." He grinned and moved to feed her the cake before snatching it away again.

With a narrow-eyed glare, she reached up and grabbed his wrist, lifting herself off the ground for a moment, her satin slippers swinging in the air.

His muscles tensed under her grasp. "Oh, now who's not playing fair? I can't very well let you fall on your arse, can I?"

"That's what I'm counting on," she struggled to say as she strained to reach his hand with her mouth.

She would achieve her goal and take the piece of cake from him. He'd won at their last meeting, and he would not win again. She stretched up one last time and trapped the cake with her lips, flicking her tongue out to lick the icing from the palm of his hand. That was the moment when he dropped her.

Her knees buckled and she landed on the floor in a heap of pale rose skirts. The pain in her backside was well worth it to see the stunned look in Holden's eyes. She was still laughing as she licked a bit of strawberry filling from her lip.

He knelt down beside her with slow movements. Before she knew what was happening, his hand was cupping her jaw. The laughter drained from her as she looked up into his face. Did he know now? Had her laughter given away her secret? Her lips parted to say something, although she didn't know what to say. Heat rose from her cheeks. He was too close to her, too close by far.

His thumb brushed across the corner of her mouth. "You missed a crumb." He grinned down at her.

"Oh."

"I should take you back to the ballroom before someone discovers us and gets the wrong impression."

"Yes, that would be horrible."

"I know." He lifted his voice to imitate either an old lady or a feminine troll of some sort to say, "When I found them they were in the floor eating piles of the Dillsworths' tea cakes. As if they were attending some type of scandalous picnic lunch. The outrage!"

"That actually sounds quite nice—the piles of cakes, I mean."

He pulled her to her feet and set her away from him. Grabbing one last cake from the table, he popped it in his mouth and nodded toward the door leading back to the ballroom.

"Miss Green?"

"Yes?" She laid her hand on his arm and allowed him to lead her from the room.

"If I'm not allowed to call on your friend, could you at least tell me what event she'll be attending next? I would greatly like to see her."

"She would like that, too," Sue replied with a

rueful frown, then added, "I would think. Suzanna will be at the Geddings' ball."

"Are you sure?"

"You have my word." Had she just given him her word that Suzanna would be at the Geddings' ball? What was she thinking? Suzanna couldn't attend a ball!

"Thank you, my lady—for the assistance and the refreshment." He gave a quick bow over her hand and was gone.

She stared after his retreating form. She really should avoid that man whenever possible. But somehow she didn't think that was going to be the easy task she had hoped it would be.

Seven

HOLDEN PUSHED THROUGH THE CROWD AND SLIPPED out the front door of the ball, his footfalls on the stone steps sounding like the drums of war to his ears. The chits had lied. "She'll be at the Dillsworth ball," he mocked into the hollow void of the night. He moved past the line of carriages to the section of iron fencing where his horse was tethered.

"They lied, Muley. The search continues, ol' boy." He gave his mount an affectionate pat on the cheek and took a step toward the stirrup. "But why did they lure me here if Suzanna wasn't to be in attendance?" He glanced back over his shoulder. Should he go back inside?

He could question them, ask them why they lied… or perhaps it had been an honest mix-up. Suzanna could be across town, ill with a cough, right now. He sighed and swung up onto his horse. At least he knew she would be at the Geddings' ball. She couldn't run from him forever.

As he gained speed down the quiet street toward home, he began to relax. With every gust against his face, the wind ripped away his agitation at not finding his quarry this evening. By the time he turned the corner to the mews behind his home, he felt quite calm.

In fact, the only thought left on his mind was the odd exchange he'd had with Miss Green. She had a familiar quality about her, as if they'd been friends for years, yet there was something else about her. There was a mysterious element that had caught his mind and wouldn't let go.

He couldn't quite put his finger on what about her he found troubling. She wasn't susceptible to his charm—that much was true. His eyes flared in the darkness, and he shook his head. Every lady found him endearing and jolly good company, every lady except for Miss Green. He neared the stable and dismounted from Muley, giving the horse a pat in farewell. Tossing the reins to the groom, Holden offered a quick nod of thanks before returning to the garden path to his home.

Miss Green, however, took issue with every statement he made. Irritating to say the least. The trouble was that in spite of these things, some part of him wanted to talk to her again.

She'd licked him. What type of lady behaved in such a manner? He traced the path her mouth had made across his hand with his thumb as he walked through the garden to his house. There'd been a moment on the floor of the refreshment room… He shook his head. The last thing he needed was another distraction; he was distracted enough as it was. And he was closing in on the source of that distraction— Suzanna. The Geddings' ball was only a few days away. Soon he would find her. He grinned into the night. Soon.

He retrieved a key from his pocket and let himself in, as he often did late at night so that his butler could earn some much-needed rest. Fezawald was dedicated to his work as leader of his staff. The maids all saw him as their grandfather, and so did Holden to some extent. Perhaps it was simply the man's age that had gained the household's consideration, or the fact that he always held the perfect piece of wisdom, pressed into neat folds, served with a side of tea, and presented readily on a polished silver platter.

Over the years on their travels together, they'd developed an understanding that Fezawald would go on to bed when Holden was out evenings. In turn, the butler would not allow the upstairs maids to begin their duties until Holden was well awake in the mornings.

He climbed the steps to the door, anxious to put his feet up for a few minutes, have a glass of brandy, and perhaps flip through a book before bed. With his mind on what book he should read, Holden swung the door open and stopped short at the threshold.

He blinked into the absolute darkness of his home. Tonight, Fezawald hadn't left the lamp burning. He'd never forgotten before.

Tossing his hat onto the table by the door, Holden dug into the small drawer in the front, feeling for one of the small pieces of wood used to light the candles. It took him three attempts of dipping the wood into the vial of acid in complete darkness to finally accomplish it. Once a flame was produced, he pulled a lamp from a sconce on the wall at his side, lighting the candle within the glass.

He sighed as a small circle of light fell on the polished wooden floor around him. He leaned his hip against the table for a moment, forcing his eyes into focus. He blinked up at the large hall around him, scanning his art collection on the walls. Everything was as it should be, except for the lack of candles left lit for him. Extending his arm before him, he lit the way through the pitch black.

When he reached the foot of the stairway where it wrapped around the back of the room, he glanced up. Not a single candle was lit on the stairs either.

Something was wrong.

Perhaps Fezawald had fallen ill. Did he need to send for a doctor? He was only a few paces beyond the stairs, on his way to the kitchen to see if any of the household was still awake, when he saw it. The flicker of light danced across the rug before him. His head snapped to the right. A fire was lit in the parlor grate. He stepped toward the doorway just as Fezawald was leaving, almost colliding with the tea tray in the butler's hands.

"Fezawald, I feared you were ill. Why is the house dark? Where are the candles?"

"I'm well, my lord, thank you for asking. However, I do need to speak with you about a matter of some urgency."

"All right, but can we have some light to discuss household matters?"

"That is but a small portion of what I must tell you, my lord. You see we…"

"Who the devil are you serving tea to in the dead of night?" Holden interrupted, eyeing the tea service in his butler's hands.

"Our company, my lord."

"What company?"

At Fezawald's hesitation, Holden pushed past the man, stepping into the parlor.

Her back was to him where she sat before his fireplace. Flames leapt around her silhouette, defining the small knot of hair on the very top of her head, dancing off her knitting needles, and showering the rest of the room in the shadows of her thin arms. Her loose gray dress hung on her shoulders and draped to the floor at her feet.

Turning back to Fezawald, Holden mouthed the words, "Who is she?"

His trusted butler and friend answered with a single raised brow, but Holden didn't need an answer to his question. He knew.

He only had a vague memory of her—her smile and the set of her eyes—as if he'd long ago memorized a portrait. But still, he knew who this woman was. The soft clicking of her knitting needles paused as she looked to the side of the room.

Holden tensed. Was she aware of his presence? He couldn't remember talking to her in the past, even though he was sure that at one point he had. He did know, however, that he wasn't prepared to do so now. But neither could he leave.

"You needn't linger by the door." Her voice rasped as if lack of use and age had scraped raw any softness that once existed. "The fire is warm. Come in." Her head dipped back to her knitting, the click, click, click of the needles beginning once again. "I'm pleased I found you. It wasn't easy with you not living in the family's home across town."

Holden cleared his throat and took a step into the room. "I've never lived at Pemberton House." He watched the firelight dance across the side of her face. There was so much she didn't know, so much he didn't know... "How did you travel here?"

"Carriage." A muscle in her cheek twitched as she spoke.

"And are you...well?"

"As well as can be expected, I suppose." She turned to look at him for the first time, her eyes the same dark green he recalled from his youth, but her skin had grown thin and her once-dark hair was now streaked with silver. "You've grown. You look like Monty the day I met him. He was so handsome." The memory must have turned sour in her mind, for she glared at him for a moment before turning her attention back to her knitting.

He turned back to Fezawald where he hovered by the door still holding the tea tray. In a whisper, he asked, "Is anyone looking for her?"

"Not that I'm aware, my lord. She arrived on foot a few hours ago in...quite a state. The maids drew her a bath, repaired her hair, and found the knitting for her. It seemed to calm her a bit. The conditions she must have come from..." Fezawald shook his head.

Holden nodded in understanding. Perhaps she wasn't of sane mind, but he couldn't send her back to a place that left her in this state. What had his father been thinking with such arrangements? Five and twenty years. He set the candle in his hand down and crossed the room, kneeling at her side. "You may stay here for a time. But I must ask that you stay within this home and the back garden."

"Anything for you, Holden. I knew you would care for me, just as I once did for you."

"Of course." He paused, the next word sticking to his tongue with a foreignness that made him take a small breath before it could be stated. "Mother."

❧

Suzanna will be at the Geddings' ball. You have my word. Sue rolled her eyes and shook her head, wishing she could walk backward into yesterday's ball, scoop up the words, and shove them back into her mouth. What *had* she been thinking? This was the problem with being so loquacious. Sometimes whole sentences flew from her mouth before she knew she was thinking them. Now, what was she to do? Suzanna couldn't very well show up in the middle of the Geddings' ballroom. And even worse than that minor issue, now she must see Holden again, perhaps even speak with him.

She looked down at the hat in her hands. The delicate peach flowers around the rim were now crushed on one side from her fretful grip. Her eyes widened. Tossing the hat back onto a display table, she turned and took a large step away from it. Thankfully, the shop owner was too busy fussing over her sister to notice the destruction of his merchandise. Dusting off her hands, Sue joined her family, but her mind

couldn't be further from the hats and ribbons surrounding her.

She'd had a plan last night, and she'd failed miserably
at her goal. She needed to find a husband, not spend
half the evening at the refreshment table chatting with
Holden. Had he almost kissed her there on the floor
of the refreshment parlor, or had she imagined that?
Not that she cared, because she most certainly didn't.
Drat that blasted man, she needed to focus on finding
a husband. And her quest would begin anew right
now...for the second time.

"We'll take the yellow as well," her mother stated
as she handed a hat that looked somewhat like a large
yellow bird back to the man in the apron.

Evangeline glanced up from her study of a simple
dove gray bonnet that was, ironically, in a style she
would never wear. "I already have a yellow hat, Mama."

"Not one trimmed with feathers. Really, Evangeline,
you can't have too many hats. You never know what
occasion might arise that would call for a yellow hat
with feathers."

"I suppose." She set the gray hat down on a table
and ran a finger over the rim before stepping away.

"Mother, isn't this green hat nice?"

"That's ghastly, Sue. Put that down at once. You
have plenty of hats."

Sue raised the green hat in her hand for closer
inspection. It was bright, but she wouldn't call it
ghastly. "I thought it was different."

"That it is, dear," her mother stated with an
upturned nose as she turned back to the shop owner.
"Have this sent to our home."

"Yes, m'lady."

"I'm Lady Rightworth of Rightworth House." Oh dear. Now, as usual, Mother would take a moment to inform a perfect stranger of Father's title, their land holdings, and her resulting rank in society. Sue tossed the hat down on the table and moved toward the door.

"Yes, m'lady."

"That's in Mayfair," she added.

"Yes, m'lady."

"We're neighbors of the Marquess of Elandor, you know."

"Yes, m'lady."

"Very well, then. As long as you know. Come along, girls."

Sue rolled her eyes toward the plaster ceiling and pulled the door open. Stepping out into the warm afternoon sun after her family, she breathed in the fresh air. It wasn't as sweet as the air in the country, but it was better than the inside of any shop on Bond Street. They were passing a window displaying an assortment of jewelry when her mother bellowed from her side, making Sue jump.

"Lord Steelings! Lord Steelings, is that you?" Her mother flung a hand up into the air and began waving as she dipped through the crowd.

Sue froze. She wasn't prepared to see him. Not now. Not yet. She'd only just renewed her efforts to find a husband. He was a distraction. A handsome distraction, but that only served to make him a more annoying distraction.

He slowed his pace, and with a sigh visible from the

shrug of his shoulders, he turned. "Lady Rightworth, I believe." He offered a nod of his head and a smile that didn't quite reach his eyes. His eyes…he looked troubled. Or was that weariness from the late night at the ball?

"Lord Steelings, it's so nice to run into you this afternoon."

It seemed more like chasing him down the street than a chance meeting to Sue. She had to look away to keep from giggling at the image now planted in her mind of her mother diving on passing gentlemen and pulling them to the ground in an effort to find a suitor for Evangeline.

"Yes, it's a fine afternoon for shopping."

"Quite right, my lord. Although it is rather warm. We were just going to get ices. Won't you escort us? You must be warm in all this sunlight as well."

"I rather enjoy the sunshine. I'm out for a stroll, actually."

"Then you can certainly use some refreshment after your exertion."

"Actually, I…" He looked around, clearly searching for some excuse to be away from them, but his gaze returned with a sigh. "I would enjoy your company for ices."

"Oh, wonderful! This is my daughter, Miss Evangeline Green. It's her company you would enjoy most, I'm sure. Come, Evangeline. Lord Steelings wants to take you for ices."

"I don't think that's what he had in mind, Mama." Evangeline's blush lit her cheekbones as if brushed on by an artist.

"Oh, Evangeline, always so modest! Isn't she a lovely lady, my lord?"

"Mama!"

"What? Lord Steelings knows a thing of beauty when he sees it, dear. Don't you, my lord?"

Holden cleared his throat, covering his mouth with his fist for a moment. Was that a smile he was hiding? "I would greatly enjoy all of your company for ices. Why deny myself the pleasure of conversation with more lovely ladies than one this afternoon?"

"Oh, my lord, you do flatter, you rogue."

"I have to keep the society matrons on my side, now don't I?"

Her mother tittered with glee as they made their way down Bond Street toward the carriage. When they reached the conveyance, Lady Rightworth asked, "My lord, have you left your carriage in this area as well?"

"I arrived on foot."

For a moment, Lady Rightworth looked as if he'd grown two heads but she quickly recovered with a smile that said she'd just been given a large stash of candies. "Why don't you ride with us, Lord Steelings?"

"Only if your driver doesn't mind the company. I find I like the fresh air this afternoon."

"Oh, yes…fresh air is quite healing to the spirit, isn't it?"

Sue glanced at her mother in disbelief. She'd never heard her utter such a phrase. This was the same woman who refused to leave the house when there was a chance of rain and complained of bugs at a picnic. She must really want Evangeline to marry

Holden. Sue's throat tightened at the thought of him as family—always around and looking handsome. Of course, she would be either shipped away to Scotland or, with any luck, married by then.

He handed them up into the carriage and swung up to sit beside the driver. It struck her as peculiar that he was a titled lord and yet he chose to ride with the driver. It was a fine day, but she'd never seen a lord riding alongside a carriage driver—ever. Was that truly his reasoning, or did he not want to spend even a second longer than necessary in her company? If that was the case, the feeling was mutual.

Sue wasn't the wagering sort but if she had to bet on his reason for sitting with the driver, it wouldn't be in favor of a sunny afternoon. She stewed over his avoidance of her for the entire trip through the busy streets, while Evangeline and her mother discussed hats and how Lord Steelings must be faring in the elements of nature. By the time they reached Gunter's Tea Shop at Berkeley Square, she'd come to two conclusions: one, she hated hats, and two, she wished it would rain on his head.

Her mother and Evangeline emerged from the carriage like birds rising from a field, a gentle breeze tugging at their artfully arranged hats and making their dresses billow behind them. Sue was pleased she didn't trip and fall into a mud puddle. She tried not to think about Holden's hand wrapped around hers as he guided her to the ground. She tried, but she was unsuccessful. Dratted man.

By the time they sat around the stone table in the park across from the tea shop, she was sending him silent curses encased in pleasant smiles. *Blast his golden hair. Blast his smooth talk and charm. Blast his swoon-worthy green eyes. Blast it all.* She needed sweets or she would surely not survive this afternoon.

Therefore, when the tea room's staff approached them, Sue and Holden both opened their mouths to speak. "I'll have the elderflower…" They broke off, looking at one another. *And blast his taste in sweets.*

Holden glanced up at the waiter. "It appears the lady and I will have elderflower ices."

"With an extra bit of honey on top of mine," Sue added.

Her mother made a tsking sound from across the table. "How you can stand such sweetness I will never understand, Sue. Positively disgusting. Extra honey, indeed."

Holden shot Lady Rightworth a daring look and said, "Extra honey on mine as well. Thank you."

Her mother coughed into her handkerchief and muttered, "We'll both have vanilla in the shape of roses."

"Yes, m'lady," the man said as he left.

"Lord Steelings, your aunt tells me you have an interest in antiquities. We have quite the collection at our home. You'll have to come and take a look one day."

"Yes." He looked away in the direction of the tea shop. He appeared to be attempting to will their ices to arrive quickly so he might leave. He sighed and turned back to her mother. "I do enjoy collections of interesting items. I've been focused on my art gallery of late."

Evangeline leaned forward to join the conversation. "Oh? Did you know Sue is interested in art as well?"

"Evangeline, he doesn't want to hear about your sister's little drawings. I'm sure he wants to hear more about your interests. Don't you, Lord Steelings?"

They broke off their conversation when the ices arrived. It was an awkward moment of "Oh, thank you," and "How nice." The silence extended while they each took a bite.

Evangeline finally set her spoon on the rim of her saucer and looked up at their mother before saying, "Mama, the vanilla was an excellent choice, not too sweet at all…ooooooh!"

Sue watched as honey-covered ice splattered across Evangeline's shoulder.

"Sue Green! How could you? All over your sister's dress? We'll be back at once, my lord." With a final glaring look at Sue, her mother dragged Evangeline into Gunter's to repair her dress.

How had that happened? One minute she'd been delving into her saucer of ice and the next… She shook her head. "I didn't mean to do that. In fact, I'm not entirely sure how I managed it." Sue stared at the spoon in her hand as if it held the answers. She wiggled it between her fingers. Perhaps she'd flicked her wrist at just the wrong moment.

Then she heard it, the rumble of suppressed laughter from the opposite side of the stone table. When she glanced up, Holden's eyes were crinkled at the corners with merriment, and he was leaning back in his seat. Soon, he wasn't able to contain his amusement and released a shower of hearty laughs that seemed to shake the maple tree above them.

She stared at him, unable to believe his nerve. "You did that?"

"As if you didn't want to."

Poor Evangeline. This was perhaps the first time that thought had ever crossed her mind, yet she did feel sorry for her sister with a large stain on her day dress. Mother was most likely in need of smelling salts by now from the tragedy of it all. Sue grinned, unable to help herself. "That's neither here nor there," she countered without conviction.

"Ah, but your matchmaking mother and sister are neither here nor there as well now, so I can enjoy my afternoon in peace." He took a large bite of his elderflower ice around a grin.

Sue shifted on the stone bench. "Do you wish me to leave as well?"

"Are you going to attempt to marry me?"

Sue almost choked on the ice in her mouth. She'd once considered it, but now… "No." She hurled the word from her lips. Had she said "no" too quickly? Would he know of her past thoughts on the subject?

"Then you may stay." His voice held an air of flippant disregard.

He hadn't noticed, and somehow that grated on her even more than if he had. Half of her wanted him to realize who she was, and the other half wanted to run away from him as far as she could go.

"How generous of you," she returned, her jaw tightening around the cold bite of ice in her mouth.

"I'm nothing if not a gentleman."

"And an art collector," Sue mused, trying to put the puzzle pieces together in some logical order that would assemble this man.

She watched him scrape all of the honey from his saucer and take a large bite of it, his eyes softening with the enjoyment of the sweet taste. He swallowed, the muscles in his tan throat just visible above his cravat. "I gather you have an interest in art as well?"

She ripped her eyes from his throat and looked into his green eyes, which was a mistake since now she couldn't look away. He was asking her something. What was it? Oh, art—that was it. She pulled her thoughts together enough to mutter, "You could say that."

He froze, his eyes narrowed on her. "I could."

Silence fell between them for a moment. What was he thinking? Had she said something wrong? She took a shallow breath, waiting. He finally shook his head, tossing his golden hair in the sunshine, and laid his spoon down.

The tension seemed to ease, yet she needed to fill the void between them. It was too quiet with only a bird's distant tweeting to punctuate the silence. "I paint a bit…and sketch. Mostly landscapes…

"I like to capture the unexpected, to hold something wild in the palm of my hand." She held out her hand, looking into it as if some great treasure could be found there. Dropping her fist back to her lap, she smiled up at him. "Do you know what I mean? You probably believe me to be crazy. However, I see the greatest beauty in…"

She glanced around for an example of nature and waved one hand toward a tree branch hanging low beside them. "That leaf falling from the tree, caught on the wind, experiencing the last of its life in pure freedom. That's far lovelier than any jewel or any gown found within a ballroom."

"Where do you paint while in London? The park I suppose, since you prefer natural settings." He rested his forearm on the table, watching his spoon as he twirled it between his fingers, spinning it on the saucer.

"Oh. I'm…" Her eyes landed on the hand lying idle in her lap. "I'm actually not allowed to paint or draw while in town." She raised her chin with a slight huff. "Someone might see me with paint on my arms, and then the family would be the topic of the latest on-dit."

He looked up at her with a smirk, his blond hair falling into his face. "The horror."

"Yes, I can see the headlines now… 'Miss G. may have an untarnished image since she remains in a chair against the wall in every ballroom, but her arms are certainly marred—with red!'"

"Red?" He quirked a golden brow in her direction.

"Yes, it's much more dramatic that way because it could be blood. They do have to sell copies of the papers, you know."

"Ah, I see. So, you're either an artist or a murderer. London society may never know the truth." The corners of his mouth lifted in amusement.

"Not until they buy another edition and find out."

"Who made this clearly logical yet inconvenient rule about painting in town?"

"Who else? My mother."

"Ah, yes, she does seem to rule with an iron fist. It's a common issue with mothers."

"What of your mother? Does she rule your family?"

Something passed across his face for a moment and then it was gone. Regret? Uncertainty? Dread? He looked away, and when his gaze returned to her, his eyes were shuttered and his smile fixed. "My mother passed away many years ago."

"Oh. My lord, I'm terribly sorry to have asked… How inconsiderate of me."

"Never mind that. It was long ago. My mourning has been over for some time." He stabbed at his ice in a manner that indicated he still held on to some anger on the subject.

She watched him for a moment, wondering. How old had he been when his mother passed away? Had he cried? She couldn't imagine a man like the one sitting across from her ever crying over anything. He was far too self-assured and jovial for that. Perhaps if she asked more, he would tell her about it. "My mother says your father stays in the country. Do you ever see him?"

"No…I…" He looked at her, his distress on the subject visible as he spoke. "Can we not discuss… Miss Green, your ice is about to drip down your…"

"Ahhh!" A freezing cold spoonful of elderflower ice hit her skin just above the lace trim at the neck of her dress. She leaned forward and reached for it with fumbling gloved fingers. Too late. The sticky bit of ice slid between her breasts to land in her stays. "Haaa. That's rather cold."

"Mmm-hmm, ice is known for its coldness above all other qualities. It's quite slippery as well. It also melts on warm skin."

When she looked up at his teasing statement, she

saw his eyes were locked on her bosom. Glancing down to see what held his attention, she realized she was leaning forward with a drip of honey disappearing into her dress. Her breasts were practically displayed for him, and she was now frozen in this position, leaning over him. "I apologize, my lord."

"Holden."

"Pardon?"

His eyes swept up her neck and met her gaze. Green. So very green. He blinked. "You may call me Holden."

Her lips moved but no sound came out. Holden. She'd said it before. But now…it hurt too much to say it again after what had passed between them and then been stripped away. She clamped her lips closed. She wouldn't say it, even if she did have his leave to do so. Not today. Perhaps not ever. How often would she be alone with him after all? This would never happen again. It truly didn't matter, if she viewed it in that light. He was still looking at her. Was he waiting for her to say his name? Because she wouldn't. "Sue," she heard herself say.

"Is that short for anything?"

"No." She sat back down on the stone seat. "Just Sue, unfortunately."

"Well, Sue, it's been nice chatting with you. However, your sister and mother are returning, and I feel the parson's noose tightening around my neck with their every step. So, if you will excuse me, I will be on my way now."

"Thank you for the pleasant company as well. I enjoyed the ice, all except for the bite that went down my dress."

"Really? That part of our time together was my

favorite." He was still laughing as he walked away, disappearing into the maple trees.

The moment her mother reached the table, her glare descended on Sue like an angry cat denied a meal of fresh mouse. "What did you say to make him flee, Sue?"

"I didn't say anything." The smile slipped from her face as Holden drew farther and farther away.

"You sat in silence? No wonder he left so quickly."

"I said things. We discussed art and…our mothers."

"You brought up his mother in the conversation? You can't bring up the dead in conversation, Sue."

"She's been dead for some time. He didn't seem distraught."

"Of course she's been dead for some time. Everyone knows that. But you ought not to mention the dead over sweets. Everyone knows that as well. Or I thought they did."

"Clearly, I didn't."

"Clearly. Well, our ice has melted now. Lord Steelings has fled your company, and it is completely your fault. Let us return to our shopping, girls. Evangeline is now in the market for a new day dress."

"Yes, ma'am," Evangeline said, moving toward the carriage.

"Sue, do keep up."

"But it's just a bit of ice. Surely it can be cleaned." Sue rubbed at the sticky spot on her skin where her own ice had slipped into her stays.

"A marred appearance lasts a lifetime."

Marred for life—Sue supposed that summed it up. With a sigh she moved to follow her mother back to the carriage.

Eight

"AND THEN YOU SAID, 'HOW DO YOU GET YOUR HAIR to stay that way?' Mother, as many times as I've heard this story, I can't help but feel some pity for the insect that got involved with poor Lady Dafterly. He never asked for such treatment. I think the real story lies with the plight of the poor bug and not with Lady Dafterly's coiffure."

"Which is precisely why you will not marry, dear. No one wants to hear your opinions or your thoughts in any capacity. Look at your sister. See how she smiles at the gentleman with whom she dances. Oh, now she is giggling at some jest he made as they glide in unison around the dance floor. Is she picking apart everything he says for discussion?"

"It doesn't appear so." Sue watched as her sister made another turn around the Geddings' ballroom.

"Is she forming opinions and stating them for all to hear?"

"No. But then is Evangeline able to form her own thoughts beyond which ribbon would accentuate her hair?" She knew once the words were out of her mouth that she'd gone too far. But once again she'd spoken before she thought. She truly needed to work on this issue.

"Sue Green, you should count yourself lucky we are in a crowded ballroom—a ball I have graciously allowed you to attend."

"I do, Mother." Her jaw tightened at the reminder of her ever-nearing future. "Very lucky indeed. Yes, I'm quite fortunate this season. Please excuse me while I go find someone to marry." There was plenty more she could say, but it wouldn't be wise. For once, she needed to keep her mouth closed. Perhaps that was the way to deal with talking too much—simply walk away when tempted to speak.

She heard her mother's exhalation of air as she wound through the crowd. Was it possible to get lost at a ball and never be heard from again? She was busy smiling at the thought of her mother having to act as if she cared her elder daughter had gone missing because the *ton* was watching. It was an amusing dream, until she walked into something hard. Taking a step backward and rubbing her forehead, she looked up into Holden's face.

Of course it would be him. Arrogance wrapped in evening finery shouldn't have blended in so well that she struck her forehead on it. And now that she was looking, his eyes seemed to sparkle at her. But those eyes sparkled at all ladies, so she wasn't special. That moment at the Dillsworth ball had been in her imagination, and the ices yesterday…well, that was nothing.

"Lord Steelings, how…nice it is to see you this evening."

"Are you all right?" He lifted a hand to steady her but it fell back to his side as she stepped beyond his reach.

"Yes. Pardon me, my lord. I wasn't looking where I was going." Certainly not, for she'd walked into the very man she hoped to avoid this evening. She needed to search for an undesirable gentleman to marry, not waste her time chatting with Lord Lady Charmer.

He leaned over her and in a soft voice said, "I thought we decided to be done with the lordly greetings, Sue."

"Yes, I suppose we did. Forgive me. My mother has me a bit flustered this evening. In fact, I should go see to…" She tried to slip past him but he turned with her, continuing their conversation as they walked.

"Oh? How did she manage to upset you? You haven't been painting things red, have you?"

"No, it's not as scandalous as that. Only the constant reminder of impending doom at season's end, a lady's worst night terror realized, and a last-minute ball-gown change because I was wearing the same color my sister. Nothing to worry about, really."

"I'm not sure how to help with the impending doom. However, I could take your mind off things with a dance. Assist you in living life a little?"

She shouldn't want to dance with him and yet she did. "I would like that, but…"

"And you can assist me in locating Suzanna. She is here, isn't she?"

"Of course she is." Sue tamped down the hysterical laughter brewing inside her at his question, along with the disappointment of knowing he truly only wanted information, not to dance with her.

"Do you know what color gown she's wearing?"

"I can't recall." She needed to get away. Glancing to the side, she searched for an excuse to escape his questions. There was no help there as she only saw a group of giggling ladies watching Holden. Did ladies follow him everywhere he went? He probably enjoyed it. Rogue. She rolled her eyes.

"Where did you last see her?" he asked, craning his neck around and spying the group of ladies. He smiled and nodded in their direction before turning back to Sue.

He was beyond annoying. There he was, grinning over other women and asking about someone he thought to be another lady entirely, all while talking with her. She was truly last on a long list of ladies who had come before her, and the list would go on well after her. She was a number. And to think she'd enjoyed his company over ices! She needed to remember his true nature. Her lips twisted with agitation as she answered, "I saw her when I first arrived."

"Did she say where she could be found?"

"No. We…didn't have time to speak." When would he lose interest in Suzanna and move on to some other conquest? There certainly seemed to be plenty he could choose from.

"Very well. About that dance…"

"Will you excuse me for a moment? I need to go… speak with someone."

"The next country dance is ours. Until then." He bowed over her hand.

An entire dance where she would be asked questions about Suzanna in rapid succession, all while allowing Holden's hands on her? She'd looked into his despicable green eyes and said yes. "I am such a blasted idiot," she mumbled, turning away. "Stupid, stupid, stupid." Well, if he couldn't find her come time for the country dance, then he would have to move on to torment some other poor lady and Sue could get back to finding a husband.

She'd spied a gentleman earlier who barely fit in a single chair in the corner, and another in the main hall who seemed to perspire profusely at all times. Both were excellent candidates for a husband. Unlike Mr. Country Dance with the eyes, who was only looking for a night's amusement and taking up far too much of her time. His moments of friendly chat were only carefully crafted attempts to find Suzanna. She needed to not think about him, for she had husband-hunting work to do.

The music changed and she jumped, diving behind a large tiled planter containing a tree. Was it a country dance? She sighed at the sound of a waltz and stood from her crouched position. She plucked a leaf from the tree's canopy and peered out to make sure she was alone. From her concealed location she studied the room, scanning for unfortunate-looking lords. However, there didn't seem to be that many gentle-men around at the moment. Even the perspiring man seemed to have vanished.

She dropped the crumpled bits of leaf in her hand and started toward the refreshment table. If she was going to find a husband tonight, she was going to need something to drink, and if they had the strawberries covered in chocolate this year like they did last year, she was certainly going to need one of those. She caught a glimpse of Holden across the room laughing with yet another lady. Make that two chocolate-covered strawberries.

Skirting the edge of the dance floor, she was almost past the crush of people near the door when she spotted Lillian. "Lillian, I am so happy you've arrived. I thought I would have to chat with my mother all evening. You know I do love chats with my mother." Her words dripped with sarcasm. "But at a ball, who wants to endure that humiliation? Not I." Sue beamed as she grabbed Lillian's gloved hand, dragging her across the floor toward the refreshment table.

"I am always pleased to be of assistance. May I ask where we're going?" Lillian called out as Sue pulled her across the floor.

"I spotted Lord Steelings entering the ballroom"—more like she'd banged her head on him, but Lillian didn't need to know the details—"so we are leaving it. Shall we escape to the terrace or the hallway or perhaps the ladies' retiring room? Yes, that will be just the place. Don't you think so? He couldn't possibly find us there. Can you imagine the look on the ladies' faces if a gentleman entered the ladies' retiring room?"

"Or we could slip into this parlor." Lillian gestured to the doorway they were passing with a long-limbed wave of her arm.

Perfect! He would never find her here. Come time for that dance, he would be wandering around the ball alone. And she would be here, sipping lemonade with ladies at least three times her age. She smiled at the brilliance of the scheme.

"Why don't you wish to see Lord Steelings?"

"His incessant questions, his annoying sense of humor, his looks…" Sue ticked off reasons on her fingers as they entered a side parlor and passed several prominent matrons, all of whom eyed them as if they'd stepped onstage for a performance.

"Does he have a poor sense of humor?" Lillian asked, her brows drawn together as she tried to understand.

"No, but that has nothing to do with it."

"Oh." Lillian fell silent, which was just as well because the last thing Sue wished to discuss was Lord Steelings.

They found two seats against the far wall and sat down, trying to blend in with the ocean of graying hair and elaborate gowns. It had always struck Sue as odd that the older a lady became within the *ton*, the more jewels and plumes of feathers she was expected to wear. Her eyes landed on a frail woman in the corner with a back that seemed to round over, leaving her head much lower than it had once been, Sue was sure. "It's most likely from the weight of her necklace. A shame, that."

"What's a shame?" asked the tall, thin woman beside her.

"Oh. I wasn't aware I spoke aloud."

"Not to worry, dear. I can hear voices that most cannot."

"That's an interesting ability." Sue turned to regard the lady sitting beside her. Her gray hair was tied up in a tight knot on the very top of her head that pulled at the corners of her green eyes. There was something familiar about her face. Had they met before? At some past season's ball, perhaps?

"Unfortunately it stems from living in a madhouse for five and twenty years."

Sue tilted her head in thought. What an original sense of comedy this lady possessed. A madhouse indeed. She smiled. "I'm terribly sorry to hear it. Sometimes I feel as if I live in a madhouse as well."

"It's quite all right. I escaped it to go visit my son. And now here I am chatting with you."

"Visiting family can be a nice retreat from daily life. I spent the past month in the company of my cousins and it was wonderful. Granted, my immediate family was in attendance as well, but nothing can be perfect." Sue chuckled.

"Is that who you're escaping this evening? Your family?"

"No, not at the moment. There is this gentleman…"

"There always is. All ladies of your age are concerned with finding a husband." The older woman's face twisted at some bitter thought on the subject. And when she referred to her home as a madhouse, Sue couldn't blame her.

"I do hope to find happiness one day in marriage." Sue glanced down at her hands lying in her lap. That fate didn't seem likely, but she would never give up on the dream of a husband.

"I'm sure you will, dear. And when you do, keep a wary eye. One day you'll believe yourself to be in love, and the next he will betray you. The only true love you'll have in your life will be your children. Protect them at all costs."

"I'll keep that in mind, my lady."

"It's Henrietta, and I only say this from the experience of life."

"Thank you for the wisdom, Henrietta. I'm Sue Green."

"A pleasure, Sue. Just remember, never trust your future husband. And your household staff will be of no assistance. Be rid of them, I say. And hold your children close. Live by those rules and things will work out fine."

"Well, that is…interesting advice. I'll remember that."

"See that you do." The older woman went back to sipping her lemonade.

What an odd lady. Sue turned in her chair to focus her attention on Lillian, only to see Lord Steelings striding into the room. He looked concerned. And he was looking in her direction. Had she missed their dance already? Did a missed dance really have the ability to worry him so? But as soon as she noticed the fierce look in his eyes, it was gone, replaced by a smile. Although she didn't quite trust that smile.

His gaze swept to the side, landing on Henrietta. "My lady, you look overtired. You must allow me to escort you to your carriage."

Sue gasped. What was Holden doing? Telling a lady she looked tired was never a good idea. She wasn't sure why, but she was quite sure it shouldn't be done.

"I'm quite fine, thank you," Henrietta stated with a raised chin.

"I disagree." He stared at her, waiting for her response.

Did they know one another? Sue's eyes narrowed on Holden. This entire encounter was odd, to say the least.

Henrietta settled deeper into her chair in defiance of the arrogant man. "I will remain here for a time. Thank you, however, for your concern."

Holden's jaw ground on a retort for a moment before he glanced around the room and sighed. Turning his attention to Sue, he bowed and offered a nod of his head in Lillian's direction as well. "We meet again, Miss Green."

Sue shot a quick glance at Henrietta. Whatever had happened only a minute ago seemed to be forgotten by all—except for her. She watched Holden as he attempted a casual stance before her but failed miserably, a muscle in his cheek still twitching in agitation. "Is it time for our dance already?" she asked.

"Soon." His response sounded more like a threat than a promise.

What about their situation, or more specifically the woman at her side, had him so out of sorts? Sue wasn't foolish enough to believe his irritation had anything to do with missing a country dance. She was studying his expression for clues when she heard a voice ring out from beside Lillian.

A well-dressed and bejeweled lady at Lillian's side stated, "Lord Steelings, do not act as if you do not see me here simply because I am with these two eye-catching young ladies. You are not too old for me to take in hand, you know."

"Your Grace," he offered with an elegant bow. "I would not dream of cutting you in such a manner. I was only temporarily distracted by your company this evening. I do hope my knuckles will stay intact."

"As long as you stay out of my tea biscuits, your fingers are safe."

"Ladies, the Duchess of Thornwood is known for rapping knuckles if you put one toe out of line. Do beware, especially if you think to sneak and eat her sweets." He laughed, his eyes crinkling at the edges, all of his ire from moments ago lost with the action. "Or is the rapping of knuckles reserved only for mischievous boys of ten years of age?"

"Dear boy, I have not seen you nearly often enough in recent years," she admonished. "You must come around for a visit now that I am in town. Have you seen my son this evening? He claimed to be attending, which I found most interesting."

"I have not. I haven't seen Thornwood in a few days. He said he would attend this evening? That is curious."

This woman was the Mad Duke of Thornwood's mother? She seemed quite sane, unlike the lady at her other side. Sue gave a mental shrug. You never could tell what was going on under the surface with members of the *ton*. She supposed that was why everyone was so content to discuss the weather and current fashions; it allowed for more secrets to lie dormant. Unfortunately, Sue didn't have the ability to discuss damp English weather for hours on end, lest she fall asleep.

"Indeed." The duchess shot a look at Lillian. "Dear, you are looking a bit pink. You are not overheated in this warm room, are you?"

"No, Your Grace. I am quite all right. Although perhaps some air would do me good. If you will excuse me." Lillian stood to leave. "Sue, I'm going to the terrace. Would you like to come with me?"

She did look flushed. Lillian had danced with this lady's mad son at the last ball. Perhaps she was fretful over being associated with him. Sue could understand her friend's hesitation. She was about to agree to leave with her when she was interrupted.

"I was coming to collect Miss Green for our dance." Holden held his arm out for her, not allowing any argument.

"Go ahead, Lillian. I'll catch up with you later." Sue watched Lillian leave before standing to join Holden. "It was nice chatting with you," Sue offered to Henrietta as she laid her hand on Holden's arm. She felt his arm tense under her touch. Glancing up at him, she saw what looked like concern filling his eyes.

When they were away from the parlor, he stopped and spun to look down at her. "You chatted with that woman?"

"The one you insulted for no reason? Yes, we spoke."

His jaw clenched and he glanced away for a moment before looking back at her. "What did you speak of?"

"How is that any business of yours?"

"It isn't. What did you speak of?"

Why did he care? And furthermore why should she defend her conversational actions to him? The over-bearing… "I was under the impression you were supposed to play the handsome and charming rake. Well, you are most certainly not charming, in case you were wondering. And I don't desire a dance with you."

He drew back in surprise. "I wasn't wondering, but why do you say that?"

Was he truly so unaware of his actions? "Because you…"—she huffed in anger before continuing—"you, my lord, are dense as well as blind. I would rather be hit over the head with flatware than dance with you."

"Flatware?"

"Yes, forks and such. You do know the definition of flatware."

"Yes." He was grinning now. Grinning! Oh, the infuriating man, grinning when she was trying to insult him. "Pardon me, I'm only wondering why you would want to be showered with forks and spoons to begin with."

"Because plates are heavy. And as much as I do not wish to dance with you, I don't want to die for the decision."

"Why not pillows, then?"

"Well, yes. In hindsight, pillows would be the best option. I'd like to pound you with a pillow or two." She clamped her jaw closed. How had this conversation gone so wrong? Spoons and pillows? She cleared her throat and looked away for a second before turning back toward him. "What were we discussing again?"

"I believe you just challenged me to a pillow fight." He began to laugh in deep rumbles that vibrated the tension from her bones.

"Blast it all. If my mother thought dead relatives were improper, I hate to know what she would think now."

He laughed harder and shook his head. "I have

no idea what you're talking about, but I admit I find it amusing."

"You would," she grumbled through a smile.

"You realize we've missed the dance I collected you for."

"Did we?" *Good!* She gave a small satisfied nod of her head.

"We're making somewhat of a habit of this. One day I will dance with you, Sue Green."

"You, my lord, assume too much. I have no desire to dance with you." There. She'd said it. She was strong. She had a plan, and it did not involve dancing with Holden.

"I thought you were jesting. I've never been turned down by a lady before." He ran a hand over his chin in thought. "I suppose I didn't think it possible."

"Other ladies find you charming."

"But you don't. I believe we've established that fact. Why, then, are you standing here talking to me? You could have left before now if you dislike me so."

Sue opened her mouth to offer some retort, but no words came to mind. Why was she here talking to him? This was the very thing she'd sworn not to do. And she thought herself strong. She wasn't strong at all. She should be husband hunting. Instead she was in a shadowed corner of the ballroom, laughing with the one man she should be avoiding. "I'll take my leave now."

He looked as if he might say something, then fell silent watching her for a moment with narrowed eyes. The moment stretched on between them, neither quite sure what to say or how to walk away. When he finally spoke, it was with slow deliberate words. "I should take you back to your family."

"I can find my own way."

"I'm sure you can."

Sue offered him a fleeting smile, turned, and sped as fast as her feet would move into the crowded ballroom.

⁂

This was silly. He was no stranger to shadowed corners of terraces and had experienced more garden benches than he'd like to admit, but waiting alone in a library for a lady he hadn't even seen this evening? There wasn't anyone at this ball that neared his memory of Suzanna.

Only a handful had her lack of height, and of those, only Sue came close to her coloring. But Sue could never be the brazen seductress Suzanna had been. A bark of laughter came from his throat at the thought. That simply couldn't be. The fact was, Suzanna wasn't in attendance tonight.

Yet here he stood.

He shook his head and looked down at the note in his hand once again. He shouldn't have trusted the Fairlyn twins again.

Come and find me. I'll be in the library during the supper hour, cloaked in darkness and alone. —Suzanna

P.S. No candles allowed.

The last line was in a different hand, and neither was written in the sweeping penmanship he would have imagined for Suzanna. Of course, how would he know about her penmanship? He rolled his eyes at his sick desperation over this lady and blew out the candle at his side with one quick puff of air. This was a bad idea.

He should leave.

He was reaching for the door when it opened. Light from the hallway spilled into the dark room, silhouetting her ample curves and nipped-in waist. His breath caught for a second. Her face was in shadow but her hair shown in the lamplight at her back like it was made of fallen stars. He'd finally found her.

"Isabelle? Are you in here?" she asked into the quiet library as she took a step forward, releasing the doorknob. "Victoria said you…"

"Suzanna," his voice came out in a rough whisper. He was close enough to hear her intake of breath, and it sent a ripple of awareness through his body.

She stepped to the side, away from him but also away from the door. "You're not Isabelle."

"Not last I checked." He kicked the door closed with his toe and took a step in her direction. He wasn't going to lose her again. There would be no escaping him this time.

"Is she here with you?" She took another step away from him, backing toward a wall of books.

He had to mentally shake himself to keep track of what she was asking. Was who here with him? He had no idea, but he did know they were alone. "No, but you are."

"You'll have to excuse me." She tried to move past him but he blocked her path.

"Not a chance." He stalked closer to her, a grin tugging at his mouth as he watched her take another step back away from him, her silhouette moving in the darkness. She thought she could slip away again? Not likely.

"I have to go see to Isabelle. I got a message she was ill in the library and in need of my assistance. If she isn't here…" Her head turned toward the closed door.

"I believe your friend is quite well. I was lured here with a note as well. Only my note is true." He crumpled the note held tight in his hand with a victorious grasp before dropping it into his pocket.

She bumped into the arm of a chair and scurried around it. Clearly, she thought a leather chair would stop him. She was wrong. "What did this note say?"

"That I might find you here." He stepped around the chair in one swift move, drawing nearer to her with every breath.

"Oh."

"Suzanna, why did you leave? Wait." He threw up a hand. "Don't answer that. I don't want to know. I only care that you're here now."

"I shouldn't be," she muttered, her face tilted down level with his cravat.

"I've heard Lord Geddings is almost as proud of his book collection as he is his hunting trophies. So many hard edges…" He heard her back hit the bookshelf with a little thud. "Not like you. Soft. Beautiful," he finished in a whisper to himself, but he knew she heard him.

He closed the final gap between them, leaning one hand on the shelf above her head. The leather-bound volumes shifted under his fingers as he moved over her. She was so close. Her hair smelled like sweets stolen from the kitchen. He inhaled, but her scent wasn't enough of her. He needed to touch her, but he waited so as not to frighten her away—not this time.

"I shouldn't…" she began, but the words became lost, clinging to her lips, full lips he wanted to trap beneath his.

"Nor should I. Yet here we are, together." He found the lace trim at the shoulder of her gown and twitched it between his fingers.

"Indeed."

Leaning in farther above her, he followed the line of lace with the backs of his knuckles where it met her skin. Up over the slight bump of her collarbone and across her shoulder, he drew a line to her neck. "I've longed to touch you ever since that night."

She swallowed and took a ragged breath. "Truly?" The word was only half spoken.

"You had a doubt in your mind?" His fingers drifted up the column of her neck, lifting her chin. She was finally within his grasp. Her soft skin burned under his touch. The shadow of her lips parted as she looked up into his face.

Darkness shrouded them but he could still see the outline of her mouth, soft and calling to him. "I thought…"

"And now here you are." His hand traced the line of her jaw, drawing a shaken breath from her as his fingers slipped up to frame her face.

"Yes," she whispered.

They fell silent for a moment, locked together in the promise of something—a kiss? Perhaps more. The darkness didn't matter anymore for she was here with him.

When he couldn't wait any longer and met her lips, she whimpered and wrapped her arms around him. She pulled him in with her strawberry-flavored mouth and her small hands on his back. He couldn't get close enough to her. With a groan he ripped his lips from hers to wrap his hands about her waist, lifting her and pinning her against the stacks of leather-bound volumes. Her hands snaked around his neck as one of the books from the shelf fell to the floor with a thud.

Her fingers delved into his hair just as he began to plunder her mouth. Her sweet mouth, oh how he'd missed it. How would her lips feel wrapped around the length of him? He pressed harder into her hips at the thought. Her tongue tangled with his with an urgency he didn't remember from before. She wanted him. And she wasn't going anywhere this time.

He slid his hands over her hips to cradle her in the palms of his hands. As if reading his mind, she wrapped her legs around his waist. Her large breasts pressed into his chest with a softness that almost made him groan. He wanted her naked, wanted to taste her—all of her. Overwhelmed with the need to dive into her and consume her, he pulled her closer still. He wanted to tumble with her for days until he'd finally had his fill of her.

Walking with her wrapped around him, he managed to find a chair and dropped into it. Their kiss was broken for a second as she settled into his lap. She was straddling his thighs, her soft weight resting on his knees.

"Too bad it's so terribly dark in here. I'd like to enjoy the sight of you atop me. So lovely." He slid his hands up the outside of her breasts and across the exposed creamy mounds to her neck, pulling her closer. "These lips." He kissed her full mouth before finishing, "I would recognize these lips anywhere."

She pulled away with a gasp, shoving him back into the depths of the chair with the palm of her hand. Her lips were parted, but on a question, not in invitation.

He stroked her side, attempting to draw her back to him. "Suzanna? Did I say something wrong?"

"Yes. I mean, no. It's only that... What am I doing?" she whispered as she began shimmying off his lap, wrestling with her skirts to do so. "I must leave."

"Wait. Don't go!" He reached for her but she'd vanished like smoke on a windy afternoon. Only the traces of her scent remained. "Not yet," he complained.

"I must." A pained whisper returned from amid the darkness. There was a rustle of skirts and a screech as a chair slid across the wooden floor, accompanied by a muttered, "Blast it all."

Then came silence.

His fingers were still grasping at the air before him when the door to the library slammed. He stood to chase after her but, damn, the chit had made him hard as rock.

He fell back into the chair to cool his blood for a few minutes—and not by choice. Offending half the partygoers wouldn't do, and considering his condition, they would most certainly be offended. He'd let her slip away again. And after that kiss... He cursed a long string of oaths he was certain would have offended the other half of the *ton* in attendance this evening.

Finally, he stood to rejoin the party, stalking across the dark library toward the door. If Suzanna was still here, he would find her and finish what they started...twice.

Nine

S<small>UE WAS STILL STEAMING WITH INDIGNATION WHEN</small> she found her mother at the edge of the ballroom watching Evangeline dance. *I would recognize these lips anywhere.* "Blind horse's arse," she mumbled as she snatched a glass of champagne from a passing footman's tray and drained it.

"Did you say something, Sue?"

"Nothing, Mother." She stared at the movement around her as everyone returned from the dining-room buffet, not really seeing anyone. His lips. His hands. And still he hadn't known her. She was foisted to the side as Evangeline arrived on the arm of a gentleman. She didn't care. They could push her down to the floor while they were about it. Her lot couldn't get any worse. What did it matter? He'd seen her again, this time with no mask on, and he still didn't know her. Granted it was rather dark in there… but truly, how dense was he not to know her? And she'd done exactly what she'd sworn she wouldn't do and fallen right into his arms. *Did I swoon?* "Blast it all, I do hope not."

"What was that, dear?"

"Nothing, Mother."

She touched her fingertips to her lips. Why had she allowed that man to lay a finger on her again? Much as she tried, her plans seemed to disintegrate into dust whenever he was about. As if summoned by her thoughts, there he was before her again.

"I see you found your family earlier with no issue, Miss Green."

"Do you? Do you see that? Shocking."

His head tilted to the side as he regarded her, his blond locks catching the candlelight from above. "Have I offended you in some manner, Miss Green? I thought we were getting on rather well this evening."

"You were mistaken. It seems to be a common problem with you."

"Is it? I'll have to make an effort to improve upon my mistakenness."

"You should. Oh, look, here is my beautiful sister. I believe you are next on her dance card. I'm sure you don't want to be mistaken about that. She's perfect, you know. Some say 'unforgettable.'"

"Yes, I suppose it is time for our dance." He extended an arm to a confused Evangeline and led her away.

Sue didn't stay long enough to see them on the dance floor. Watching them glide away together looking the perfect couple was hard enough. Mother was beaming with pride, of course. With the murmured excuse of a headache, Sue was out the door and in their carriage before the music began. She wasn't even sure what she was upset over anymore. The list was simply getting too long to keep track: Victoria's lies, the twins luring her to the library, her mother's reminders of where her season would no doubt end, Holden looking her over once again after their kiss. That kiss…

She sank further into the carriage seat as if someone might see her in the window and know what was on her mind.

⤜⤛

The waltz had barely come to an end when Holden deposited the younger Miss Green back with her mother. She was pretty enough but agreed with him to an annoying degree, unlike her sister who seemed perpetually angry with him. In this instance he preferred anger. What was wrong with him? He shook his head.

In the past, the exotic beauties who laughed at his jokes had always held his attention the longest. Granted that attention span was somewhat short lived, but this was the first time he'd ever been pleased that a dance with the most beautiful lady in the room was over. Perhaps it was the interlude in the library that had him rattled this evening. That must be the issue—Suzanna had slipped from his grasp once more. His mind steadily avoided the horror at seeing his "deceased" mother chatting with Sue earlier. He sighed and tugged on the cuff of his coat, even though it already sat perfectly on his shoulders.

His mother had made it plain earlier that she couldn't be pried from this ball without a scene, drawing even more unwanted attention than if he left her here. He supposed he had no choice but to do just that and hope no one discovered her identity. Where had she found a bloody ball gown anyway? He would have to have a word with Fezawald when he returned home. His staff must be more vigilant if he was to keep his mother hidden in London. It was ill advised to keep her about, but so were many of his actions these days. He almost chuckled. No good could come of any portion of his daily life and he knew it.

No longer in the mood for dancing and chatter about the weather this evening, he made his way toward the door. There, beside an exceedingly large potted plant near the base of the main stairs, he spotted the one person who could make leaving even more difficult—his mother.

"My lady, why don't I escort you to your carriage," he said as he gripped her elbow and began pulling her through the main hall.

"Yes, I should be getting back. I'm quite weary from all the excitement."

"If you feel that way, then perhaps you shouldn't have come." *As I asked of you*, he finished to himself. He bit his tongue, however. If they were to argue at a ball, half the *ton* would know of her existence by tomorrow. He pasted on a polite smile. "I must admit I'm surprised to see you here this evening." Almost as surprised as he'd been to see her at his home.

"I'm flattered you noticed me at all with the way you were fussing over that Green girl."

"Leave her out of this," he snapped before placing a carefully crafted smile on his face. When he'd seen his mother talking to Sue earlier… He pushed the thought away. Now was not the time to dwell on the contents of that little conversation.

"Oh, have I upset you? Are you interested in her? She doesn't seem your type, Holden."

"I'm not, and how would you know of my interests?" he hissed at her as a footman handed him his hat and top coat.

"Just as well. You don't have room for a lady in your life anyway since I only recently arrived and we need to become reacquainted." She reached up and patted his cheek before he could move out of her reach. "How I've missed you, my dearest boy."

"Yes, this is all so very…nice." He leaned away from her and shoved her out the door in one swift movement. Had anyone seen her touch him? He led her away from the entrance toward the line of carriages, stepping farther into the cloak of darkness.

Once they were beyond earshot of the door, he added, "But you know you cannot stay with me forever. It's only temporary, until I can make arrangements of some sort."

"I don't know about that. I'd forgotten how much I missed society." A bland smile covered her face as she looked at him. Surely, she didn't mean to repeat this evening, but he could see by the set of her jaw that indeed she did.

"Mother, you can't come to another ball. I do apologize, but you simply cannot."

"So forceful, my son. When did you grow up and learn to speak in such a manner to your mother?"

"I was forced to come of age far before my time, and that was many years ago."

"All the more reason for me to stay. We can do all the things I've missed over the years. Where shall we start?"

"*We* can start by going home and not attending any more balls." He led her along the line of carriages until he spied his rig.

"That sounds perfect! We can stay home and chat in the evenings…"

"I won't be there. You will stay at home. I need a drink."

"You're leaving me? Alone? With that butler of yours? I don't trust him one bit, Holden. There's something unsavory about him."

"He's two and eighty! Even if he had an unsavory bone in his body, which he doesn't, he wouldn't have the energy to take advantage of it."

"Perhaps I need to set some things right for you in your home. You need a woman about to handle these things. I haven't been here as I should have, my dearest."

"Leave my staff be," he stated in a tone that could not be misunderstood. "They're my family."

"I'm your family. Only me."

"Mother…" He turned away, running a hand through his hair. He couldn't discuss her future here in the Geddings' drive. He needed air and apparently there was none to be found, even outside on a crisp night such as this one. Turning back, he handed her up into the carriage. "Good evening. I'll be home late."

She gasped as he shut the carriage door, closing her in darkness as he walked away. Would that keep her away from the next event he attended? Most likely not. He exhaled a slow breath and stepped away from the line of carriages, watching as his vehicle rolled away. There was a long row of wrought-iron fencing running the length of the front garden, and he braced his hands on it behind his back.

Closing his eyes, he waited there for some answer to come to mind, yet it didn't. He'd never understood why his father sent his mother away. Even now it seemed a harsh punishment. But his father was a harsh man. If he heard that Holden had allowed his mother to stay even one night with him, his father would be furious. So he mustn't find out. The sound of barking dogs caused Holden to open his eyes.

Were those Lord Geddings' hunting dogs making such a racket? He bragged of their superior training to anyone willing to listen, but surely he wasn't showing them off in the middle of a ball. Holden sighed, leaned back onto the fencing, and looked up into the cloudless night.

With the drama of his mother dropping in at balls, perhaps he should give up the idea of seeking out Suzanna. It was all a bit too much, and he was coming off as rather desperate anyway.

Would she ever not run from him? He either needed to abandon the hunt or get more information from the devious twins who led him here to begin with. As muddled as his mind was, this was no time for decisions. And the footmen would begin to talk if he loitered here much longer. Pushing off the fence, he began walking toward the street.

"Steelings!"

Holden turned to see his friend striding out the door of the Geddings home. "Thornwood. Just the man I was in need of this evening."

"Oh? Is there something you need?" The duke slowed as he neared Holden.

"No, it's mostly the fact that you are not female that speaks in your favor tonight."

"Ah. I agree with your sentiment entirely. In addition to a lack of women, I require a strong drink."

"As do I. What a mess of an evening." Holden shook his head.

"A pack of hunting dogs in the middle of a ballroom do tend to make a mess of things, don't they?" Thornwood chuckled and clapped his friend on the back.

"A pack of dogs? And I thought my night was interesting. It seems I missed the true excitement of the evening." They started off down the street toward the heart of town.

"Indeed. I shall tell you of it over a large glass of whiskey, and you can relate the ongoing saga of your avoidance of a leg shackle."

"There will be no leg shackles, ever. Just so we're clear."

"No. Of course not. Let's go have that drink." Thornwood grinned.

⤞⤝

Victoria arranged her skirts around herself on the blanket in Hyde Park. "I was only trying to enliven your season a bit, Sue. There's no reason to get angry."

"You told me Isabelle was ill and in need of rescue in that library. You knew who would await me instead of a sick cousin." Sue accepted a plate of cold chicken from her cousin's maid and sat back against a tree, squinting into the sunlight.

It was a bright afternoon, an oddity in London

that had to be celebrated with a picnic. Or so she'd thought. Evangeline was locked away inside to protect her cheeks from freckling. But Victoria and Isabelle were with her and they had some things to discuss. Namely, the library stunt at the Geddings' ball.

"My involvement was never in question, Sue. Of course I lured you to the library. Am I supposed to feel guilty now? Because I don't." Victoria popped a bite of apple into her mouth.

"How can you not feel guilty? I could have been compromised. He might have…"

"Were you? I want details. Did he kiss you?"

"That's not important." Sue focused on picking at a piece of bread on her plate to avoid her cousin's gaze.

"He did! You must tell us!"

"I will not!" The heat was already rising in her cheeks, betraying her secrets.

Isabelle was practically bouncing with excitement as she interjected, "But don't you see, Sue? This is wonderful news. Now he knows who you are. After he came all the way to our house to find you, then followed you to London, now he's found you. You can be together. I bet he'll make arrangements with Uncle soon. Oh, Sue! You're going to be married! And to such a handsome gentleman."

"That's not quite how events transpired, Isabelle. I'm no closer to marriage now than I was a week ago, further in fact because there are two fewer balls now."

"He won't marry you? The rake!" Isabelle's mouth made a perfect "O" in her shock.

"We never discussed marriage, Isabelle."

"But he kissed you." Isabelle shook her head in dismay.

Victoria rolled her eyes. "Isabelle, sometimes I wonder how we're related."

"We're twins," Isabelle returned as if that settled all discussion.

"Thank you for the reminder." Victoria sighed. "I meant how can you be so terribly naïve?"

"I am not! I believe the best of people. There is goodness all around in life. You simply refuse to see it."

"Goodness all around us?" Victoria threw her head back in laughter. "I suppose all gentlemen have honor, rainbows line the skies, and wildflowers spring to life in your footsteps."

"All gentlemen do have honor. Papa told me he'd see to it."

"You didn't notice the way he was cleaning his hunting rifle when he said that?"

Sue stood and shook out her skirts. "Would you mind if I slipped away for a few minutes? I need to walk to clear my mind."

"I'm sure you do after an evening in Lord Steelings' arms."

"I was not…"

"Don't lie, Sue. You know you're a terrible liar."

"I…I'm not…" Sue huffed and kicked at the blanket where it was tangled with her foot, then stalked off across the grass.

Victoria was right. She was a terrible liar. So why did it feel as if her whole existence was a lie right now? She followed the path around a bend where the large clearing became more wooded. She slowed down, kicking sticks with the toe of her half boots. Isabelle's words were still ringing in her ears: *You're going to be married.* If only.

Even the undesirable men in town seemed to be spoken for. And as for a certain handsome gentleman, that wasn't possible. It was odd that she'd considered marriage when they first met at the masquerade, but since then it hadn't crossed her mind. He would never marry her. Evangeline? If Mother had her way in things, then yes. But not her. He didn't want to recognize her. He didn't want the dream of Suzanna shattered, only to be left with Sue. She couldn't blame him; she wouldn't want to be left with her, either.

Pulling the small notebook from her pocket, she sat down on a bench and began to draw. Nothing settled her mind like escaping into a picture for a few minutes. Wouldn't it be lovely if all problems in life were as easy to navigate as lines on paper? Sue sighed and became lost in her drawing.

She smudged the line of charcoal across the page of her small notebook, watching as the tree in Hyde Park came to life on the parchment. Sue smiled down at the notebook in her lap, pleased with her own cleverness. A piece of pocketed coal from the fire in the parlor and a notebook small enough to fit inside her pelisse pocket, and she was able to sketch when Mother wasn't around. Brilliant! It wasn't the same as being able to paint all afternoon, but it was keeping her sane while in town.

Leaning closer, she began to add definition to a few leaves. That was when she felt it—heat running up her spine like fire. Someone was watching her.

Before she could turn her head, she heard the rumble of Holden's voice as he leaned over her park bench. "You're breaking the rules."

Her heart pounded as the warmth of his words swirled around her ear. At the sound of his voice, the remnants of her anger at him from the night before drained away, leaving only the memory of his sinful kisses. She turned and smiled up at him. "You won't tell on me, will you?"

"Never. May I look?" He came around the park bench and sat beside her.

"It's only my drawings, notes of this and that…"

He ended her excuses with a glare and an out-stretched hand.

"Very well." She handed him the notebook, trying to act as if she didn't care if he pried into her thoughts on the world around her. He collected her paintings but these drawings were rough sketches, unfinished. Would he think her talentless now that he saw her work incomplete and in pieces? Her muscles tensed as he slowly flipped through the pages, and she flinched with every blink of his eyes.

"Are these all from the park?"

"No, there are a few random scribbles here and there from elsewhere in town. Anytime my mother wasn't around. It's mostly sights that inspire me. Thoughts I have for paintings so I don't forget. Whatever is on my mind…"

"You have a lovely mind."

She swallowed the compliment. At least he thought one part of her appealing. "Thank you." Her voice came out in a whisper.

"No, really. You're quite talented." He turned another page, his head tilting to the side in thought. "It's chocolate cake."

"Did I draw cake?" She tried to lean close to see what he saw.

He pulled the notebook away from her with a playful smile.

"I can't say that I'm surprised, but I don't recall sketching any sweets."

"No. It's just…when I was a small boy, our cook would bake chocolate cakes. The smell would flood the house. I always spent the last hour before the cake was cooled enough to eat sitting in the kitchen. Mrs. Cuppings—she was our cook—would tell me stories of knights and castles. Then we would eat cake together. Some of my fondest memories are from that kitchen. Even today, when I bite into a piece of chocolate cake, I think of Mrs. Cuppings and sitting in the kitchen with her."

"I'm afraid I still don't understand."

"Your drawings are like chocolate cake. They remind me of something I can't quite place, and yet there's an element of comfort in these lines of coal."

"Oh. I thought they only brought me comfort." Was she imagining it or was there some connection between the two of them?

"No, Sue. It's not all in your mind." Although he was speaking of her sketches, she wondered if he could read her thoughts about him, for their relationship seemed to be all in her mind.

He returned his attention to her notebook, flipping to the last page and flinching at what he saw. What had she drawn there? She couldn't remember.

His voice was rough as he asked in a deliberate tone, "Why do you have a page of your notebook covered in script of the name Suzanna?"

"I…think it's a pretty name. I've never been fond of mine." *Idiot, idiot, idiot!* When had she scribbled "Suzanna"? She pulled the notebook from his grasp and shut it, trying to ignore the way her hand grazed over his. She also attempted not to think about how close he was sitting to her on the bench. She was failing miserably, but she tried nonetheless.

"So, you practiced writing Suzanna's name?"

"Yes. Ladies do this sort of thing, if you must know."

"Practice signing other ladies' names?" His brows drew together as his emerald gaze sliced through her with a brightness that made her quite wary indeed.

"Yes," she bluffed.

"Do they? Just when I think I know all there is to know about ladies." His brow was still furrowed while he clearly considered the truth of her statements.

"Yes, well, I'm happy to impart some information to you today." Her voice was higher than usual as she smiled to cover her sudden fit of nerves.

"It's…interesting." His lips quirked up into a smile. "Thank you for sharing your sketches with me. If I put my finger on what your drawings remind me of, I'll let you know."

"No need to put too much thought into it. You shouldn't dwell on art, I always say." You shouldn't dwell on art? Was that the best cover story she could think of?

"That's an odd thing to always say. I always say, dwell on the pleasing parts of life and pretend the rest don't exist. Art is pleasing."

"Is that easy to do?"

"Thinking about art? Yes."

"Pretending the unfortunate parts of life don't exist," she clarified.

"Sometimes more than others, but I endeavor to try." He looked deep into her eyes for a moment before stating, "I must be going now. Until the next ball." He rose and gave her a cheerful nod of his head before he began to walk away.

"The next ball where I won't be dancing with you?" she called after him.

He paused and tossed a smile over his shoulder. "I look forward to your refusal"—he chuckled—"very much indeed. I shall see you there."

She was still smiling after him as he wound down the path with the long, relaxed stride of a man in complete control of every aspect of his life. His life seemed to be charmed and without even a hint of strife. How did he manage it? How could she attempt the same? Just as the smile started to slip from her mouth, she heard the crunch of footsteps across the grass behind her. Turning, she saw the lady from the ball who'd warned her away from marriage. Henrietta? Had that been her name? And why was she stumbling out of the bushes?

"Miss Green, how nice it is to see you again."

"Likewise, Lady… I'm terribly sorry. I don't believe I caught your title when we last chatted."

"Yes, I do seem to be forgetful like that. Lady Pemberton. You may call me Henrietta, though. I can tell we are going to be fast friends, even if I am twice your age."

"Oh, surely not. You look quite young," Sue lied. Henrietta's gray hair, which was wound into a tight knot on her head, gave away her age more than the wrinkles around her eyes. But even with the social graces of a turnip, Sue knew not to tell the truth in this situation.

"Thank you, dear. Can you stay and chat this afternoon?"

"No, I'm afraid I have to go meet my cousins. I've been away too long already."

"That is a pity. You'll have to come by for tea with me, then."

"Yes, that would be…nice. Good afternoon, Henrietta."

"Good afternoon, dear."

Sue gathered her skirts and made her way toward Isabelle and Victoria. Something about the woman seemed a bit off. Was it the assumed friendship simply because they'd spoken at a ball? Or the way her eyes pierced through Sue's skin? Either way, Sue wanted to be away from Henrietta as fast as possible, and if it could at all be helped, she would not be taking tea with Lady Pemberton. What was it that Holden had said? Pretend the bad parts of life don't exist? Of course with Sue's life, if she imagined away all the bad, she'd have nothing left.

❧

"Holden!" Aunt Penelope's voice rang out as he stepped into the library. "I'm glad you were able to come to call today." Her eyes were a bit too bright as she stood from her seat by the fire.

"Sorry for the delay. I was"—he smirked and ran a hand though his hair at the thought of his afternoon—"in the park when your note arrived." And what a delightful and interesting afternoon it had been. Could he have finally unraveled the mystery of Suzanna? But, Sue? It couldn't be. His mind refused to accept the conclusion. Why would she have kept it from him all this time? He would have to think about it later when he was not being summoned to tea by his aunt.

He closed the door behind him and moved into the room. Slowing as he took in the desperation in his aunt's eyes, he asked, "Is something wrong? Is it one of the girls? Do I need to duel some young lad to protect their honor? You know I will, and I'm a far better shot than Uncle Joseph. Who is he?" He sized up an invisible enemy with a playful snarl in an attempt to improve her mood. Unfortunately, it didn't seem to work.

"The girls are fine. However, you need to sit." Aunt Penelope indicated one of the chairs before beginning to wring her hands.

"This can't be good news if I must sit to hear it," he offered with a grin as he rounded an armchair in his path.

"Tea?" She perched on the edge of her chair as if she was forcing herself to remain still. She always paced the floor when upset.

He raised one brow as he asked, "And it requires tea? What's happened to bring us to such a place?"

She blinked at him, her fingers twisting into a knot in her lap. "Last night I saw your mother."

"Oh, that." Damn. He hadn't removed her from the ball fast enough. If only he'd been able to get his mother away when he'd first spied her, but there had been no way to do so. And then he'd received the note from Miss Fairlyn. Damn, damn, damn. He sighed, fell into the chair behind him, and braced for the impact of the verbal lashing he was about to receive.

"*Oh, that*? This is all you have to say? Holden, everyone believes her to be dead. In general, deceased people do *not* attend balls."

"Did anyone else see her?"

"Not that I'm aware. I saw her leave with you, Holden," she scolded.

"I'm sorry?"

"What are we to tell people? What if someone did notice her presence last night?" She bit at her lip and shook her head.

Holden leaned forward and lowered his voice. They were alone, but he was always cautious, always. Caution had been the one constant in his life. "I'm handling the situation."

"How are you handling it, Holden? How? With Henrietta attending balls in town?"

"She…turned up at my home a few days ago." He gritted his teeth against his aunt's reaction before adding, "I told her she could stay with me."

Her mouth fell open as she stared at him. "You can't allow her to stay under your roof! Are you mad? She could hurt you, Holden. She isn't well."

"She had no place to go. What was I to do?"

"I don't know. Instruct her to leave?" Her words rushed out in an urgent whisper.

"And go where? Back to Brooke House?"

"If it would remove her from your home, then yes, back to Brooke House."

"In the middle of the night?" He couldn't do that to his mother, and Aunt Penelope knew it.

She shook her head and searched his face for answers. "How did she escape? Does your father know? Oh, when he hears of this…"

"He won't be hearing of this."

Aunt Penelope sighed. "You can't go the remainder of your life not speaking to your father. At some point you have to…"

"No. I will not have dealings with that man. If he wants to believe I'm gallivanting about France with loose women and plenty of drink, let him think it. Meanwhile, Mother will stay with me while I find a suitable living situation for her. I wouldn't send my worst enemy back to that place, let alone my family." Days later and he still couldn't erase the starved look that had pulled at his mother's cheekbones when she first arrived at his home. He shook his head. "Father was wrong to keep her there."

"In his own way, he does care, you know. He claimed she was dead and sent her away because he had to, Holden." She watched him for a moment before continuing. "Whatever the state of things between you and your father, I know he would want to know of this."

"He will want nothing but to lock her away once more."

"She can't live with you, Holden."

"I know that." He ran a hand over his eyes and leaned back in the chair. "I won't have Father deciding her fate, though."

She poured a cup of tea and glared at him over the

rim in silent disapproval before asking, "Then what will you do?"

"She's been gone from my life since I was a child. The family had claimed she was dead for so long that I began to believe the lies. And now she's back." He looked up from his study of the arm of his chair with a sigh. "Do you have something stronger than tea by chance? I believe I require a beverage for this conversation after all."

"In the decanter on the table. It's your uncle's favorite." She waved to the crystal container at his side. "Holden, you can't retrieve a lost lifetime of memories over a few days' stay. And certainly not with a woman like Henrietta. It isn't safe."

"I'm safer now than when I was a child in her presence," he reasoned as he filled a glass with the brandy.

"I understand that she is your mother. She's my sister-in-law. But she also ended your brother's life."

"I'm well aware. Father has never let me forget it." He looked into the depths of his glass, mocking, "*Samuel wouldn't have acted in such a manner. Samuel would have made good decisions.*" He'd spent his life in the shadow of an older brother he could hardly remember. He wished Samuel had lived as well, but his father had an unfortunate way of grieving—blaming Holden.

"It was a terrible event."

"Indeed. I lost everything that day." He took a sip of the brandy, letting it burn away his past.

"And you think you can get it back by hiding your previously murderous and currently ill mother within your home." It wasn't a question. She sliced him open with a glare, making him wince.

"Some part of me is curious about her, I admit. She is my relation, after all. I won't allow her to stay with me forever. Only…for now."

"It isn't safe. She's killed before."

"I'm perfectly safe, Aunt Pen. Her actions in the past don't matter, not now."

"Don't they?" she countered.

"I'm fine. I've been fending for myself for many years, and my mother's presence isn't going to change that fact."

"Henrietta is appearing at *ton* events, and you are not fine. None of this is fine."

"All I need do is keep her under wraps while she's about. Not to worry, Aunt Pen. She'll remain dead and everything will continue on without note—as always." He certainly hoped so anyway.

"Holden, think of your cousins." She tilted her head in that way he always struggled to refuse, like a puppy begging for table scraps. "If Henrietta is recognized in town, their season will be shrouded in scandal."

He ran a hand through his hair as he tried not to look at her. "I'll handle it properly. You have my word."

"Perhaps I can help." She bit her lip, clearly considering their limited options. "We should tell Joseph that his sister has returned. He'll be upset, of course, but we must. You cannot bear this burden alone. It would be best to tell your father, but you must have assistance from some corner of the family."

He pulled away, struck by her words. This was his burden, and his alone. "I can't let you do that. The more people who know of this…"

"Holden, he can help you. He already knows what

happened all those years ago," she urged, her hands entwined again, making her knuckles turn white. "You can't keep this secret forever. I see that now. It's too difficult. If I tell your uncle of Henrietta's whereabouts, he can…"

"No! I can do this alone. No one can know of this. And no one will."

"Holden," she pleaded, her head tilting to the side once more in the look Holden couldn't refuse. But this time he must.

"Aunt Pen, we can't allow this situation to be known, not even by Uncle. If the truth finds a way out, every salon in London will be buzzing with the family's secrets. 'Didn't you know? He claimed his own mother was dead. He should be in chains. And did you hear about her? Mad as a March hare.'" He sighed, the weight of his situation settling heavier on his shoulders—his cousins' chances at a good marriage, his own reputation… "I'd planned to stay after this visit, but if word gets out, I'll have to leave. Back to *France*, I suppose."

Ha. France. Someday he would actually visit the country. Scotland, Belgium, and even Iceland he knew quite well. If things fell apart here, he would simply pack his belongings and leave.

It would be easy. He'd done it before.

And yet…and yet he couldn't imagine truly stepping onto a ship bound for foreign soil. If he did that, he would miss the next event on his schedule and this time Sue Green might dance with him. The promise of Sue twirling around the dance floor with him and laughing up into his face made him smile. He shook his head.

He blinked away her image with a whispered, "I can't leave. Not now."

There was a sharp intake of breath across from him. "Why, Holden Ellis! You're taken with someone."

He lifted his gaze at her sudden change of tone. "We were discussing a rather important matter, Aunt."

She waved the issue away with the back of her hand. "Promise you'll see her to proper accommodations for someone in her condition—soon! And that she won't make any more public appearances."

"I will see to it that no scandal befalls us. Do not doubt it."

"Very well, then. I suppose there's no sense in arguing. It doesn't change the situation for us to be at odds." She settled back into her chair on a sigh as the door burst open from the hallway. His cousins spilled into the room just as his aunt instructed him, "Tell me of the special lady who's caught your eye!"

"Oh, Holden has a special lady?"

"Who is she?"

"Tell us! Oh, you must!"

Holden stood and faced his cousins. "I don't have a special lady!"

"You most certainly do. Your grin betrays you," April stated.

"Truly." He held out his hands in surrender. "It isn't what you believe it to be. She…"

"Oh! There *is* a she!" May exclaimed, clasping her hands together over her heart.

Damn. There was no escaping this discussion other than to say, "I should be leaving."

"And deny us our afternoon of entertainment?" June complained as she sank into a chair beside his aunt.

"More like afternoon of sport...in ancient Rome. I believe I'll be on my way before you release the hungry lions."

Just then Jan walked in with her puppy in tow. "Holden! I have a new rabbit! Do you want to meet him?"

"I would love to, Jan. I'll leave through the back garden. Good afternoon, ladies."

As he moved to leave the room, Jan's dog pounced on the side of his boot before running into the hall-way. Holden turned. "See? Hungry lions. I knew it."

"Take care, Holden. And look into that situation we discussed."

"I will."

Trailing after him as he accompanied Jan from the library were echoes of "What situation, Mama?" and "Who is his lady?"

He shook his head and followed his cousin down the stairs leading to the back garden. His mind was flooded with what lay ahead in the coming days. He wasn't looking forward to telling his mother she must return to a hospital. Her actions were a bit off, but was she still as dangerous as his aunt believed her to be? Surely not. He needed time to find a new doctor in a private house where she would be fed properly and given suitable attire. None of that could be accomplished within a day. And his nights were filled with balls at the moment—he grinned.

As long as he kept his mother inside the walls of his home, no one would be the wiser. That would give him the time he needed—and the time he was ashamed he desired. He would simply have to be more careful she didn't escape while he sorted things out.

"Holden, are you coming to see my new Angora bunny or not?" Jan's voice called out, pulling him from his thoughts. "He's an *Oryctolagus cuniculus* and he's beautiful!"

He cleared his throat and descended the remainder of the stairs toward Jan, who was standing in the light of the kitchen fire. She looked the picture of innocence with her long dark braid falling over one shoulder. He contained a curse within a sigh as he neared her.

Beneath all of his wishes on the subject of his mother, he knew as he looked at Jan that his aunt was right. If he didn't hide his mother away for good, it would bring scandal on the family for some time. Even years from now when Jan came of age, she would be the subject of talk. He had to repair this situation. If only for Jan's sake. "Yes, let's see this new pet of yours. What does this make? Twenty? Thirty?"

"Only nine."

"Is that all?" He smiled down at his youngest cousin, knowing what he must do. He would hide his mother away for good. She would be cut from his life once again. And he would go on without a backward glance, just as his father had done. But he wouldn't do it today. He had much to think through on a variety of subjects at the moment. He finally had his mother back. And today everyone was safe. He would simply have to keep everything in check…for now.

Ten

HOLDEN STEPPED INTO HIS PARLOR. THAT MUST HAVE been where he left his book, for he'd certainly searched everywhere else. He doubted he would be able to settle into a book for distraction from his circular thoughts, but he planned to try like the devil. He stilled at the creak of the chair in the corner of the room.

"Oh. Mother, I didn't know you were…" He watched his mother's chest rise and fall with sleepy breaths. Her knitting lay abandoned in her lap as she dozed in the warmth of the small room.

He lingered by the door for a moment, not wanting to disturb her. He'd let a day slip past already with similar reasoning. Soon he would find a home for her and tell her she must leave his house, but not just yet. Holden ran a hand through his hair and glanced over his shoulder at the open doorway. He could leave. He didn't really need…

"I was looking for a book," he whispered, taking a step farther into the room. Although he came look-ing for his latest read, his eyes never strayed from her sleeping form in the chair. "I started it a few days ago, but now I can't seem to place it." When she didn't stir, he raised his voice to a soft level. "I suppose Fezawald could have borrowed it. However, I can't quite see him interested in *The History of Art in Eastern Europe.*"

His mother's chest rose, then fell without a twitch.

Holden shook his head. All of chattering London and he was here talking to a napping *deceased* woman. "I'm not sure why I'm explaining this to you since you're asleep. You are asleep, aren't you?" The silence in the room seemed to extend to the whole world, as if everyone in existence had ceased what they were doing for a moment to listen. Nothing.

"That's what I thought." He moved closer, sitting on the edge of the tea table near her chair. "It really is too bad, you know. You've missed so much of life being locked away. It's where you had to be, but sometimes I can't help but wonder…

"God! Why do things have to be this way? If you were of sane mind, things would be so different." He dropped his head to his hand, trying to rub his troubles away from his temples. "You can't come to any more balls, Mother. I don't know if you understand that. Aunt Pen wants me to place you back in Brooke House, but I told her no. Yet you can't stay here forever. She says it's not safe, and I admit when I saw you talking to Sue…" He exhaled on a ragged breath.

"Of course Sue didn't suspect anything, but that doesn't matter. Your very presence puts those around you in danger." He thought of Sue and shivered. "I wish you understood the position I'm in because of you. Aunt Pen saw you the other night. And if she saw you, so could another, and then all of the well-crafted lies to protect everyone would be exposed.

"I was wrong to think I could do this, have this life. Keep you here even for a time. Hell, my entire return to England has been a mess." He motioned to the room around him before settling back into his stance with his forearm resting on his knee. "You have no blame in this, not this time anyway. Aunt Pen mentioned contacting Father when we spoke over tea, and I find I've been ill at ease ever since. Father and I haven't spoken for some time. I don't know if you knew that." He glanced to the window, half expecting to conjure up the man by the mere mention of his name.

His mother shifted in her sleep and her knitting slid to the thick rug at her feet.

He leaned over and scooped up the knitting, laying it aside. "He believes I've been living in Paris for years, squandering my life and resources. The truth? I've never even seen France. As soon as I was old enough to leave school, I went to the harbor and boarded the next ship leaving port—a fishing vessel bound for Iceland."

He chuckled. "Iceland. Can you believe that? That's where I spent the first four years I was away. I eventually saved up enough funds to find my way back as close as Brussels. Then I raised sheep in Scotland for a bit. The ironic part is that I've been fairly success-ful. Enough to keep me fed, clothed, and with a roof over my head, anyway. I've never touched the money Father puts in my account—I refuse to. I don't want his assistance, financial or otherwise. Yet he still sees me in a poor light. And so I've let him."

His father had never been fond of him, and at this point in Holden's life, the feeling was mutual. There had been a time when he was young when he desired his father's approval, but he'd grown weary of the effort when he was still school aged. In recent years he'd kept his distance from the man, encouraging the rumors that spread of his own reckless actions in France. The talk of his rakish behavior kept his father far from his life—as Holden preferred him to be. He huffed into the silence of the room. "Anyway, now I'm back. And as long as you stay out of sight of the *ton* and I am able to avoid Father, I believe I may stay for a bit.

"I wasn't expecting this—any of it. You. Sue…" He sighed. "And I'm not quite sure what to do on that score. I'm fairly certain she has concealed a rather large truth from me. Until I'm sure, I don't know… and even if I knew for certain…

"She must have had her reasons for playing this game with me, mustn't she? After all this time, I don't want to frighten her away. I don't think I should say anything until she admits her deceit. If indeed there is any deceit. The question is how I will know for certain." Everything came into focus in an instant, causing him to sit up straight. There was one way to know for sure if Sue was only Sue. He grinned, thinking of Sue's lips, usually so busy berating him for some slight.

"Thank you for this little chat, Mother." He stood and left the room. He would find his book another time. Yet he'd only made it to the base of the stairs when there was a knock at the door. He called out, "Fezawald, are you about?" But no one answered. With a shrug, Holden went to the door and pulled it open.

"Father," he muttered in greeting as he looked into the face of the man he'd been running from for eleven years. He'd aged, his once blond hair now threaded with silver at his temples. It surprised Holden to see they were of the same height and frame. The man who loomed in his memories was now on equal footing with him. He looked well enough, with a finely tailored coat hiding most of the evidence of his large appetite.

"So this is where I find you."

"Indeed. I came back to England only recently." Holden took a step out onto the front step instead of allowing the man entrance.

"I heard as much. Is this the home of one of your French friends?" his father asked, with a sneer at the facade of Holden's home.

"Why did you come here, Father?"

"Whoever she is, she keeps you well dressed. Of course, I'm sure that's to her advantage."

"The house is mine, as are my clothes."

"Hmmm. When I heard you were in town, I thought I would call. Some issues have arisen of late in the family."

Holden shut the door at his back and ushered his father back down the steps into the small garden. "Issues?" Had Aunt Penelope contacted him after all? Holden's jaw clenched at the thought. He'd trusted her.

"I received word from the doctor at Brooke House

that there was an escape effort." He glanced around before saying, "Your mother is unaccounted for."

Holden nodded. "I appreciate the information." Aunt Penelope had kept her silence for no reason, then. That damned doctor.

His father gave him an uncomfortable nod of his head. Glancing around the garden, he seemed to be searching for words. When he finally looked back to Holden, it was to say, "I should be on my way."

"Very well." Holden crossed his arms across his chest.

"Holden, you can come stay at Pemberton House, if you so choose. If things don't work out here…" He glanced away.

"That won't be necessary, Father. I'm quite comfortable as I am."

"You know it shames the family for you to live as you do. Living off some French lady's benevolence is no life at all. You don't have to…" He seemed unable to say any more on the subject.

"If I see Mother, I will inform you."

His father nodded and turned, moving toward the garden gate. His hand paused on the latch. Turning back, he asked, "You didn't have anything to do with this recent disappearance at Brooke House, did you?"

"No. I don't make it a habit of breaking ill people out of hospitals. Don't you know I'm too busy with loose women and drink for that?"

The familiar hardened look in his father's blue eyes returned. He turned back to the gate, swung it open, and stepped up into his carriage without another word.

✥

Sue walked out into another beautiful sunlit afternoon. What an oddity to have two days in a row of perfect weather! May was right—she certainly didn't wish to spend such a day in a parlor sipping tea and discussing fashions. The Rutledges were a delightful group of ladies, yet her mother and Evangeline never allowed the conversation over tea to stray too far from convention. Somehow, she thought if her mother hadn't been in attendance today, tea would have been quite different and rather enjoyable. As it was, Sue had been stifling yawns for the past hour.

May must have seen the wistful look on her face as she gazed out the window, for she made excuses and ushered Sue out the door to the garden a moment later. "Now that we're out of that obligation, would you like to tour the garden? I would show you around, but I need to go back to the mews and check on my horse before anyone notices I'm gone. She was set to be reshod this afternoon. Do you mind?"

"Not at all. I'll take a turn about the garden and enjoy the day. I'm simply pleased to not be discussing waistlines on dresses."

May laughed. "As am I, Sue. I'll return in a bit. You should start with the rose garden beyond the maze. It's my favorite."

"Thank you. And don't feel rushed with your horse. I'll be fine here."

May smiled and disappeared around a trellis of purple flowering vines.

Sue had a feeling they would be fast friends. Too bad they'd only just met during Sue's final season. Sue sighed and stepped out onto the gravel path. Skirting the maze hedgerow, she moved toward the back corner of the garden.

Stepping through a doorway cut into the green of the hedgerow, she was overwhelmed with a profusion of blooms stretching in every direction. Lilies, mixed with tulips, rested under the shade of rosebushes of every color imaginable. Flowering trees leaned over the paths, as if protecting them with loving arms. She moved farther into the hidden garden, her head spinning with the effort to absorb all of its beauty.

Then, rounding a bend in the path, she stopped. He was lounging on a bench. Holden would have looked like the typical devil–may-care rake, perhaps awaiting a liaison, if not for the tapping of his toe on the ground and the frown about his eyes. Of course he still looked impossibly handsome, even with troubled lines creasing his brow.

She stepped closer, catching his attention. "I didn't know you would be here." He moved to stand, but she stopped him with a raised hand.

He shrugged and settled back into his seat. "I didn't know I would be here, either."

She took a few more steps in his direction, pausing before the bench where he was lounging. "I'm here for tea with your cousins. Well, we already had the tea part of the tea and now we've moved on to the chatting part of the tea. It was rather dull with all the talk of fashion and such, and I'm not allowed to participate anyway because Mother says I bore people. I'm not quite sure how I accomplish it, though, to be honest. I consider myself an excellent conversationalist, perhaps a bit verbose at times, but never boring."

He quirked a golden brow at her but said nothing.

"Oh no, now I'm boring you with talk of not being boring. How ironic. I didn't mean to intrude." She took one step to the side, not sure what to do with her arms, first crossing them, then lacing them behind her back. "I'll go."

"No, stay." His voice was deeper than usual with a gruffness she'd never heard from him before. "I could use a distraction."

"I'll attempt to be distracting then in the more pleasing sense of the word." She threw him an unsure smile as she wobbled back and forth on the heel of one boot. "Not like an insect buzzing about one's face, or someone who desperately needs to bathe yet insists on standing too close at a ball. I'll attempt to distract instead in the way of a child's laughter or a lovely view. I've been told I'm quite distracting. Although I believe that statement might have been meant as an insult, now that I think about it. However, I will endeavor to distract nonetheless."

"I'm sure it won't take much effort." He almost chuckled, the laugh never quite reaching his eyes.

"The flowers are plenty distraction for me. I've never seen so many blooms on a single rosebush. May was right. It is a lovely garden. I'd like to sketch it, but Mother is just inside so I wouldn't dare pull out my sketchbook just now. I'll simply have to remember it."

She swept her eyes over the garden and tried to breathe in the memory of the afternoon. Her eyes, however, wanted to remember other things than flowers as they returned to Holden once more. His casual posture as he lounged on the bench with his long legs extended, his arms wrapped across his broad chest, the faraway look in his eyes...

"So, May was the one who lured you outside. I can't say I'm surprised. I think she feels as out of place indoors as I do."

"Do you? Feel out of place indoors? You never let on as much. You seem to sweep through rooms in command of everyone and everything in your path. The great Lord Steelings—envy of gentlemen, wooer of ladies, charmer of all."

"Appearances can be deceiving."

"Ha! Clearly." He had no idea, she thought as she rolled her eyes heavenward.

"And I'm never able to command you, yet I seem to find you in my path a great deal." He cracked a smile.

"I'm not easily commandable."

"May I command you to sit?"

"Only because that bench looks comfortable, unlike my shoes."

"One of the many reasons I'm pleased to have been born a man."

"Hessians do look comfortable, I must admit. I dream of shoes with room to wiggle my toes. I bet you have that luxury in those boots. These?" She sat beside him and lifted the toes of her half boots so he could see them from beneath her dress. "I can barely twitch my little toe. It's a sad state of affairs when you can't twitch a single toe. The worst are dancing slippers. They bind."

"Do they? Is that why you never want to dance with me?"

"No. But that would have been an excellent

excuse. I'll have to remember to use it the next time you ask me." She laughed. "I suppose that wouldn't be in good taste, though."

"Refusing me a dance? I quite agree."

"No, referencing aching feet to a gentleman. Come to think of it, I shouldn't have said anything about toes—wiggling or twitching. That was wrong."

"It's only wrong if I'm offended. I rather enjoyed the thought of your toes wiggling. Scandalous! Next thing you know, I'll have you barefoot in the grass."

"Only if you brought some smelling salts for my mother."

He bit back a smile, the corners of his eyes crinkling as he looked at her. "I must have left them in my other coat. She'll wake eventually, and the ground is soft this time of year."

"To bury our toes in?"

"To prevent injury when your mother collapses. But also for our toes." He laughed.

"I can hear my mother now: 'I told you, never make mention of your person or any ailments associated with your person. And what do you do, Sue Green? You discuss being shoeless out of doors with a gentleman!' Apparently I say all the wrong things in conversation. You know, I was raked over the coals for what I said to you over ices that day."

His brow wrinkled with thought. "About art?"

"No, when I asked about your mother. And now I've gone and mentioned her again. That's awful of me. Sometimes I say things before I can think better of them. My apologies. I'll be in hot water indeed over repeating this offense."

"I won't tell. And I didn't mind before. If I recall, you only asked after my well-being in reference to her passing anyway. Surely that's allowable."

"No. Horribly inappropriate…or so I've been told." He shrugged and looked off into the hedgerow. "She's been gone since I was a small child. And by all accounts she wasn't the maternal sort to begin with."

The silence following his statement surrounded them. Sue didn't dare break it. For once, she kept her mouth closed. There were only traces of pain in his voice, hidden by years of apathy. But still she knew he hurt in a place so deep that he would never allow anyone to see. Except in this moment. Would he let her see it?

"I've always wondered what it would have been like, what life is like in other families," he mused. "Games, picnics, and such… My father wasn't fond of anything that might be considered enjoyable. Thought I needed a firm hand, a hard line, and all that.

"We never saw eye to eye. I left England for France after I finished school and never saw him again. And the world has been a more cheerful place for his absence. Ah, if I could only keep it that way." He let out a derisive laugh and shook his head.

"Oh." Another moment of silence fell between them before she asked, "Was it all bad?"

"France was lovely." He tossed a wry grin in her direction.

She searched his eyes, looking for answers. "I meant when you were a boy. Was it so terrible?"

"No. Only the parts when I was at home. My holidays with friends were quite nice. And life with my aunt and uncle…well, you see where I sit now."

"I wonder if your father was always that way—stern. I've often wondered if my parents were always as they are now or if I somehow broke them." She tossed him a warm smile to ease the tension of their conversation.

"I can remember glimpses from before my mother… before my brother, but…" He shook his head.

"You have a brother?" How had a detail like that slipped past her mother? "I've never heard mention of him."

"That's because Sam passed away when he was only seven years of age. I was four."

"That's dreadful."

"You have no idea." He tried to brush the conversation away with a casual smile and a wave of his hand.

There was so much more to Holden than what appeared on the surface. She would never have guessed from his devil-may-care appearance that he had such a dark past. She shook her head. "He was older than you? That must have made receiving your title rather painful."

"I was young. I try not to think about it now." He gazed into her upturned face, making her heart beat faster. "I can remember playing with him in the nursery. He was always fair, even though I was younger. He would have been a good lord. Honest and honorable. Much better than I am." He turned away with a grimace.

"I'm sure that's not true. You're quite honorable. Well, mostly."

The corner of his mouth turned up as he glanced her way, his gaze remaining there for a perilous moment.

She was now in danger of falling headlong into those green eyes. She cleared her throat and cast her eyes across the garden for a moment. "He passed away around the same time as your mother? Was it a fever?"

Holden nodded uncomfortably. "Something like that." He ran a hand through his hair. "I remember seeing him there on the parlor floor with my mother holding him. Everything changed that day. Sam was gone. My mother..." He swore and looked away.

"That must have been dreadful."

"I saw the entire incident. I didn't understand it at the time, but I watched as..." His head lifted for his gaze to meet hers. "I've never spoken of this to anyone. And I shouldn't begin now." He ran a hand through his hair, tossing it on end before dropping his arms to his knees and slumping forward. "What am I about today? I'm not myself. I apologize. I should go."

He shifted to stand, but she stopped him with a light touch to his arm. The wool of his coat was warm under her fingers as she gently squeezed his forearm. He glanced down at her hand and she felt his muscles twitch under her grasp. It was hardly a strong enough grip to hold him back if he truly wished to leave, yet it seemed to settle him back onto the bench beside her. His eyes lifted to hers, pain warring with confusion in the emerald depths.

When she opened her mouth to speak, her voice felt small. How could she help him? She wasn't big enough or grand enough for this task, and yet... "Tell me. Please, I want to know."

"You don't want to know about me. Not really."

"Yes, I do."

He searched her face for a moment before he spoke. "At four, I watched my brother take his last breath." His normally good-natured, deep voice was pounded flat by the truth he told. "He died that day because of me."

"How can you think that? You were a child."

He nodded. "I was. And I believe now that was how it occurred. My mother lost a child in birth when I was but three years old. She never recovered from it. So when she saw my brother hit me...the youngest, her baby..." He shrugged and shook his head.

"I wasn't hurt, but she wouldn't listen." He exhaled in a harsh puff of air.

"Are you saying your mother killed your brother in an attempt to protect you?"

"She was ill."

"You are not to blame."

She wasn't sure at what point in his story she'd slid her hand down his arm to wrap her hand around his, but she glanced down to find their fingers entwined now. She should move. She should remove her hand from his grasp. Instead she squeezed his hand and laid her other hand on his forearm, attempting to rub the tension away.

With his story came understanding. A few of the missing pieces that made him whole snapped together in her mind. Not all of them, but enough for now. "Your father can't honestly hold you responsible for such a thing."

"I can't believe I told you any of this. What is it about you?" He glanced down at their joined hands, pulling away as if burned. Flexing his fingers for a moment, his gaze returned to her face with an intensity she hadn't seen since they'd met on the stairs that night.

"Holden." Her mouth went dry and she licked her lips. "This is why you try as you do to play the disreputable rake."

"Might we return to the subject of wiggling toes?" His breathing seemed harsh as he looked at her.

"You wish to confirm your father's presumptions about you. You try to sink to his expectations. I can't say I blame you. I suppose…"

Unexpected warmth flooded her senses as he reached up to frame her face with his hands, pulling her closer. His kiss was harsh, punishing, but with a desperation she matched. She heard a startled whimper escape her throat as his lips moved over hers. Her hands fluttered in the air for a moment before landing on his chest. He pulled back, watching her. There was an awareness in his eyes that she didn't quite trust, as if he remembered something he'd forgotten long ago.

Her lips parted in question, yet she had too many thoughts to ask. He'd released her lips but his hands held her head still. His thumbs brushed against the wisps of fallen hair at her temples.

Blinking up into dark green eyes and lips she wanted back on hers, she tugged on his lapels until his mouth met hers once more. He chuckled, the rough sound vibrating through her, only to be soothed by the softness of his mouth. His tongue traced the lines of her lips until she opened to him, allowing him in. Time must have passed but she was unaware of anything beyond his lips on hers.

His hands slid to the back of her neck as he tasted her, his warm skin heating hers more than a thousand suns. His lips slashed over hers, pulling her deepest desires from her, then delving for more. Exposed, in need, she bit at his bottom lip, dragging him into the spiral of longing with her. As if in a battle where neither side would surrender, she matched every movement he made. She'd learned. Whether he knew it or not, he'd been her teacher. Her hands were inside his coat now, splayed on his chest and slipping further around him with every passing second.

Nearness. That's what she needed.

His body pressed close to hers. His hand moved down her neck, sliding down her back to rest on her hip. He pulled away with a lazy smile, his eyes darting across the garden. "Where's a bedchamber when you need one?"

"Holden, we shouldn't."

"Yes, actually I believe we should." He pulled her in for one more kiss, leaving her flustered, confused, and giddy.

She touched her fingers to her lips as he pulled away. He'd kissed her. Not Suzanna, her! Sue Green!

"For someone who hasn't danced a quadrille before, you certainly are experienced," he mused.

"You. Only you," she whispered. Had she spoken aloud or only in her mind?

"You have the most intriguing mouth. I feel as if we've kissed many times over, and yet I *know* we haven't." A smile tugged at the corners of his mouth as he spoke, making her want to kiss him again.

"Everything about you feels quite familiar. I wish I could put my finger on what it is. Like the memory of a dream that vanishes before you can truly enjoy it."

Did he remember her? She had to tell him. Enough secrecy and lies. She needed to tell him she was Suzanna. "Holden, there's something you should know."

"I was only trying to make you stop talking, but I'm glad I did. That was quite unexpected, although I should have guessed. You are a passionate artist, so it stands to reason you would be passionate in other areas as well." He was grinning a broad smile that lit his eyes and made them crinkle at the corners.

She shoved him on the shoulder and stood to leave. "Only trying to make me stop talking?" He'd shared intimate details of his childhood. They'd had a tender moment! And he was in the mood to tell jokes? The blasted man!

"Wait. Sue, don't go. I didn't mean that the way it sounded."

"I will see you at the Habernes' garden party where, you will be relieved to hear, there will be no dancing. I suppose you will be forced to wait for another event for me to refuse you another dance."

Her cheeks were flushed, and it seemed as if her darkest secrets were written there. Shaking out her skirts, she took a steadying breath. He didn't care for her. He'd only shown her a small crack in his armor—most likely he hadn't intended even that much. He'd wanted a diversion in the garden to improve his mood and she'd been convenient. She took a step away from him, only daring to look back for one quick glance.

Unfortunately the quick glance turned into a long glance.

There was something in his eyes, some emotion she couldn't read. All she knew was that there was some connection between the two of them, whether he thought it just a dalliance in the garden or not. "I'll see you at the Habernes' event all the same." She ripped her gaze from his and sped from the garden as fast as her legs would carry her.

❧

His morning ride had thus far done nothing toward the goal of clearing his mind. Perhaps some sense would eventually settle into his mind, but it was clearly not going to occur today. At the moment there was quite a bit to consider.

He shook his head and increased his speed leaving the park. His mother's presence threatened everything he'd built in London. His father's return to his life had set his nerves on edge. And then there was Sue, kissing him like she was trained by the entire demimonde, and in doing so, proclaiming the truth he suspected. That last bit had the strongest hold on him at the moment.

Suzanna was Sue. Sue was Suzanna. Or there never was a Suzanna, and Sue had always been Sue. However he flipped the information, it still brought him back to the same thought: What was he to do now?

He tightened his grip on Muley's reins as he left Hyde Park, heading down the street away from his home. Sue hadn't admitted her secret to him so he couldn't have an honest conversation with her yet.

Therefore, all of his questions stewed in his mind like poorly cooked soup.

She'd been there. She'd been there all along.

It was no wonder Sue had spent so much time angry with him. He'd seen her that night, too. He'd asked her to find…her. He'd pushed past her to find…her. Then he'd gone to her cousins to find…her. And all along it was her. Always her.

He urged Muley down the street to the speed of his racing thoughts. How could he ever make amends for his oversight? Could he? This was why she'd refused all his charm. And he'd gone and followed her about, asking for dances when she must want nothing more than for him to leave. He'd pushed her out of the way that night in search of a fantasy. Suzanna wasn't real. She never had been. Sue, on the other hand…

He shook his head. He was back to wondering what to do now—again. Perhaps if he could coax a confession out of her, they could discuss things. One thing he knew for certain was that secrets had to be confessed in the guilty party's time. If a secret was let loose too early, "everything will crash down," he muttered to himself.

He'd experienced this process enough to know that the truth couldn't be sprung on someone, catching them unaware. That would only make her defensive. No, she needed to admit who she was, and he would just have to give her ample opportunity to do so.

He slowed to allow a hack to pass and caught sight of movement at his side. Glancing over, he saw another rider waiting for the street to clear.

Her eyes flashed in challenge as her horse pranced

beneath her—where she sat astride in breeches. "Fine morning for a ride," she offered in greeting.

"It is." Holden was in no frame of mind to chat with a new acquaintance.

She steadied her prancing horse and smiled. "Care to make it interesting?"

"I don't believe we've met." Who was this lady? Not only was she using a man's saddle, but her hair hung down her back in a long auburn braid. He shook his head.

Just then the hack moved past and she took off down the street with a clatter of hooves. Holden had no interest in racing a lady through the streets of London, but neither did he wish to be bested by the chit. He leaned over Muley's mane and urged him forward.

With hooves clattering down the street, he began to close the gap in the race. Buildings sped by as they moved into a quieter section of town. He was level with the lady now. Glancing over at her, he saw her grin and pull ahead of him. Holden pulled up, slowing Muley as he watched her continue down the street. He'd been beaten by a girl. Add that to the tally of confusing circumstances that had occurred today.

He shook his head and turned up the street toward the Rutledge residence. That was when he caught sight of the auburn-haired rider tethering her horse across the street from his cousins. That was Ormesby House where the Moore family had long lived. He knew Trevor Moore from school years prior, and she must be related to him with that hair.

He shook off the sight of Trevor Moore's

unconventional relative and dismounted. Pulling out his watch, he checked the time. "Perfect timing," he murmured to himself. He would stop in for a surprise visit for breakfast. With any luck they would be serving the blueberry tea cakes today. If a ride couldn't settle his mind this morning, he would simply move on to sweets. And perhaps sometime after he'd eaten all the sugar in sight, he would know what came next with Sue.

❧

The window beside Sue was thrown open not because it was a beautiful day outside, as it was actually quite dreary, but because Isabelle had dropped a bottle of perfume on the floor not fifteen minutes prior, smashing it to pieces. Now the parlor she shared with Evangeline smelled strong enough to make a prostitute run for fresh air.

Sue lifted her gaze to the room and sighed. The only evidence she lived here was a small stack of canvases leaning against the wall in the corner. The remainder of the room was an eruption of hats, ribbons, feathers, and shoes. She curled further into the corner of the settee in an attempt to ignore the afternoon of excessive preening going on around her.

Victoria, however, didn't take Sue's posture as a sign to leave her alone and continued to converse with her. "I don't understand why you're still keeping this secret, Sue. Tell him the truth."

"I tried to tell him I was Suzanna just yesterday afternoon in the Rutledges' garden." Sue turned the page in her book, focusing on the printed images of flowers in her lap.

Isabelle stopped fussing with her hair in the mirror to flop down on the settee beside Sue, jostling the book in her grasp. "You were in the garden together? How romantic!"

Sue tried to ignore Isabelle, who thought everything was romantic. Her younger cousin didn't understand how complicated things had become or what was at stake in her life. "He's difficult to talk to about such things."

Victoria dropped the ribbon in her hands to her side to glare at Sue. "Heavens, if *you* can't talk to him, no one can."

Evangeline strolled by, plucking the ribbon from Victoria's fingers on her way to the seat at the vanity. "I think it's for the best. Keep your distance from him, Sister. He's distracting you from finding a husband." She sat and held the length of ribbon up to her hair with pursed lips.

"Thank you for that reminder, Evie. I'd forgotten I need a husband. Truly I had." Sue shut the book on her lap and laid it aside. It was no use. She would look at it later when her family wasn't trying to run her life for her.

Victoria turned to the tea service and bent to refill her cup. Apparently preening for hours on end gave one a great thirst. "Why not run away with Lord Steelings while dressed as Suzanna? It would be days before he discovered the truth, and by then it would be too late."

Evangeline cast the ribbon aside and picked up another. "The 'too late' bit is the troublesome part, Victoria. She can't risk her virtue for the likes of him."

"She already has. In the library," Victoria argued.

"She has?" Evangeline spun on her chair, leveling a glare in her direction. "Sue, you didn't! You could be with child!"

"I only kissed him, and you are not in charge of my actions. If I want to kiss a handsome gentleman, then I shall. In fact..." The memory of his mouth on hers in the garden yesterday came to mind. His hands on her skin. She tried to hide the smile tugging at her lips but couldn't.

"Sue Green! What did you do?"

"Urg, you sound like Mother, Evie. Did you know that? You're like her twin, only younger."

"Just like me, Evie!" Isabelle exclaimed with a little bounce that threatened to launch Sue off the settee.

"That's not what she meant, Isabelle." Victoria rolled her eyes as she pulled out a small flask of something and poured a measure into her teacup. "And never mind all of that. I want to hear details. Sue, you're still blushing! What happened yesterday?"

She sighed, remembering Holden telling her of his childhood struggles but not wanting to share them with anyone. Some words were too private and too precious even for her to discuss. And then he'd kissed her. "It was nothing. We talked."

"It looks like something indeed," Victoria said over the rim of her teacup.

"Very well. Perhaps there was a kiss. But it was nothing," she lied. "It's become so complicated now. He still doesn't know I'm...me." And he's not at all the person I thought him to be, she finished to herself.

"Sue, you must tell him the truth," Isabelle chimed in. "Keeping secrets will give you wrinkles."

"That's not true at all." Sue smiled, thinking of

a lady she'd seen on Bond Street the week before with lines covering her face, every one looking as if it held a fabulous story. "And besides, I find wrinkles rather endearing."

Victoria snorted into her cup. "You would."

"What good could come of telling him the truth?"

Isabelle clasped her hands below her chin and beamed as she pronounced, "He could realize his undying love for you. The two of you would then run away to Gretna Green, and you would be Lady Steelings!"

Evangeline turned from the mirror with one elegant brow raised in question. "Isabelle, how many of those gothic novels have you read? You know real gentlemen don't go around in shining armor discussing undying love, don't you, dear?"

"It could happen," Isabelle huffed.

"What if I tell him who I am and he runs in horror that he could have been attracted to such a plain-looking lady? What if that's it? It's over—all of it. What if I end my season alone? What if I'm forced to..." She was surprised to realize that the worst part of that line of thought was the bit where Holden wouldn't be in her life any longer. When had she grown fond of the arrogant man? She shook her head.

"'What if' seems to be quite the terrifying phrase," Isabelle mused.

A moment of rare silence fell over the group before Victoria's voice broke the silence. "Sue? What if he cares for you?"

Isabelle was right. "What if" was a terrifying phrase.

Eleven

THE WOODEN SIGN BEARING THE FADED IMAGE OF A mortar and pestle swung in the damp air blowing in off the Thames. The shop hadn't changed a bit since Henrietta was here last. Five and twenty years. Had it truly been that long? The years she'd wasted locked away in that wretched place!

She glanced up the narrow street to ensure she was alone before swinging open the door to the apothecary shop. A small bell rang above her head, and she smiled at the memory of walking in this very door for the same purpose all those years ago. Nothing had changed.

Only this time everything would go according to plan. Breathing in the sweet smell of herbs, Henrietta moved farther into the dimly lit shop. Warm circles of light shone from lamps hanging on the cream-colored walls, lighting the shining head of the shopkeeper behind the counter. He looked up in greeting and pushed his spectacles further up on his nose. Dusting bits of the herbs he was working with off his apron, he slid the herbs out of the way, awaiting her request.

It was a shame it had come to this. Holden held ever so much potential, unlike his brother who had threatened the very life of her sweet babe. Her nose twitched at the memory of Samuel's incessant whining and fits of temper. Holden, however, was bright and handsome. He was everything a son and heir should be. Or he would be once she had influence on his life again. Now the time had come to repair things.

"May I be of assistance, m'lady?"

"Yes. I need something of a rather delicate nature."

"Is it…"—the shopkeeper leaned over the long wooden counter to whisper—"lady problems?"

"In a manner of speaking, it is. I'm glad we see eye to eye on the matter, sir." This would be easier than she'd realized.

"It happens. Ladies of your age and all. I have just the thing." He turned and began digging in one of the small drawers lining the back wall. "You'll need to mix this into a tonic. You'll want to take it with your dinner, of course. Otherwise…"

"Pardon, but it's not for me."

"Right." He winked at her. The nerve! "It's for some other lady who is, I'm sure, much older than you."

She narrowed her eyes at him. Why must men be so difficult? All men except for her sweet Holden, of course. "I'm afraid you have it all wrong. Those are not the lady problems I'm here for."

"My apologies then, m'lady. Please explain your malady."

"As I stated before, it is not for my use. I find I'm in need of…"

The bell on the door began tinkling and a brief

breeze blew through the shop as a tall, broad-shouldered man entered. She'd spied him with her son not a day ago, no doubt filling Holden's head with thoughts of abandoning her to the madhouse once more. And wasn't he one to talk since he was known all over town as the Mad Duke of Thornwood.

"Your Grace!" The shop owner straightened at the sight of him. "What can I get for you this morning? Or do you have some rare treat for me today? African herbs? The tea leaves you brought last visit made quite the unusual brew."

Thornwood strolled up to the counter beside Henrietta. "Did they have the desired effect?"

"Yes." The shopkeeper's eyes flashed beneath his thick spectacles. "Indeed. The wife wants me to acquire more…for apothecary research, of course."

Thornwood laughed and leaned one elbow on the counter. "I'll remember that next time I go on expedition. I'm afraid I'm empty-handed today."

"Oh? What can I get for you, then?"

Had the man completely forgotten she was here? She arrived first, then in walked Thornwood and she was forgotten. Her jaw clenched as a familiar pang shot through her. Thornwood. The world would be a better place without him as well, but that's not why she was here…not on this visit at any rate.

He didn't seem to notice her staring as he stated, "I'm looking for damiana."

"Ah, I happen to have some in the back."

She cleared her throat and pursed her lips in a telling way to gain the man's attention. He would not ignore her any longer.

He hesitated with a glance in her direction. "Allow me to finish with this fine lady first, if that's all right."

"Do what you must." Thornwood shrugged.

"M'lady? What did you need?"

"Atropine."

At the questioning look in the shopkeeper's eyes as well as Thornwood's turned head, she added, "In small doses it calms a fever."

"I've never heard such." The apothecary shifted with discomfort.

So squeamish. It was a disgusting character trait. Sometimes in life things must be done, actions taken, all for the greater good. She raised her chin and looked him in the eye. "Are you questioning a lady of impeccable bearing?"

"No…m'lady."

He turned and began preparing a glass vial of dark red juice while she waited. Aware of Thornwood's eyes on her, she turned. "Yes?"

"You look familiar. Not the gray hair or the wrinkles, but your eyes. I've seen you before."

"I do not have wrinkles, and my hair is as dark brown as it ever was!"

Thornwood threw his hands up in surrender. "Didn't mean to offend the lady buying poison. That wouldn't be wise a'tol."

"I am not purchasing poison. It's for a fever."

"A fever." He nodded and turned his attention back to the shopkeeper, muttering, "And they call me mad."

"Your atropine, m'lady."

"Thank you." She handed him a few coins and turned to leave the shop.

Of all the ways she could spend her morning, she did not want to spend one second more of it in the company of that man. He would steal her son away from her. She knew it. She'd finally escaped the hospital, and she refused to lose her precious Holden all over again. Thornwood would give him ideas. Troublesome ideas. Just like that Green girl. But she would fix things. This time she would succeed. She and Holden would be together forever.

It was almost lunchtime. She started up the street to the busier thoroughfare ahead, knowing she needed to get back before she was missed. Those troublesome servants were always watching her, especially after she stole the neighbor's gown and went to that ball. But it was a good thing she had gone, for now she knew the severity of Holden's circumstances. And she would deal with this situation the same way she'd handled Sam's behavior.

She patted the vial inside her reticule, taking comfort in the soft clink of the glass. It was the sound of a promising future. Reaching the busy street, she signaled a passing hack. Holden would be ever so pleased once her plans were carried out. Finally, they would be together as a family—the way they should always have been.

❦

Sue slipped behind a hedgerow when she saw her mother begin to move in her direction. Peeking out to make sure she'd gotten away, she saw her mother's large green-feathered hat melt into the crowd on the Habernes' lawn. Letting out a sigh of relief, she stood surveying the party from the cover of the bush. There were far too many thoughts rattling around in her mind this afternoon to survive an encounter with her mother, and she didn't think she would fare well with random acquaintances, either.

The one person her eyes were sweeping the crowd for today was Holden.

Funny that she'd spent so much time avoiding him only to now have trouble finding him. Her palms were sweating inside her gloves, and she closed her eyes for a second to try and calm herself. She'd decided today was the day. Her family was right. Even if he was only trying to stop her from speaking in the garden, he hadn't been too quick to pull away once she stopped talking. Or had he? No. She must stay strong.

Today she would tell him the truth about the masquerade ball...and the library. She had quite a bit of explaining to do, if she were to be honest. Fanning her flushed cheeks with the back of her hand, she turned and bumped straight into another lady. The blue muslin of her capped sleeve plastered itself to Sue's shoulder with the heat of the afternoon.

For a moment, the lady hung there in the air, her arms flailing, but not yet falling. Sue reached out to grab her arm with a gasp. The girl staggered back a step, clinging to Sue. Just when Sue thought they would both end up tumbling to the ground, the lady righted herself.

Her dark eyes widened with surprise. Was she angry? Sue truly could not manage an angry lady today, not now. Her eyes swept over the lady, sizing up her adversary. Her blue dress hung loosely on her shoulders, and her hair—dark brown streaked with flames of red—was falling around her shoulders. Why was she half clothed behind a bush at a party? Perfect. Now she must deal with an angry, half-nude woman. This afternoon was going downhill rather quickly. But just as soon as the thought occurred to Sue, the young woman began laughing.

She had a crooked smile that simultaneously put Sue at ease and made her wary. Or was her wariness because the woman was half dressed and with her hair in disarray? Sue glanced around for the woman's half-clad counterpart but saw no one.

"Oh! Terribly sorry." The lady was still giggling. "I wasn't looking where I was going. I'm sure it was my fault."

"No harm done. Do you mind?" She turned, revealing her exposed back to Sue. "I can't seem to reach to get this blasted contraption back on."

"Certainly." Sue reached for the clasps of the woman's day dress. "I'm very discreet, just so you know."

"That's nice." The woman's shoulders lifted with a small shrug.

There was a moment of silence. Blasted silence. Sue couldn't help but fill it with words. "I won't even ask your name."

"It's Katie Moore."

"I also won't ask how you came out of your dress in the middle of an afternoon garden party because it's truly none of my concern. See? Discreet." Sue pulled on the fabric at Katie's back to finish the job.

"I got dreadfully hot."

Hot? Is that what she'd said? Sue scrunched up her nose in question at Katie's back. "Hot?"

"Yes, it's awful out here with not a whisper of a breeze. And, for the life of me, I don't know how you ladies wear these things." Katie lifted the hem of her day dress as if it was contaminated with some disease before dropping it back to the ground. "I don't think I've taken a breath since yesterday."

Sue finished and stepped to the side to see around Katie's turned shoulder. "What do you mean by 'you ladies'?"

"You know, girls who prefer salons and frills of various sorts." Katie turned as she spoke, waving to the bushes as if they were all made of said frills.

"I am not one of those girls. I'm Sue, by the way."

"Thank you ever so much, Sue." She gave Sue a slap on the shoulder that made her stumble to the side. "Now if you'll excuse me, I think I'll try to find a hidden door to the stables. No one would have such a large, utterly wasteful garden unless they had stables as well."

"I can't say that I know where the stables are. Will no one miss you if you leave and go to the stables?"

Katie pulled a face of confusion and shook her head. "Father will guess I've found something more amusing than a bunch of flowers."

"Stay in your dress or he'll think you've found something a bit too amusing."

"Fresh air and the ability to inhale it?"

"No. I was referring to…never mind. I hope you find the stables."

"Not to worry. I think they're that way."

"How do you know?"

"I can smell the shite. All right…well, have a nice

time…you know, sipping punch or whatever you do at one of these things."

Sue watched her go. She was still staring after the young girl when Holden stepped around the far corner of the hedgerow, nodding toward Katie as she passed.

"Who was that?" he asked as he neared Sue.

"A very odd lady, but I think I like her."

Holden's hair caught the sun as he stepped closer. He looked impossibly handsome today. Blast him. Why must he make this so difficult? Her mouth went dry as she looked up into his green eyes, crinkling at the corners as he offered her a smile. *Say something, Sue. Now is your chance. Tell him. Tell him!* She swallowed and dropped her gaze to his cravat straight in front of her. That helped. "Holden…"

"You were right."

"About what?" She looked back up into his face— which proved to be a bad decision. She couldn't stop looking at his lips, quirked up in an easy smile. Two days ago those lips had been pressed to hers. *Get hold of yourself, Sue. He only kissed you to shut you up.*

"Not an orchestra anywhere in sight." The shoulders of his tan wool coat shook with his chuckle.

She tried to laugh along but it came out as a breathy smile. What was he talking about? She'd lost her handle on the conversation. He was still watching her. Could he read her jumbled thoughts? If he could, he certainly had the advantage.

"Your habit of refusing me dances?" he supplied with a smile. "There's no need to do so today since there is no dancing…and now that I've explained my jest, I've successfully removed all charm from my words." He glanced away down the path and shook his head before turning back to her. "Of course you've never found me charming anyway, so I suppose that's neither here nor there." There was a look in his eyes. What was it? What did it mean?

She could only give a halfhearted chuckle in response as she looked up into those eyes.

He cleared his throat when she didn't answer. "I spotted some apple tarts on a passing tray a few minutes ago."

She regained her senses at the mention of food. Shaking her head and glancing into the green of the bush beside her instead of his blasted eyes, she retorted, "Apple tarts are better than a waltz any day."

He held out an arm to escort her across the gathering toward the buffet set up under a large tree. "You haven't waltzed with me. I put apple tarts to shame."

Yes, he did. Their dance at the masquerade would live forever in her memory. He needed to know. She should tell him now. However, when she opened her mouth, all that she said was, "That would depend on the apple tart in question."

"You wound me, Sue. I'll have you know that ladies delight in dancing with me."

"If you have your choice of ladies in any ballroom, why do you wish to dance with me?" The question was out of her mouth before she could stop it. It was barely a thought before it was released into the world. And once it was there, she couldn't take it back. She didn't want to know the answer to the question. Or maybe she did but she didn't think she could bear to hear it. She looked away. Her mouth opened and closed, but now no words came out. Her cursed mouth!

He ran a hand through his hair, and she almost heard his own curse released under his breath. Or had she imagined that? "Take a stroll with me? After the apple tarts, of course—we must have priorities. I believe I saw a sculpture garden around the far corner. I'll act the perfect gentleman and it isn't a dance, so no need to refuse me on principle."

"Very well. I have something I need to discuss with you anyway." As they wove through the crowd on the lawn, she tried to calm herself. All she needed to say was "I'm Suzanna." How difficult was that? She took a breath and glanced up at him to see he was watching her, a smile tugging at the corners of his mouth.

"You're quiet. You're never quiet—or nearly never."

"I know." She bit at her lip. "I have something I need to tell you."

"Then say it. I know you couldn't possibly be carrying some dark secret...could you?" He raised an eyebrow in question. "I know you would never hide anything from me."

"And if I did have such knowledge of which you were unaware..."

"There is no reason not to tell me, Sue. There never was."

"I..." She looked away, biting her lip.

"Hmm, now I'm intrigued. May I guess your secret?" There was a mysterious gleam in his eyes as he looked down at her.

"I'm not sure that you can." She almost laughed.

"That's not very sporting of you."

Her heart was racing. Surely at her next statement, he would guess her truth. *It must happen, Sue.* She licked her lips and said, "You may ask me two questions. Isn't that how this game is played? Or so I recall." Heat rose in her cheeks at the memory of their game on his bed that night.

He paused, his eyes crinkling at the corners with his apparent enjoyment of her situation. Then with a twitch of his lips, the look was gone, replaced by a piercing glare.

Did he now know? Had he taken her hint? Did that bring her relief or further worry—she didn't even know.

He flashed a grin as he asked, "Do you secretly sell your artwork?"

She scrunched up her nose in confusion. Her artwork? He didn't remember their game? Had he forgotten about Suzanna? It was true he hadn't asked after her in a few days. Perhaps only she remembered that night now. Where relief should reside there was only disappointment. Perhaps it wasn't as prized a memory for him as she'd thought. She twisted her hands together before her. Her artwork. In comparison, that secret didn't seem to matter anymore. "Do I secretly sell my artwork? Yes, yes I do."

"Ha! I was right. You sign your work SAG, don't you?"

"I do, but...wait... How did you know? I suppose I shouldn't be surprised. I knew you collected my paintings. I simply thought... Was it the sketchbook? Did I sign something?"

"No, it struck me when I walked past one of your

paintings this morning. There was a distinct sameness, a familiarity."

The irony that he could connect her with her artwork, but not with the woman he tussled with in his bed a fortnight ago, was not lost on her. Perhaps he didn't remember her anymore, but she remembered him. *Secrets, always so many secrets.* She was done with it—all of it. She was going to tell him about Suzanna and make him remember her. "Speaking of familiarity…"

"I know. We need to talk about what happened in the garden. That's the true reason I wished a walk with you today. Sue, I hope you can forgive me. When I kissed you…"

"Stop. I need to tell you something. Now. It's important. About who I am."

"You're an artist. That's all you wanted to say, correct?" He glanced away and she thought she saw a trace of laughter when he turned back to her. "I won't tell anyone, if that's what you're worried about. I'm actually quite pleased to discover I'm friends with an artist whose paintings I collect. That doesn't happen every day."

"Friends," she repeated. Is that how he saw her? Had it all meant nothing to him? Even yesterday afternoon?

"Yes. You are my friend, aren't you? When I said I wanted to shut you up in the garden, I only partially meant it."

"You meant it?" She crossed her arms before her as she stared at him.

"Only partially." He laughed as he grabbed two tarts from a passing footman.

"I suppose we're partially friends, then."

He turned back to her and leaned closer to whisper, "Can I purchase the other half with an apple tart?"

"Perhaps." She smiled in spite of herself and accepted the sweet from him, taking a bite. She must tell him now. Her opportunity was fading; soon it would be gone. He only considered them friends, nothing more after all. What did it matter if she was Suzanna? It was just another secret.

Their kiss didn't seem to mean as much to him as it had to her anyway. Friends. Would they laugh about this later? Or would he be revolted by her and cut her from his life? The bite of apple tart in her mouth turned bitter and she had to choke it down.

"You do know that I never mentioned which paintings I collect. It's interesting to me that you *assumed* I collected yours."

"You mentioned it once. I'm sure of it." She looked down at the small plate in her hand, fixated on the tiny pink roses winding around the edge. He'd mentioned it. Only it was on the night of the masquerade ball. *This is your chance, Sue. Tell him.*

"Did I?" he asked around a bite of tart.

She glanced up in an attempt at innocence, cursing her nerves. "Oh, certainly."

"When?" The intent look in his eyes made her heart race.

Not for the first time this afternoon, she wondered if he already knew her secrets. She blinked. Her lips parted. She needed only say the words, yet her confession refused to leave the safety of her mouth. Instead she said, "I believe you're out of questions."

"You're using that as an excuse. Why, Sue?"

"Another question. Oh look, there's my mother."

"You're seeking out your mother now?" He nudged her elbow to move to the side of the party where they could continue their discussion. His fingers lingered a moment longer than was respectable, leaving her skin warm. "Is my company so horrible?"

"Yes, but I rather enjoy it." *And that is the problem,* she finished in silence with a glance up into his face. Her heart pounded in her ears.

"As do I." He seemed ill at ease as he shifted on his feet. "Sue?"

"Yes?"

"The reason I pester you for dances—dances you refuse, but dances nonetheless…" His gaze seemed to look through her to her core. "I enjoy this. You."

"And I refuse you because I enjoyed our dance too much," she finally blurted out, emotion welling up behind her eyes the moment her words were set loose. *Don't cry, Sue! You ninny!*

"Ahh, this must be your big secret… When did we dance, Sue? Just say what you mean to say."

"In a dream, Holden." She sniffed away the threat of tears and continued, "I wore a dark rose gown tied with ribbons. I was quite foxed, you see…"

"Dreams can seem quite real, can't they? I've experienced the same inexplicable fantasy. Do go on."

He didn't understand. He thought she was teasing. How could she explain? "That night in your bedchamber…"—she attempted to clarify—"it was me." Had she said that last bit aloud or only declared it in her mind?

His face was unreadable. Just then her mother walked up, shoving Evangeline in front of Sue like a prize pony at a harvest festival. Her opportunity had come and gone. She'd failed. Why was she able to say everything else in the world except the very thing that needed to be said? Or had she said too much already?

∽

"Yes, the weather is warm this afternoon," Holden agreed with Evangeline as his eyes swept the garden for the girl's sister.

As he led Evangeline past a row of roses, he caught sight of Sue standing by the table laden with food. Her fingers were poised over a bowl of chocolates as she made her selection. She lifted the sweet to her lips and popped it into her mouth.

"I do hope the weather cools a bit, don't you?" Evangeline said at his side.

"I suppose." He craned his neck to see over the people milling about the lawn for another glimpse of Sue. Finally, he spied her. She was sucking on the piece of chocolate while a satisfied gleam filled her eyes—eyes the color of autumn leaves. He wondered yet again how he'd been so dense as to not see who she truly was. And now he was trapped strolling about this garden with her sister when Sue had as good as admitted she was Suzanna only minutes ago. "Damn it all."

"I know. I find the sun rather bright today as well. And look at my sister…lifting her face to it and allowing herself to tan or, worse, freckle. What can be done with her?" Evangeline laughed.

"I find I'm wondering the same thing." As they grew closer, he caught sight of an escaped lock of Sue's hair stretching out in the breeze like a banner announcing Suzanna's arrival. "Burnished gold," he muttered to himself.

Sue had been right all along—he was blind. "Bloody hell."

"Pardon?"

"I can...hardly tell...if your sister has freckles from this distance."

"I don't believe she does. I know I don't have any. Mama says they're the sign of a life lived in dirt."

"Does she?" Whatever insulting comment came next, Holden didn't know. He was too focused on his own stupidity when it came to the girl's sister. He'd been so focused on finishing what he started with Suzanna that he'd lost sight of what was staring him in the face—Sue.

"Doesn't that sound lovely, my lord?"

"What? Oh yes, indeed."

"Perfect! Mama will be ever so pleased when she sees us sitting together."

"When?"

"Dinner at the Amberstall event? You said..."

"Oh, yes. That." What had he agreed to do? He hadn't been listening to a word the chit said.

"That." Evangeline tittered and hit his arm with her fan. "You do make a nice jest, my lord."

"So I've been told by a few. I suppose I'll see you at Amber Hollow, then."

"What's this?" her mother interrupted. "Arrangements to see one another again? And after only one turn about the garden." She clasped her hands together in excitement. "It doesn't take long, does it, Lord Steelings?"

"I suppose not if one chooses to stride it out instead of stroll. It can be done quite efficiently."

"Oh, Lord Steelings, your wit is not under-estimated."

Damn, here came the tittering. He hated the tittering. Sue never tittered. Her laughter was like... He sighed. *Raindrops falling on metal.* How had he ever been so daft as to not see the truth right in front of him?

"Will you excuse me?" He needed to speak with Sue—now.

"Certainly, my lord. I look forward to our seeing one another again."

"Quite," he offered, not taking his eyes from Sue. She would not slip through his grasp again. Not today.

He moved through the crowd, closing on her position beneath the tree. He watched her pop another sweet in her mouth, then look down at her glove, now stained with melted chocolate. She pulled a face of concern, glancing to the side before her tongue escaped her mouth for a quick lick. She was still rubbing at her fingertips when he approached her.

"If it isn't paint, it's chocolate."

"Oh, Holden. Did you see? Um..." A blush spread up her neck.

"I'm seeing quite a bit lately, and I must admit I'm enjoying it. We never made it to the statuary garden." He extended his arm. Where should he begin? He'd never offered an apology and then attempted to remain linked with the lady he was in debt to before. This was all new. They passed through the gate into the small garden marked by cherubs perched on columns.

"Holden, earlier I said some things. Well, I'm quite sure I rambled a bit, which I know I'm prone to do, but I said something in particular. I think I did, anyway. I believe I've become overheated in the sun today because I can't recall if I truly said what I meant to say. But know that my intention was to say it."

"Clearly." He began laughing against his will.

"You're laughing." Her head tilted to the side as she looked at him. "Do you have the ability to ever be serious?"

"Only when losing at cards and kissing ladies."

"Both of which I'm sure you do often."

"I'm quite good at cards, I'll have you know."

"And the ladies?"

"I'm quite good at that as well."

She shot him a look of annoyance.

"I see you remain unconvinced." He turned to meet her eyes, tracing his fingers down the edge of her jaw before dropping his hand. "I admit I have some regrets when it comes to you, Sue."

She pulled away from him as if struck. "It's the kiss in the garden, isn't it? Everything else is just words, and as you said, we're friends. Good friends. Really, that's all it could be. You regret it. It's all right. I suppose I regret it, too." She looked away across the garden.

Was that true? She only desired his friendship? He'd never hated his own words more. He'd meant he regretted overlooking her at the masquerade ball. Should he keep the knowledge of his oversight to himself and allow her to find happiness without him? Continue on as friends? Nothing more? His chest tightened.

She would find some other gentleman. She would marry and bear children. Something inside him snapped. He'd finally found her. She was his. He ran a hand through his hair and exhaled a puff of exasperation before looking back in her direction. "You do? You regret kissing me?"

He watched her but her eyes were on the marble statue of a lady before them, revealing nothing.

"Certainly," she bit out through a clenched jaw before falling silent as she rounded the statue, staring up at the white fabric draped from the lady's shoulder.

"I don't," he stated as he followed her around the statue.

"What?" Her head snapped around as she looked up at him.

"The kiss wasn't what I wanted to discuss with you. I don't regret kissing you. I've only regretted one kiss in my life, and that was the result of a dare when I was sixteen. She bit me."

"Perhaps I'll try that next time."

"Now you assume there will be a next time?" he teased. "Only a moment ago you regretted kissing me. My pride may well be wounded, Sue. Have you no compassion? And how do you know that I'm not ready to move on to my next conquest by now, rake that I am? I could have a rule about multiple kisses with a lady."

"Your pride seems intact to me." Her face contorted in disbelief. "And you have no such rule."

"Don't I?" He stepped closer and lowered his voice. "And how would you know that, Sue? What if…I simply can't endure ladies who are so clinging that they follow me into a dark library at a ball to have relations with me, for example?"

"I would never follow you into such a clandestine location." Her gaze dropped to her feet, her hands twisting into a knot at her waist. "Not to mention that if I did go to such a place, it would be because I was lured there under false pretenses."

"But you would never do something so…scandalous. Would you, Sue?" He tilted his head to the side, trying to see her face. "You, Sue Green, would never find your way into my bed in the middle of a ball to which you had no invitation." He needed to see her face. He lifted her chin with a light touch until her eyes met his. "Would you, Sue? However, a kiss on a garden bench, that's allowable. Isn't it?"

Her eyes were wary as she regarded him. "Holden…"

He loved the way her lips moved when she said his name, like a small plea to be kissed with every syllable. He slipped his hand up to cup her cheek. "Yes, Sue? Or should I say Suzanna?"

She took a ragged breath before speaking. "About you not wanting any more secrets…"

"I believe I'll make an exception for this one."

The distinctive sound of a society matron clearing her throat rang out in the warm afternoon air. "Lord Steelings, you must be lost in this garden with such oppressive statuary." Disdain dripped from Sue's mother's voice as she moved closer.

His hand fell away from Sue but he couldn't look

away. Their eyes locked together as challenge met dread and wrapped itself in wanting. He needed to leave. Her mother was here after all—her marriage-minded mother. He took a step away with a practiced smile. "If you'll excuse me, ladies, I must go. Miss Green, I look forward to your refusal of my dance." With a bow, he left without a backward glance.

Twelve

HE KNEW. SUE'S RAGGED BREATH FOGGED THE carriage window as she stared out at the buildings they passed. He knew of the masquerade ball and the library; he knew her cousins had lied to hide her. But what did any of it mean? She needed to talk to him, to explain. Or perhaps he was the one who needed to explain. She couldn't keep track anymore. Everything with Holden had become so blasted complicated.

"I'm quite pleased with your progress today, Evangeline. Lord Steelings is certainly a difficult catch, yet catch you did."

Sue's head spun with a speed that sent a pain up her neck. "What happened?"

"Lord Steelings asked me to go in to dinner with him at the Amberstall event. Mother is quite happy."

"And what of your happiness, Evie? Are you happy?" Sue studied her sister.

"Of course she is, Sue. Don't be silly."

"Is inquiring after my sister's happiness silly? I suppose so. Dining with a gentleman like Lord Steelings, she must be thrilled."

Evangeline turned troubled eyes on her. "Sue…"

"I'm not quite sure when he found the time today to ask you, though. You certainly make quick work of things, don't you?"

"Indeed," her mother boasted.

Holden and Evangeline would now be sitting together at dinner. Their names would be put together by every matron in attendance. And Sue would watch as she always did. When had he arranged it? One minute she was hoping for her own happiness, and the next her sister had stolen it away once again.

It could be for the best. He knew her secret now. She should be able to free herself of her connection with him. She could move on—to what, she didn't know, but on somewhere nonetheless. And he could move on as well. But hadn't he said he enjoyed her company? Hadn't there been heat in his eyes as he gazed at her? Surely, she hadn't imagined it.

The carriage stopped before their house, and a footman assisted her to the ground. What was real and what was illusion? She was beginning to understand Holden's confusion over her identity. After all, she couldn't keep track of him, either. Evangeline was floating up the steps to the house beside her. She was perfect. Sue could never compete with her sister for a gentleman's affections. Clearly, a union between Holden and her sister was Mother's wish, and no one went against Mother's wishes—Evangeline least of all. If this was a contest, Sue would lose. And yet…

And yet there had been a glimmer of something in Holden's eyes today when he looked at her. Was it hope? She wasn't sure, but as long as there was a speck of it there when she saw him next, she would cling to it. She took a breath and followed her family through the front door.

"You'll need all new ensembles, of course," her mother stated as she removed her hat and handed it to a maid.

Evangeline shot an apologetic glance in her sister's direction. "Sue will need at least one new dress, don't you think, Mother?"

"Sue will look fine. You will be the one catching Lord Steelings' eye, not Sue."

Sue swallowed the words but they didn't sit well in her stomach. Her eyes narrowed on her mother as her hands began to shake with anger.

"He only wishes to sit with me at a dinner," Evangeline replied. "That's hardly a proposal."

"It's not a proposal *yet*, my dear. These things take time."

Something inside Sue snapped like an overextended twig from the garden. She ripped her hat off and threw it on a table, having heard enough for one day. "Mother, what would you think if I caught Lord Steelings' eye instead of Evangeline?"

"You? Lord Steelings would never look twice at you, dear. He's only being kind to you because of your relation to Evangeline."

"I see." Sue swallowed, watching her mother remove her gloves as if not a thing was amiss, not a single thing.

"Good. It wouldn't do to get your hopes up in that regard."

"Yet it is good for Evangeline to expect a betrothal?"

She glanced at her sister, who was making a thorough study of the inside of her reticule.

"Evangeline is the sort of lady Lord Steelings is looking for as a wife. She would complement his good looks, title, and money."

"And I wouldn't."

"Simply because a gentleman shows you kindness does not mean he is interested in you, Sue." Her mother shot her a sympathetic look.

"I didn't think that. I only…"

"He looked terribly weary from your company when I saw him today." Mother turned from her with a sigh and began fussing over the state of Evangeline's hat. "That was why I decided to rescue him from the awkward situation of showing you statuary. He appeared quite relieved to see me, in fact. You've never understood how to read these things in gentlemen. That is part of your problem, Sue. Albeit a small part of your problem, but a problem nonetheless."

"Rescue him? He was not weary. I will never understand, Mother, how you think it right to hide me away to protect gentlemen, only to throw Evangeline at those same gentlemen."

"Jealousy doesn't suit you, Sue."

"Neither does being tossed aside in favor of my sister. If you'll excuse me, I'm feeling quite weary from *this* conversation."

Sue ran up the stairs, not pausing until she heard the soft click of her bedchamber door, indicating that she was alone. Jealous? Her mother thought her jealous? She didn't want what belonged to Evangeline, only what was hers. Was he hers to lose, though?

You? Lord Steelings would never look twice at you, dear.
The words refused to leave her mind. She recited
them in her memory as if practicing for one of her
mother's dreaded poetry readings. Over and over the
words rang in her ears, burning her every time.

Feeling thoroughly singed, she crossed the room
to the wardrobe in the corner. She shoved her shifts
and a pair of gloves aside and pulled a box of paints
and an unfinished painting from the back. Mother and
her rules could jump from a high cliff. She needed to
escape her situation, and the best way she knew to
escape was through art. Glancing down at her dress,
she sighed at the thought of changing. What did it
matter if there were a few paint splatters on her skirts?
No one would notice anyway.

She opened her paints and began to mix the colors.
The night sky in her current piece needed to be
finished. Purples swirled with blues into a storm of
darkness trapped on canvas. She paused to look out
her window into the growing nothingness of evening.
The painting needed to be deeper than London's skies
at night, enough so that she could disappear into its
depths. She whipped the brush in long strokes. It had
to be bold, bolder than she could ever be. Larger than
she could ever be, more beautiful...beautiful. The
word sank like an anchor in her stomach.

It had to be beautiful—something she would
never be.

Pushing a tear from her cheek with the back of
her hand, she slashed her brush across the canvas once
more. Holden had once thought her beautiful—before
he'd seen who she was beneath her mask. Could he

see her that way again or was that moment lost forever? She would know soon enough.

❧

Holden descended the main stairs of the Amberstall
home still shaking his coat into place. He'd ridden
with Thornwood all the way here at the breakneck
speed his friend insisting on maintaining. Holden still
wasn't sure why they needed to arrive in such haste,
but one never knew when it came to Thornwood's
ideas. Yet, he'd been glad of the wind on his face
today. That was until he'd caught sight of himself in a
mirror after arriving.

He'd left Thornwood in the stables to come clean
up before seeing Sue. Sue. What would he say? It had
been two days, and still he had no idea how to proceed
with her. He only knew he needed to see her.

He slipped past the hosts of the party while they
were busy greeting a new arrival. If Sue was here
already, she would be with the other guests on the
terrace. He moved through one of the drawing rooms
toward the wall of glass doors thrown open to the
terrace. Outside, a few guests milled about munching
on sandwiches. For once he couldn't spare a thought
for the food served.

As soon as he stepped out into the sunlight, he saw
her leaning against the half wall overlooking the large
expanse of grass. Her head was tilted up as she chatted
with her friend. What was her friend's name? Phillips,
Lillian Phillips—that was it. Sue turned back to the
lawns before her. She looked like a sugared lemon
today in a yellow dress bound in white, and just as

with any sugared lemon, he wondered if she would be sweet or tart. He supposed it was time to find out the answer to that question. With a sigh, he took a step closer. *Be charming, Holden. You're nothing if not charming.* He smiled and moved behind Sue, who was still chatting with her friend and oblivious to his arrival.

"I would like to try and find the hidden lake I heard was here," she was saying.

Perfect! Fate was shining on him at last! "I shall take you to see it, then."

Sue turned at the sound of his voice, the tension visible in her shoulders. Her lips parted to speak before closing again.

Miss Phillips cleared her throat. "That is very kind, Lord Steelings. However, we were about to partake of some of those lovely sandwiches over on the buffet. I've heard wonderful things about the cucumber sandwiches. Have you tried them?"

"Yes. Dreadfully dry. But I wouldn't want to stand in your way if you wish to try one. Come along, my lady. I'll show you that hidden lake you wished to see. I've been there many times." Perhaps many times was an exaggeration since he'd never set foot on this estate until this afternoon, but if there was a hidden lake, he would find it. He offered an innocent smile as he read the hesitation in her eyes.

"I shouldn't go just now," Sue rushed to say. "I was only thinking…"

He took half a step forward, his eyes never leaving hers. "Tomorrow all of our moments will be planned for us as the party begins in earnest. It's not far." He extended his arm to Sue and held his breath, hoping she would take it. She stared at his arm for a second before her eyes lifted to his face, beautiful eyes filled with warmth.

"Yes, all right." She pulled her gaze away to toss a parting smile in her friend's direction. "Lillian, I'll return shortly."

"I believe the nature walk begins over there in that grove of trees." He pointed to a far point on the lawn that seemed a likely place to conceal a body of water.

"And that leads to the hidden lake?"

"I certainly hope so."

"You can't recall?"

"You could say that." He grinned down at her as he led her down the stone steps to the lawn.

"You don't know the way, do you?"

"Of course I do."

"You've never been there, have you?" Her nose scrunched up in disbelief as she gazed up into his face. "I'd wager you didn't find the sandwiches to be dry, either. Do you even know the direction of the lake? Or are we to walk in circles until we stumble upon it?"

"It's a lake. How hard could it possibly be to find?"

"I hate to point out it's called the 'hidden lake.'"

"Ah, but take comfort in the fact it's not called the 'hidden mud puddle.' For that would be considerably more difficult." He led her into the grove of trees, relieved to see a beaten path leading away from the lawn.

"Why hide a lake in the first place?" she mused at his side as they moved farther into the shade of the forest. "On most estates, the owners seem as proud of the lake as they are of the family title. I've seen entire homes oriented around a lake that's really more of a pond, yet here they hide it away and put the stables on display for the world to see. Do you find that strange?"

He chuckled. "Have you met Amberstall?"

"We met a few years ago." There was a hardened note in her voice that said there had been more to it than that, but she didn't elaborate.

He quirked a brow in her direction. "And you still question his pride in his stables?"

"I believe his pride goes without question. I was merely speaking as to the wisdom of that pride."

"Again, have you met Amberstall?" He smiled down at her as they rounded a bend in the path. Stepping over a tree root sprawled in front of them, he glanced around. The woods were growing denser as they walked, yet the trail ahead remained. He could almost see sunlight in the distance, dripping down like golden rain between the leaves above. For all his flaws, Amberstall did have a nice estate. Holden nodded in satisfaction as they moved through the trees.

"Is your estate a reflection of you, too, then?"

Her question stopped him. His estate? He hadn't been to his childhood home since he rode away at eighteen. What would it look like today?

He picked up a tree limb from the ground and tested it as a walking stick. His house in London was his home now, not rented rooms in Iceland, not rooms above a shop in Belgium, not a cottage in Scotland, and certainly not Pemberton. He would have to go back there one day, but that would not be any day soon. For now, he wanted to stay. He'd never tried that before—staying.

If she wanted to know about his home, he would tell her of his house in London. "I do try to keep a nice home. I have perhaps too many pieces of art. My butler complains about the clutter but he's rather disagreeable to begin with, so I don't think he minds overmuch."

"Why not let him go if he's disagreeable?"

"Fezawald is family. Not in truth, but the only truth I've ever known."

"He's very fortunate to have you. Mother sends servants away almost weekly for less. I never know who will be gone by morning. Soon I think it may be me." She laughed, but the laughter didn't reach her eyes.

"You have her at an advantage, though. Don't you see?"

"Do I? How is that possible?"

"You're tiny. You can hide. She'll never find you to toss you out."

"Oh!" She shot a glare in his direction.

"Surely there's a drawer you could tuck yourself away within." He laughed as she shoved him. "A hatbox? Oh, come now. You're short. You must know it. I can't make a jest?"

"You are a giant who…is too tall."

"That was pitiful. Try again." He turned to face her. She tapped her lip with the tip of her finger for a moment before dropping her hands to her waist with a dejected frown. "I can't insult people on command." She shrugged. "Your ears are uneven on your head."

"No, they aren't."

"No…they aren't." She studied him for another

moment before shaking her head. "Your nose isn't even crooked, and I kicked you in the face."

"That you did." He began laughing.

"Do you have flaws, Holden? Is there any hidden, soiled part of you? It's quite disconcerting for a lady, you know, to be around someone so…so…"

"I'm plenty soiled. My life is positively black with it." But he didn't want to speak of anything other than the two of them here in this forest. Nothing else mattered more than this afternoon with Sue. He grinned down at her. "And I rode here, so I'm fairly certain half the road to London is still in my hair."

With one quick movement he dipped his head and shook his hair in her face, glancing his cheek off the exposed skin at her neck. She smelled of sweet bread baking in the kitchen. He tossed his head at her again, chuckling at her flailing complaints.

"No!" she mocked, leaning away from him in laughter.

To his surprise, a moment later her hand slipped into his hair, the strands falling around her fingers. He sucked in a breath as she brushed against his scalp, raising the hair on the back of his neck in the process. He began to straighten, enjoying the fact that Sue's hand had to trail down his chest to fall back to her side. What had been laughter a moment ago lingered on her lips, full and rich with untold pleasures. "Filthy," she stated.

He stood gazing down into her face. He was standing too close for friends, as he'd claimed they were only days ago. But now they were alone and he didn't care about friendship. He'd chased her all summer, and now she was here. "I could teach you filth."

"I'm guessing you could."

And he planned upon it, but now was too soon. He tamped down the flames she'd stirred within him. First, he had some details to resolve, beginning with discussing their past together and then finding an apparently damn-well-hidden lake. He cleared his throat and looked down the trail. "Perhaps. But just now we should find that hidden lake and hope the person who named it lied."

They walked in silence for a minute, keeping on the beaten path as it led out of the woods and into a sun-drenched clearing. The grass brushed against the sides of his boots, making a pleasant swishing sound, yet it was too quiet. And Sue was never quiet.

He took a breath and dove into the conversation they were both avoiding as if it were icy water on a cool summer morning. "I should have known it was you that night at the masquerade ball. I'm not sure what I was thinking. Sue, you have my sincerest apologies."

"It's all right. You were expecting…someone else. Someone like Evangeline, my cousins, your cousins… anyone but me."

"I don't know who I was expecting, but I know I would have been disappointed with anyone but you, Sue."

"You don't have to appease my vanity—I have none."

He stopped, pulling her around to face him. "I'm not exaggerating or making up stories to make you feel better. What I did was wrong, and I must accept the consequences. But Sue, I tell you the truth when I say I'm glad it was you. No one else would do."

"Do you mean that?"

"Did I not prove it when I kissed you in the garden?"

"What of your interest in my sister, then?" she asked in a rush of words and then looked away from him.

"What interest in your sister?" He pulled her around so she faced him. "I have none."

"You're escorting her in to dinner tonight. My mother is thrilled."

"Unfortunately, I'm not quite so pleased." He tried to catch her eye but she stared straight at his cravat. "Sue, I'm here with you. The invitation to your sister was a mistake." How could he make her understand?

"Evangeline would be quite the match for any gentleman. And you could have any lady you desire."

"Not anyone." He bent his head to meet her gaze. "You."

She shook her head. "I've heard the stories of your French sweethearts."

"Right." He cursed the day he'd thought it a brilliant idea to allow on-dits to link him to France. What once had hidden him from his father was now going to kill everything between them. "Many stories about me aren't entirely factual. You should know that."

"There's a kernel of truth in every falsehood."

"Not always." He shook his head.

"You don't have to lie to me. We're friends, remember?"

Friends. He was beginning to hate that word. "I'm quite aware of our friendship, such that it is. Tell me, Sue. In your experience, do friends touch each other...like this?" He moved his hand, tracing a line up her neck with his fingers.

"I believe they do," she murmured with a tilt of her head, inviting his touch.

"Do friends on occasion do this?" He wrapped his hand around the back of her neck, pulling her closer. His lips met hers in a tide of heat and wanting. As she slipped her hands around his waist, he broke their kiss, gazing down into her upturned face. His fingers danced in small circles on the back of her neck. He didn't want to let her go, yet if he didn't stop now, they would be on the hard ground in minutes. Sue deserved more than that. He needed to at least find soft ground. He smiled at her dazed expression.

"I've never had a friend like you."

"Nor I you."

"Do you think we will remain friends?"

He dropped his hands from her and guided her ahead of him on the path, his hand lingering on her lower back. "Until we're old and decrepit? Covered in wrinkles?"

"Yes."

"I'll be a doddering old man with aching joints who complains of the weather. Will you want to kiss me then?"

She laughed. "Of course. As I said before, I have no vanity."

"I suppose one day your husband will take issue with such behavior."

She snorted. "That, Holden, is extremely unlikely."

"You don't plan to marry? Why do you attend the balls and such?"

"I'm told to attend balls and so I attend. I don't expect anything to come of it. At this point, it would be folly to think I will marry. So I will continue to do what is expected of me." She shook her head. "Whatever that may be."

"You make it sound like a sentencing in a dungeon."

"Sometimes it feels that way. You're a gentleman so you wouldn't understand. You have the freedom to live as you choose with no burdens."

"Indeed. It's nice not to have a single problem in my life."

"One day I hope for similar circumstances."

"As do I."

They rounded a bend and came upon a grouping of boulders on the side of the path. The tall grass of the clearing became shorter, clearly maintained for picnics and so forth. They must be close to the lake. He grinned with a mischievous idea. "We have to stop here. I apologize but it must be done."

"But we haven't yet reached the hidden lake. Must we return so soon? You aren't injured, are you?" Her eyes swept over him.

"No. We only need to stop a moment. Sit. There on that rock." He indicated the boulder nearest her.

"All right. I suppose a rest would be nice."

"Give me your foot."

"*What?*"

"Your foot. Lift it up."

She sat unmoving for a moment before complying. Catching the heel of her half boot in the palm of his hand, he began to remove it.

"What are you…" Her voice trailed off as he tossed her boot aside into the grass and reached for the other. "Barefoot. We can't, Holden. What if someone sees us? I already don't have a chaperone."

"Shhh. No one will know." He pulled his boots off and laid them beside hers, where he noticed she had laid her stockings as well while he was busy. The look of bliss covering her face made him chuckle. "I believe the hidden lake is just around the next bend. Not far a'tol."

"How do you know?"

"Close your eyes and listen. Can you hear it?"

"No."

"Neither can I."

She laughed and wrapped her hand around his arm. He could listen to that laughter forever. Would they remain together until they were old and feeble as they'd teased earlier? He wanted to keep her in his life that long. What did she want? He would have to answer that question in time. Right now, he knew two things: she was with him and they were alone. Fate had indeed smiled on him today.

As they rounded a hill, Sue exclaimed, "It's beautiful!"

He looked down the path as it wound to the edge of a small lake with foliage cascading to the edge of the water. "I knew it was this direction."

"You knew no such thing."

"Are you suggesting my sense of direction is based on luck?"

"Yes. That is precisely what I'm suggesting." She laughed and went to the grassy bank overlooking the water.

The lake was indeed hidden from view of the house. As the destination for the nature path carved into the hillside, it was perfectly manicured and designed with boulders placed around to form seating. He stripped off his jacket and tossed it onto one of the large, flat rocks and began rolling up his sleeves.

"You aren't going to go for a swim, are you?"

"I wasn't planning on it, but I could be coerced into it if you wish."

"Ladies don't swim," she stated with a rehearsed quality to her words.

"Another of your mother's rules?"

"Yes, although I heard that one at finishing school as well, so it's most likely true."

"Do you ever wish you could break the rules?" He stepped into the cool water and turned back to her.

"I did. Once, if you recall."

"Care to again?" He held his hand out to her and watched indecision flash through her eyes. "Take my hand. It's slippery on the wet stones, and if I return you covered in mud, people will talk."

"Indeed." Her fingers slipped into his, sending a tremor up his arm. "You must promise not to look at my ankles, though."

"Sue, I've already seen your ankles."

"I suppose you have. How do I allow you to convince me to break so many rules?"

"I'm charming, remember?"

"Your charm doesn't work on me, remember?" She hiked up her skirts and held them in one hand, giving him a view of one leg up to the knee.

"And yet I'm the lucky gentleman who is allowed to see your ankles."

She shot him a dark look in response.

"I'll be honorable. You have my word. They're only ankles, Sue."

"I forget you've spent so much time in France, becoming used to their customs. Ankles are nothing to you, are they?" She lifted her skirts up her legs and looked down at her wiggling toes.

Must she keep mentioning France? The country of France had nothing to do with his thoughts on ladies. He wanted to pull her skirts up higher. *Patience, Holden.* "I admit ankles aren't my favorite part of a lady." He couldn't stand watching her prance on the embankment with bare legs and not touch her for much longer. He reached for her in one movement, his hands wrapping around her waist. "Are you ready?"

Before she could answer, he lifted her off her feet and set her before him in the cool water.

"Oh! It's cold! I was imagining cool, and it certainly didn't disappoint."

"Am I to assume you don't want to swim with me, then?"

"I'll freeze! And what of my gown?"

"That can be remedied." He dipped one finger into the capped sleeve of her gown, slipping it down one shoulder in invitation.

"Someone might see us. It would be the talk of the party. I would…"

"Today, there are only you, me, and our muddy toes. That is all." He brushed a lock of fallen hair from her face. He waited, not wanting to rush into things any more than he already had.

With a small nod and a crooked smile, she lifted to her toes. His heart slammed into his chest beneath her small hands as she placed her full lips on his. He allowed her to kiss him with slow burning desire for a moment. It was a sweet kiss. One made by young girls behind the stables, not one for them.

When she pulled back with a dreamy look in her eyes, he leaned in with one reckless movement, pulling her close and slashing his mouth across hers. His tongue slipped past her teeth to tangle with hers. She tasted of strawberries plucked fresh from the vine, warm from the sun and moist from a sweet rain. He wanted more. He bit at her bottom lip, then soothed it with his tongue.

Her hands drifted up around his neck. Her breasts pressed into his chest. A small whimper escaped her mouth as she opened to him once more, mimicking his kisses as she tugged on the back of his shirt.

He picked her up and settled her against his chest, her feet dripping water down his shins. With careful steps he moved toward the grassy shore. Her arms were entwined around his neck, stroking small circles between his shoulder blades while he plundered her mouth. He broke their kiss to set her down in the shade of a tree. She pulled at the front of his shirt, tugging him back down over her.

"Patience, Sue," he murmured against her lips before ripping his shirt off and tossing it on the ground. He needed to touch her, to be touched.

She hesitated beneath him, apparently not sure where to land her hands. Her pink lips parted to speak but no words were said. No words needed to be said. The question was clear in the concern in her eyes.

"You can touch me, Sue. I believe I've told you that before."

"This isn't like before."

"Because you aren't foxed?"

"Because you called me Sue." Her eyes were wide on him as she placed her hands on his chest with a feather-light touch.

He leaned over her and rumbled into her ear, "I want you, Sue Green."

Her resulting shiver ran up his spine and sank all the way to his bones.

Grazing the light stubble of his face against the soft skin of her neck, he found where her pulse beat like drums in some foreign land. *Bum-bum. Bum-bum.* Capturing that rhythm with his mouth, he met it and challenged it.

She arched into him as her hands wound around him, pulling at the cords of his muscles. He moved his lips down the exposed skin above her dress, breathing in the scent of her skin. With a flick of his fingers, he loosened the fastenings of her gown, releasing the yellow fabric's hold on her body. Shifting over her to tug her dress down with his teeth, he pulled the rough lace trim across the hardened peaks of her breasts. He grinned against her skin as she gasped and tightened her hold on his back. He pulled her exposed breast into his mouth as he shifted her skirts higher on her hips.

Releasing her breast, he rose up on his elbow, his other hand drawing small circles on her hip now. He placed a kiss on her forehead before burying his mouth in her hair. His erection throbbed, screaming for the warmth of her body. He ground his hips into hers as he said into her hair, "Do you feel how much I want you?"

Her hips arched into his for more contact as her knees fell apart a fraction. Her lips grazed his shoulder as she spoke, "I want to touch you...there."

"You don't even need to ask." He released the placket of his breeches, watching her eyes swallow him whole the same way he longed to disappear into her body.

She moved a hand down, grazing her fingernails across his stomach and making his muscles jump in response.

It took all the control he had to remain still as her small hand wrapped around his length. She looked up into his face, her soft brown eyes round with wonder as she slid her hand down to the base, testing the power of her touch.

His breath grew more ragged with every movement of her hand. When she rubbed her thumb over the tip, something resembling a growl escaped his throat. "Sue," he begged as his lips met hers in a kiss of desperation.

He needed her, more of her. He wanted to feel her writhe beneath him in pleasure. He nudged her legs farther apart with his thigh and sank one finger into her depths as he took her mouth. Coaxing her with the flick of his wrist, he pressed his thumb to the center of her sex. He stroked the small bud there until she arched into his hand, her grip on his member tightening.

He thrust another finger into her as he dove into her mouth, the pressure of her hand intoxicating as she moved over his length with expertise he knew she couldn't have. His hand met her body with increased force as she arched to meet him. He broke their kiss to look down at her, flushed cheeks below half-closed eyes, lips swollen from his kiss.

He thrust into her again and again, enjoying the pulse of her grip on him as she found her pleasure. She lifted her hips to meet him as she exhaled heated puffs of air. His body was rigid with need, and she seemed to need him as much as he did her. He wasn't going to last much longer.

"Come for me. You're beautiful, Sue. So beautiful." He pushed into her again, feeling her tighten around him.

She cried out beneath him as he gave her one last flick of his hand, pulling her over the edge into oblivion. He rolled from her, spilling his seed in the grass before settling back beside her.

She was watching him with lazy interest. "Did you mean that? About me being…"

"Beautiful? Yes, love." He ran his hand down the porcelain skin of her stomach to rest on her hip. He did mean it; she was lovely. Sue had a beauty all her own. He wasn't sure how he'd overlooked it before, but he was thankful no other gentleman had discovered her secret.

"Holden, you wouldn't lie to encourage me to do scandalous acts with you, would you?"

"I would never lie to you, Sue." He closed his eyes and rested his head back against the soft grass so she wouldn't read the truth written there. He did think her beautiful, but any truth he possessed had been lost long ago and would never be spoken. "Now, about that swim…"

Thirteen

"You're painting?" Evangeline shut the door to their bedchamber and leaned against it. "If Mother sees you…"

"Then what, Evie? Will she remove me from London? Force me to serve as a companion to Great-Aunt Mildred for the remainder of my days?" Sue glanced up from the small canvas she held in her hand, the brush hanging from her fingers and threatening to drip emerald paint on her dress.

"She'll have a fit. Do you know you have black paint on your nose? You can't be seen that way—not here! It was Lord Amberstall whom you offended by being covered in paint, after all."

Sue rubbed at her nose with the back of her hand, flicking a trail of green into her hair in the process. "Hang Lord Amberstall and his notions on propriety among ladies. He isn't interested in me, so why should I spare a thought for him?"

Evangeline was wide eyed as she stared her sister down. "You're under the man's roof, Sue. We must show respect for his position, or Mother will…"

Sue turned her attention back to the painting she held. Tiny emerald eyes stared back at her. The hair needed work, however. "I'm weary of worrying what Mother will think, Evie. In fact, I mean to cease all thought of Mother."

"How can you do that?"

"Someone once told me, 'Dwell on the pleasing parts of life and pretend the rest don't exist.' Painting pleases me."

"And Mother doesn't exist?"

"Precisely." Sue placed her brush back on the small tray at her side and retrieved another, determined to capture the light in Holden's hair as she'd seen it yesterday afternoon.

"Sue, may I sit?" Evangeline asked, already moving toward the edge of the bed. "I find I'm out of sorts this morning."

"Should I send for a maid? We could get tea and something to eat. Have you eaten? I always feel wretched if I haven't eaten properly."

"No, thank you. It will pass. I'm sure of it." She settled back on Sue's bed, leaning her head against the large panel at the head covered in pale green silk. "Tell me, Sue. How will you pretend Mother doesn't exist?"

"In the same manner she plans on ridding herself of me."

"You plan to go along with her ideas for your future, then?"

"No. Yes. Perhaps. I don't know. What I do know is that I will walk away from her and never look back."

"Where will you go?"

"That remains to be seen." Sue smiled up from behind the small canvas. Where would she go? She knew what she wanted, and for the first time, she thought it attainable. Her eyes dropped back down to Holden's familiar face.

"How can you be so cavalier? Your future is terribly uncertain."

What would Evangeline have her do? Wallow in self-misery while following Mother's every whim? Her life was worth more than Mother's accounting of it. Whatever her fate, she would be the one deciding on it. "Don't think badly of me for rising above Mother's fits and choosing to be positive about my future."

"I don't. I only hope I might be so bold one day."

"You're always bold." She glanced up at her sister in confusion. "You turn heads with every step you take. Bold and beautiful. That is you."

"Jewels made of paste are those same things."

"Evie, is something the matter? You don't seem yourself."

"I'm quite all right. I should go. Mother will be expecting me repaired and ready for the day ahead by now."

"Evie."

"Yes?" Her sister paused with her hand on the doorknob.

"You're made of stronger material than paste. Don't allow Mother to destroy you, too."

With a nod, Evangeline left the room.

Sue was as surprised at her words of strength as her sister had been. She was even more surprised to discover how true the words were. Holden had been right that day in the park. Mother held too much control over her life. She wanted freedom from it all, freedom to choose her own future.

Setting down the canvas, she rose and went to the basin in the corner to clean the paint from her face. Her hair had fallen from its confinement and was stuck to a dot of green paint on her forehead. Black was smeared across the ridge of her nose, making her smile. For the first time in her life, she looked in the mirror and saw beauty. Perhaps not perfection, but just as in nature, the beauty was one with the flaws.

She was beautiful.

She could see it now—what Holden must see when he looked upon her. He was right; she did deserve better fare than her family was serving. She deserved happiness. Happiness and love. Did she already possess both? She wasn't sure yet, but she was enjoying the path to discovering the answers.

❧

A horse exhibition. Of course this event of pure horsey adoration would dissolve into a horse race. Sue blinked into the brilliant sunlight of the afternoon as she stepped out the front door of Amber Hollow. It was nearly time for the festivities to begin. With her eyes sweeping the front drive for Lillian, she walked out onto the raked gravel. Her friend would surely be in attendance since the duke had instigated the entire event. Last night at dinner, Lillian had kept looking at the duke—looking and blushing.

A knowing smile curved Sue's mouth upward. She

knew that anxious yet excited look well, for it was plastered on her own face as of late. Lillian would never admit to having an interest in a man, but her actions spoke volumes. Would her friend finally be the one to tame the mad duke? Hopefully Lillian knew how to control the fire with which she played.

Two gentlemen passed Sue with nods as they strode ahead, exchanging money and speaking in hushed tones. She let them pass as she moved in the direction of the paddock but at no great speed. She was sure Lillian would join her for the exhibition; until then she was alone. Evangeline and Mother refused to spend additional time in the sun "watching animals run in dirt." On this occasion, she understood their point, but she left the suite in spite of it. She needed to walk, to think. Would Holden be there too? Her chest tightened. What was happening between them? She dreaded the answer to that question as much as she anticipated it.

Sue's toe had barely touched the grass on the far side of the drive when she was tugged sideways through an opening in the bushes. She gasped, glancing around to find herself on a small path through the rose garden—with Holden.

She stared up at him for a moment while trying not to think of the way his fingers were curled around her wrist, stroking the skin at the edge of her kid glove. "I was going to watch the horses."

"As am I." His lips curled up into a smile. "I'm merely suggesting the scenic path to the paddock."

"Dragging me through the bushes is hardly a suggestion."

"Consider it repayment for pulling me through half the ballrooms in London." He wrapped her hand around his arm and began moving down the path at a leisurely pace.

"I did no such thing. All right. Perhaps I did tug a bit on you once, but we were going to get cakes. I do have my priorities, you know, and cake is at the top of my list. Especially the ones at the Dillsworth ball."

"That wasn't quite my meaning, but it's nice to know that the order of your life's concerns begins with sweets." He chuckled and gave her shoulder a gentle shove with his elbow.

"Of course it does. Eating sweets is the most pleasure we're given in this life. Hmm, perhaps not the most, but..." She blushed, thinking of yesterday afternoon in the grass. She cleared her throat. "What was your meaning before? About being hauled through ballrooms?"

"It wasn't hauled; it was pulled—as if you could haul me. I'm at least twice your size. But my meaning was figurative." He paused, turning to her. His brow creased into a deep vee as he gazed down at her. "Sue, I've followed you from ball to ball this entire season. I know we began on improper footing, but I've been seeking you since I met you. It's always been you. Always."

"Holden, I wanted to tell you of it all. I..."

"Never mind that." He reached up to tuck a stray lock of hair behind her ear, his hand lingering on the side of her neck with a gentle caress. "I'm simply glad to know now. I'm glad I know you, Sue. Not Suzanna. Sue. Sue Green."

She couldn't breathe. What was he saying? His eyes shone with a soft intensity that created as many questions as it did answers. Did she dare ask? And if he was leading to some grand decision involving her future, shouldn't he know what her family's intentions were for the end of the season? It was only fair to tell him. "Holden, I don't know where this is leading, but I should tell you…"

"I don't know where it's leading, either." After a barely perceptible shake of his head, his expression cleared to a lazy grin. "Let us continue walking, and we will see when we arrive where we were heading when we began. You never know, we could find another lake."

She could feel the heat rising in her cheeks. Although they were in a rose garden, she wished there was another lake. Yesterday would live forever in her memories. The smell of the sweet grass, his hands on her body, his lips…

"What did you want to tell me?"

Her mind refused to function, remaining rooted to the clearing by the lake yesterday. Had she wished to tell him anything? She glanced up at him.

"You aren't, in secret, anyone else I know, are you? One of my many cousins?" He pulled a face of horror. "Thornwood?"

"No. Nothing like that." She was through with secrets. Her smile dropped to the ground. "It's actually my family."

"Oh? Has your mother set another rule? I hope it isn't against walks through gardens with gentlemen."

"No, although I'm sure she wouldn't approve."

"Good. I like being the means of your rebellion."

"As do I." The smile on her face fell as she took another step. "Holden, my family has plans for me at the end of this season. You see...I've been not dancing at balls for several seasons now."

"That was your decision this season, Sue."

"I know." She looked away. "But I'm quite on the shelf in my family's eyes. As such, I was told this season would be my last."

His eyes were on her now, but she couldn't meet his gaze. "Where will you go? Back to live on the estate and grow into someone's matronly aunt?"

She swallowed and turned to look up into his eyes. There was no turning back now. "Sent away to Scotland to live out my days as a companion to my chocolate-loathing great-aunt."

He stopped, staring at her for a moment before asking, "What?"

"Mother thinks that is the only life I'm suited for. She became angry when she saw me dressed once in an ensemble she deemed less than appropriate." She couldn't tell him that her night as Suzanna had sealed her fate. He might believe her to be a manipulating wanton which, despite her mother's assessment, she was not. "She'd long given up on the possibility of my finding a husband. And now, with this being my last season, I must live with my fate."

His hand tightened over hers where it wrapped around his arm, his fingers grasping hers through the layers of their gloves. "How can they even consider it?"

"I know, it's awful. A lifetime without chocolate."

"I meant abandoning you to the wilds of Scotland. I've…been there. It's no place for you."

"That, too. I'm told no man of sane mind would want me—not in that way, at any rate." She bit out the words, her jaw hardened against the pain of being so worthless in her family's eyes.

"I want you." His breathing was harsh and so were his thoughts, if the warning in his eyes were any indication.

"You're Lord Steelings, confirmed bachelor and charming rake of the *ton*."

"Yes, I suppose I am those things. Just as you are a lady who doesn't dance at balls. But I still want you." His grip on her fingers loosened and he turned to face her, pulling her close.

"About where this path is leading…" she murmured against his chest, taking comfort in his steady heartbeat.

"I still don't know, Sue. But I know this: I can't stand by and watch as your family sends you to a place where I can't reach you." His arms kept her safe as he rubbed the tension from her shoulders.

"I didn't tell you this so that you would save me. I know I face uncertainty; I only wanted you to be aware of it. I can find my own way out of this muck. My purpose in all this is…" She looked up into his face. "I don't want any more secrets between us."

"No more secrets," he repeated, his jaw tightening on the words.

She sighed on a contented smile. "No secrets."

❧

The gentle clip-clop of horse hooves on the dusty road turned to pounding heartbeats against Holden's ears.

The sight of Sue lying in the grass beneath him burned in his mind. How had he ever believed he could see her again and satiate his desire for her? Once wouldn't do—not with Sue. She possessed a well-contained wildness that he wanted to set free and watch run. Her response to him went beyond response and well into action. When her hands had touched his skin…

"I don't understand them, Steelings," Thornwood said from the seat of his horse at Holden's side.

"Who?" Holden blinked, shooting his friend a confused look while shifting in his saddle to ease the tightness of his breeches.

"Ladies," Thornwood grumbled.

"Ha! And you think I do?"

Thornwood shrugged. "No, I suppose not. After all, you never even found your Suzanna."

Holden couldn't keep the grin from his face. "Suzanna was an illusion, it seems." And he'd never been so pleased with the secrets of an illusion. Sue was nothing she seemed to be and everything he wanted. He glanced at Thornwood. Was he watching with those annoyingly perceptive eyes of his? Could he guess Holden's thoughts? But his friend looked troubled, his gaze distant. Perhaps he wasn't the only one on the trail of a lady. Holden had seen Thornwood speaking with Sue's friend on a few occasions. But this was Thornwood after all; he would claim he didn't have time for ladies.

Holden's eyes narrowed on him. "I saw you speaking with Miss Phillips yesterday after the horse exhibition," he led in, hoping for some details to distract him from the memory of Sue.

"Yes, Lily and I were discussing…"

"Ah, so it's Lily now, is it? How very interesting." Holden raised a brow at his friend with a chuckle.

"It's not so amusing at the moment if you must know, since she's angry with me."

Anger and ladies did seem to go hand in hand—or was that only in *his* dealings with ladies? Sue certainly spent plenty of time angry with him. Of course, in that instance, he deserved her wrath. "It's difficult to keep them happy, isn't it?"

"Who?" Thornwood asked with a confused glance.

"Ladies," Holden supplied.

"Yes, quite."

Clearly Thornwood didn't wish to discuss matters regarding the lady. To be honest, Holden didn't want to discuss Sue, either. For now, she was his secret passion. When would he see her next? The Peppersforth ball? It was too bad, really, that the ball wasn't this evening. What would come next? Would he chase her from ball to ball, hoping for a private moment with her, until the end of the season? And what then? If her claim was true, she would no longer be within his reach come the end of the season. He couldn't allow that to happen.

She was his. The thought stunned him.

He blinked into the patchy sunshine shining through the trees. When he told her yesterday he wouldn't allow her to be carted off to Scotland, he hadn't been sure how true his words were. After all, how would he save her? But now that the seed of thought had taken root in his mind, it wouldn't leave him. She was his.

Everything seemed so simple now. Why hadn't he seen it before? She belonged with him. He wouldn't need to wait and hope for a private moment with her. He could have her at his side every night. Of course there would be preparations to be made before he spoke of it with her, but surely he could have things in place by tomorrow night's ball. He urged his horse forward. He had plans to see to and not many hours between now and tomorrow. Soon Sue Green would be his—forever.

❧

"Fezawald, I trust you survived my absence." Holden handed the man his hat with a smile.

"Only just, my lord."

Holden began walking toward the library door. He would wash the road dirt off and change later. Right now, there was much to do and little time. He turned back to the butler with his hand on the doorknob. "Would you send for my man of business? I find I'm in need of new living arrangements."

"Oh? Are we leaving, my lord? So soon? It wouldn't hurt you to stay somewhere longer than a fortnight, you know. The world would not indeed end, as you believe."

"We are staying, Fezawald, so you can end your lecture. Thank you."

"Very well, my lord. You know my dislike of packing."

His mother stepped out of the open parlor door. "I won't go to another hospital!"

"Mother," he grated as she entered the hall. "It

is true that you cannot remain in my home forever. You will receive far better care with a doctor than I can provide. However, I was speaking of another residence here in London."

"I am your mother! You can't send me away! Why, you ungrateful…"

"Ungrateful?" he snapped at her. "For what, precisely? The destruction of my life?"

"Everything I've ever done has been for you."

"No, you will not cast that charge on me," he grated. He'd been pushed too far. His hospitality had its bounds, and she was several steps over that line. "My own father has blamed me for your transgressions my entire life. You show up here seeking shelter, and when I take you in, you take advantage of the situation by attending a ball? And you call me ungrateful."

Her eyes narrowed on him, creating deep lines of disapproval on her face. "How you disappoint me, Holden. I came here only to be close to you, to know my own son."

He took a step closer to her, his eyes never leaving hers. She'd cast a dark shadow over most of his life, but she wouldn't be doing such a thing any longer. Enough with his desire to understand her. This was too high a price to pay for knowing one's mother. "Father was right about you."

She swallowed and backed away from him half a step. "I can see I am no longer welcome here."

"This arrangement was never permanent."

"Let me know the house you find for me, and I will begin to staff it properly. If you insist on sending me away, I suppose I will comply," she returned, her chin raised as she shot Fezawald a look of disgust.

"The house isn't for you. I have a friend in need of new arrangements."

She turned her attention back to Holden. "One of your whores?"

He pushed her against the door casing, holding her there with his forearm.

"You will never speak that way of anyone of my acquaintance again!"

"Oh, I see." She smiled. "It's that little chit, isn't it? That's who you've chosen over your family."

He released her and stepped away. "My cousins are my family. Fezawald is my family. My staff is my family. Unfortunately, you are nothing but a bad memory."

A silence fell in the hall, yet he knew the echoes of this conversation would be felt for years to come. He didn't move. He'd said what needed to be said, and he was wasting precious time on her—time he didn't have.

"I can see now I have no place here. If you'll excuse me, I have some things I need to see to."

For the first time in his life, Holden stood still and watched as someone walked from his life. Her hold on him was gone and soon she would be gone, too.

Fourteen

THE PEPPERSFORTH BALL WAS ALWAYS A GRAND AFFAIR, but tonight Sue didn't have a care for the garlands draped across the ballroom ceiling, had barely noticed the orchestral music in the air, and had yet to try the sweets in the adjacent parlor. Her eyes swept the room in search of blond hair and sinful eyes. Sue smoothed her skirts out again and bit at her lip.

She hadn't seen Holden since the Amberstall party, and that had been days ago. She'd lain awake nights since then, the same questions rolling about in her mind and knocking all other thoughts away. Where were things headed with Holden? Did he love her? Would it matter if he did? Even after ripping the situation apart from every angle, she still wasn't sure of the answers. She touched her hair to ensure it hadn't escaped the confines of the pearl-tipped pins.

Evangeline glanced in her sister's direction over the rim of a champagne glass. She'd been at Sue's side thus far this evening since Mother was at home feeling under the weather. "What are you fussing over?"

"Evangeline, do I look presentable this evening?"

"Yes. The cream silk actually brightens your eyes a bit."

"Truly?" Sue looked up from tugging her glove into place.

"Why are you concerned over your appearance tonight? You would attend balls in your artist's apron, if allowed."

Sue folded her hands before her and scanned the room again. "No reason."

"Very well, keep your secrets. I have plenty already," Evangeline stated and turned to walk away.

"I will, thank you. Wait. Evie, what secrets do you have already?" But she was gone before Sue could find out more.

She only stared after her sister's retreating form for a moment, watching her round the corner into the main hall, before she turned back to the dance floor. Colors swirled before her eyes as ladies twirled around the floor in search of some existence beyond their own. Hope. Was that what flooded through her veins this evening? Perhaps. She smiled out across the dancers. Maybe they would all find what they were looking for tonight.

Warmth spread down her arm as someone trailed fingers across the exposed skin above her glove. "I thought I might find you here."

She turned and grinned up at Holden. He was always devastatingly handsome in formal wear. "Well, go on and ask me for a dance so I might refuse you."

"I'm counting on it. Let's go to the terrace." He reached for her elbow.

"Aren't you getting a bit ahead of yourself?"

Sighing, he muttered, "Very well." He offered her a bow with an extra flourish of his arm, the charm of which was lost with the roll of his eyes. "Miss Green, may I have the pleasure of this dance?"

She raised her chin in perfect imitation of her sister. "You don't seem very sincere, my lord. Therefore, I'm forced to refuse you."

"Thank you. Now let's go to the terrace." He grabbed her elbow and pulled her toward the doors.

"What's on the terrace?" she asked as she scurried behind him in an effort to keep up.

"We are." He grinned down at her as he pulled her out the doors into the chill of night.

"Indeed." She glanced around to see who was enjoying the air as well, only to discover they were alone. As the cool air began to blow through her gown, she realized why they were the only ones braving the terrace this evening. She wrapped her hands across her chest in an attempt at warmth.

Holden shed his coat and draped it around her shoulders in one fluid motion. "Better?" It was far too large for her, swallowing her whole. She was surrounded with the spicy scent of him and the warmth of his body. She inhaled a slow breath, trying to memorize the moment. The crisp breeze on her face, his eyes fixed on hers. She could see the tension in his muscles. Her questions would be answered tonight; she could feel it in the air.

"Sue, I've given much thought to the issue you spoke of while we were in the country."

"You mean the small issue of my future falling apart within a matter of weeks?" Her voice sounded tight, but he didn't seem to notice.

"Yes, that issue. I have a solution."

"Do you?" Her heart threatened to beat out of her chest. This was it. Her entire life had led her to this moment.

"Indeed. Sue, as I said before, I've given this a great deal of thought. I think I've known I desired this longer that I care to admit. The truth is, Sue, ever since I saw you that night dancing down the stairs, I've wanted to keep you in my life. The very thought of you leaving to spend the rest of your days chatting with some distant relative in the north…" Anxiety mixed with determination flared in his eyes. He stepped closer, running his hands down her arms as if to assure himself she was still there. "Sue, it cannot happen."

"What are you saying?" She wanted to be in his life as well. Yes! This was everything she wanted. Holden, day and night, Holden.

"Sue, I've come to care for you, your constant chatter, the way you see beauty in everything." His thumb rubbed across her wrist where her pulse beat with wild abandon.

This was it. Holden was offering her marriage. Had he spoken with Father yet? He cared for her. It wasn't love but perhaps one day it would grow to be so. She would wake to his face every morning and fall asleep in his arms every night. They would have children and a life together. She could hardly believe it.

"I want to feed you chocolates in bed, Sue. I want to go to the theater with you on my arm. I want to lie on blankets in the grass while you paint in the sunshine."

"Yes," she whispered.

"Sue, I want you in my life." He lifted one hand to tuck a fallen lock of her hair behind her ear. "I want everyone to know you are mine. Any oversight of you in the past will never happen again. Sue, Suzanna, whatever you wish to be called, I don't care. I want you—the real you, red paint up your arms and all."

"Yes." She'd only said one word but within that word was an idea. She loved him. She loved this man. Had this love fallen on her like a heavy rain, or embraced her over time like steady mist? She didn't know, but she knew the truth of it now. She loved him and they would be married.

"I'll protect you. Your family will never hurt you again. I bought you something this afternoon in hopes that you would want it as much as I do."

She only nodded, her eyes filling with unshed tears.

"I can't wait to show it all to you. It's a bit cozy, but there's enough room for an art studio on the third floor. It's near the park and just around the corner from my home. I'll be able to visit you as often as you like."

His home? Wouldn't it be their home? "We wouldn't live together?"

"As much as I hate convention, it simply isn't done to live under the same roof as one's mistress."

"Oh. I see." She ripped her hand from his grasp. His mistress? That's what he wanted? The air was sucked from her lungs, and she struggled to find room for it there again. His mistress. She'd thought he wanted…that he was going to ask…

"Sue, I'll be with you almost every night. And you'll be free to paint during the days."

"That is true." She needed to leave. She pulled at his coat weighing heavy on her shoulders, the wool now scratching her skin. The dark of night was closing in on her. She needed air. Suddenly she couldn't breathe.

"Is something wrong? I'm sure once you see the house you'll feel better about things. I can take you there tomorrow. Perhaps even tonight?"

"No."

"All right, tomorrow then. I suppose I can wait *one* more day to be with you."

"No!" She heard her voice pierce the night, tearing with it shards of her heart.

"No?"

"No." She ripped the coat from her shoulders. With another "No," she slammed it into his chest. "No, no, no," she stammered with angry punches to his arm. How could he do this to her? Was that how he saw her? How he would always see her? She was such a fool. She turned and stepped away from him into the cold of the night. Tears now fell down her cheeks, leaving cold trails in their wake. She didn't bother brushing them away. It didn't matter. Nothing mattered, for all was over.

"Sue," he murmured at her back.

She turned to face him one last time. Shivering, sniffing, and with tears falling in a steady stream down her face, she spoke. Her words were as hollow as her heart. "Holden, there was a time not too long ago that your offer would have been grand, and I believe I would have said yes."

"But not now."

She shook her head, feeling strands of her hair slip

as she did so. "And it's your fault." She inhaled on a gasping sob. "You made me see my life for what it is—what I possess and what I deserve. And I deserve more. I want more."

"I want to be with you. I'll come to you every night if you wish it." He stepped forward, pulling out a handkerchief for her, but she pushed his hand away.

"That's not enough, not for me. Not now. Can't you see that?" Her voice was strained through her tears.

"What can I offer you to make you come with me?" Desperation showed in his eyes as he reached for her.

She took a step away from him. "If the answer to that question isn't clear, there isn't anything I can say to make you see. That's your problem, you know. *You never see!*"

"Marriage? Is that what you want? I thought you'd given up on that idea." He shook his head in confusion.

"It would appear I haven't," she cried.

The moment strung out between them, colder than the night around them and colder than the sea in winter. His face was colder still as he said, "I can't marry you."

There was no recourse. No turning back. He'd left her no choice. "Then I must leave."

"But we belong together. You're perfect when you're in my arms. You know I'm right."

"Am I not perfect just as I am?"

"Of course you are. I didn't mean… Damn it all, Sue, I need you."

"I can't!" she exclaimed as she turned for the door to the ballroom. She needed to be away from him.

It was over, and staying for another minute wouldn't change that. She was shaking as she stepped through the door to the warmth of the ballroom.

"Sue, wait. Sue! *Sue!*"

She didn't stay to hear any more. She was already running.

⤫

The cool air blew pieces of Sue's hair across her face and lifted her hat from her head. With an adjustment to the pin holding the flowered thing to her hair, she rounded the bend in the path leading back to the park's entrance. She'd hoped the brisk walk and fresh air would clear her mind, yet her thoughts were just as muddled as they had been earlier.

She'd only taken a few steps when she saw a familiar figure ambling toward her. Drat her luck. It was that crazy Henrietta woman. Lady Pemberton, wasn't that her name? Why did she think they were friends? There was nothing wrong with Henrietta, but there was something not quite right. This was what Sue got in return for talking too much to people she didn't know. "Good afternoon, Lady Pemberton. I didn't expect to see you here."

Henrietta's mouth drew up into a pleased grin as if she'd just been handed a large slice of cake. "You would do well to be more observant. I see you here every day. You always walk clockwise around the path twice before returning to your home for tea."

Sue shifted on her feet and glanced around. That sounded like the woman had been following her, but surely not. She was being ridiculous. "Henrietta, I find it rather disconcerting to discover I'm so predictable."

"Pattern and routine are the foundations of life."

"I've always thought the foundations of life were art and chocolate."

Henrietta chuckled in a forced titter. "Yes, you enjoy drawing, don't you? I've watched you sketch in your notebook."

"Have you?" Sue glanced behind the woman blocking her path, counting the seconds until she could get away.

"Oh indeed." Henrietta tsked through pursed lips. "You don't remember the last time we spoke in the park?"

"Certainly, I remember," Sue bluffed with a smile. "I'd simply forgotten I had my sketch pad with me that day."

"Cavorting with gentlemen will do that to a lady's mind."

Cavorting? That sounded awful. She had to be referring to the afternoon with Holden, for no other gentleman ever spoke to her. However, she'd only chatted with Holden that day. Of course, none of that mattered anymore. She didn't want to think of him, and she certainly didn't want to discuss him. "I'm fairly certain I didn't cavort. And he is no longer my friend anyway."

"Is he not? The two of you looked quite cozy on the bench that day." She gave Sue a coy wink that would have turned heads thirty years prior.

"That was before...and much after..." She didn't want to talk about this, not now, not ever. "It's a long story with an unhappy ending."

"I don't believe that for a second. I saw the way

he looked at you." Henrietta's hands were clenched before her in a white-knuckled grasp.

Sue didn't want to ask the question flying to her lips. She didn't want to know. But she was already speaking before she regained control of her tongue. "How? How did he look at me?"

"With desire, of course." She looked disgusted by the thought, but then Henrietta was a bit off when it came to the subject of relationships. "Pretty young thing like you should be used to such attention."

"Unfortunately, I discovered later that desire was all that existed with that particular gentleman."

"Many a marriage has been built upon less."

"If you don't mind, can we speak of something else?"

Henrietta's tone softened in an instant. "How inconsiderate of me, dear. You must be distraught. Clearly you still have feelings for the man. And I would wager the air you breathe that he has feelings for you as well." Her jaw twisted up into a smile. "My home is just down the street. Come and have a cup of tea with me. You'll feel right as rain after a cup of tea."

"Thank you, but I need to return home." Tea with Henrietta was too much on a day like today. She truly couldn't imagine a worse fate at the moment.

"Your mother and sister passed by in a carriage not ten minutes ago on their way to see and be seen along Rotten Row. No one waits for you at home."

"Oh." *Blast it all.* "I suppose I have no excuse to refuse tea then, do I?"

"My home is just there." Henrietta pointed to a spot beyond the row of trees inside the wall encircling the park. "Come along."

Sue trailed along beside the woman. She was in no mood to take tea but didn't see a way to politely refuse, either. It wouldn't take long. One cup of tea and she would be gone. They crossed the street just outside the park gate and made their way around the corner.

Henrietta led her to a handsome brick home with cream-colored trim. Orderly flowers marched down either side of the stone path leading to the front door. Above them, windows had been thrown open to allow the sunshine inside. Somehow the home didn't fit with her impression of Henrietta. This was a cheerful home. And if there was one thing Lady Pemberton was not, it was cheerful. She shook off the thought and ascended the stairs to the front door.

Stepping inside beyond an ancient butler, she stopped to stare in awe. Gilt-framed paintings in a variety of sizes covered almost every inch of the red wall above the dark-stained wainscoting that ran around the hall. Lord Pemberton must have an interest in art. She glanced up the stairs where they arched up the back wall of the room and saw that the paintings extended as far as she could see.

She turned back to Henrietta, noticing the large statue of a Grecian lady at the woman's shoulder. Her head spun. There were handcrafted urns flanking one door and another sculpture of a young girl in the front corner next to a side table. The house was exquisite. It was one part museum, one part home, stirred together into a delicious concoction. Again Sue wondered that someone like Henrietta lived somewhere so beautiful. Her dress was frayed at the edges, and yet her entry-way rug was imported from some exotic market.

"You must excuse the décor. It's my son's home. He enjoys paintings. I plan to redecorate for him. Just after I relieve him of his nosy staff," she said with a pointed stare at the butler.

"I'll fetch a maid to ready your tea."

"That would be lovely."

When the man was gone, Sue turned to ask, "You have a son?"

"Certainly, I do. He's the dearest thing in the world to me. Let's go into the small dining room. It's a better location for our private chat than the main parlor, don't you think?"

"Very well." She almost walked past it. Almost missed it. What caught her eye were the tiny dots of grazing sheep on the hillside in a painting she passed. Those dots had taken her nearly a fortnight to master. Her heart was slamming into her chest.

How did one of her paintings come to hang here?

Was Holden not the sole collector of her work? There were others? She still struggled with the idea that anyone would want her paintings. This season her paintings seemed to be in every home in London. Perhaps this was a sign. She would survive in life as an artist. She was no lady's companion. She was an artist—a starving artist, perhaps, but an artist none-theless. Maybe it had been a good idea to come here today. She needed to be reminded that she could earn wages on her own. She didn't need the crumbs Holden offered. She didn't need her family. She didn't need anyone.

"You like this one?" Henrietta asked from over her shoulder.

"Yes, it's different. How did you come across it?" She couldn't tear her eyes away.

"No accounting for taste, I suppose. I'm sure it's from a shop in France. My son has lived there for several years. He only arrived home a few months ago. I'm quite pleased, as I'm sure you can imagine. We've been busy becoming reacquainted…"

France. Sue's mind raced to catch up with the rapid fire of her thoughts. She turned to face Henrietta, blurting out the one question spinning around in her head. "Lady Pemberton, who is your son?"

"Holden Ellis, Lord Steelings, of course."

No. Sue stumbled back one step, her gaze frozen on Henrietta, Lady Pemberton. Was that his father's title? She couldn't remember. But Henrietta's intense green eyes told the truth.

The truth.

What did she know of the truth? She knew Holden's mother was dead. He'd said so. They'd spoken of her on multiple occasions. On all occasions she'd been deceased. Her mother even believed the woman dead. How could this very alive woman standing with her be Holden's dead mother? His dead mother was standing here with her in *his* home. He'd lied. There was no other explanation. She shouldn't care. It wasn't as if they had a future together anyway. She never wanted to see him again. But she did care.

"You look as if you've seen an apparition. Come, let us have some tea. The tea will make everything better."

"Yes, tea would be lovely." Sue sank into one of the chairs set around the small table. Tea with a dead woman. She found that thought didn't distress her nearly as much as the threat of seeing Holden again inside his home. Yet there was no way to leave. Not now.

The old butler supervised the delivery of the tea tray to the table before her.

"Thank you, Fezawald. I can see to it from here."

"Very well, m'lady." The elderly man cast a wary glance over her before turning for the door.

Fezawald was Holden's butler. She recalled the name. He'd told the truth about his disagreeable butler but lied about his mother's death? Of course, none of it mattered. Not to her. She would never get tangled with that man again.

Henrietta sat across from her and raised the teapot from the tray. "Sue, you know I have the most delicious berry juice that, if added to your tea, is said to make all your troubles with a man disappear."

❧

"Holden," Aunt Penelope offered in greeting over the top of her book. "What are you doing here at such an early hour? I'm afraid I'm the only company to be found this morning. The girls are still abed and your uncle is out for a ride."

He closed the heavy library door behind his back. "I have to leave."

"You just arrived. Have some tea at least. I'll ring for a tray." She closed her book and tossed it onto the sofa seat beside her.

"I have to leave London." He moved away from the door to stand in the center of the room. "Today."

She froze halfway to her feet, her wide eyes never leaving him. "What do you mean, you have to leave?"

She stood, turning to face him. "You said you would stay this time. What about…"

"I must. I can't stay here." He ran a hand through his hair and looked away, unable to meet the accusation in her eyes.

She turned and began pacing before the fireplace. "What of your mother? She isn't back within Brooke House, I know. Your father told me of it. You know what that woman's presence means for this family." She paused, placing her hands on her hips. "My family."

He twirled the large globe on the table, watching it spin at top speed. "She's also leaving town."

"With you?" Aunt Penelope shook her head. "Have you lost your mind as well?"

"No, not with me. I made it fairly clear she couldn't stay with me, even though she refused to return to the hospital."

"Then what shall we do? We can't very well have her on the loose in London."

He looked up, watching his aunt struggle with the riddle that had kept him awake all night. "Then let her leave London as well."

"And trust her to do so?"

"If I leave, she won't stay."

"Send her to Brooke House and stay, Holden. She isn't worth you uprooting your life once more."

"I don't have a choice. Staying here and watching as life continued would be too difficult."

He turned away, walking to the front window. "I spoke with Mother this morning. She won't hurt anyone. You have my word on it."

"Your word. The reputation of this family on your

word." He heard her sniff into the silence. "I'm sorry. I didn't mean that. It's just… Holden, you cannot leave when Henrietta is still about."

"And yet I cannot stay."

"Why? Why would you risk the good name of our family?"

"It's no risk. No one will learn of my mother's existence if she leaves town."

"Then why must you go as well?"

"I've stayed too long already. I thought I could manage things this time. Have a life." He closed his eyes, still seeing Sue's face shining with tears in the moonlight. "But that's not to be."

"Is this about a lady? You're risking everything to run from some girl with notions about you?"

"It isn't like that, Aunt Pen," he ground out, watching the silhouette of his jaw move on the windowpane.

"Then tell me. Why are you fleeing when your family is here, your life is here?"

"Because I can't watch her," he said, his breath fogging the glass.

"Watch who? Perhaps I can help."

No one could help. It was over. He'd lost Sue all over again. "You've done enough, Aunt Pen."

He could feel her approach behind him. She was the closest thing to a mother he would ever know. Not that woman across town. He knew that now, and what did he do? He burdened her with his situation. At least she was safe and alive at the end of things. If his mother knew of his fondness for Aunt Pen, she would be killed just as it happened with his brother. The same would have happened with Sue. He couldn't be close with anyone. He was damaged, and that's the only truth he knew.

"Holden…" Aunt Penelope began at his back.

"God! Why must I destroy everything I touch?" He pounded a fist on the window frame, relishing the rattle of the glass. Maybe it would shatter. Everything else in his life shattered; why not this, too? He pounded the frame again and sneered at the glass sitting unaffected and shiny.

"Holden, you are a good man. You simply never allow anyone to see that side of you."

He spun around to face her. "I can't very well run around town telling the truth of my life, though, can I?"

"Is that the problem? Have your secrets pushed this lady away?"

"No," he bit out. "I never let her close enough for that to be an issue."

"You could trust her."

"To what end?"

"Happiness. Peace. Marriage?"

"I won't endanger her life. I won't. Sue has a pure soul. She's better off without me."

"Perhaps she is stronger than you believe her to be," his aunt offered with a smile.

She thought she'd won, but she didn't understand. He could never marry.

"Strong enough to endure attempts on her life? You know it would only be a matter of time. As long as my mother lives, I can't have anyone in my life. It wouldn't be safe for Sue. And I would never rest, knowing I'd caused this danger she would live under. No. It isn't right."

"Then send your mother back to the hospital where she belongs, Holden. Be happy."

"Even then, you know the truth of my life. Will I take her with me when I run out of funds and go in search of work abroad? I can't provide a life for her."

Aunt Penelope shot him a disapproving look at the vague mention of his relationship with his father. "And what is to come of this lady if you leave? If you abandon your family, what will that accomplish for her?"

"For her? Nothing. But it would save me from seeing her again. Knowing how close I came. How I almost…" He'd almost found it. Almost found the love he'd spent a lifetime searching for.

"Holden, dear. You already have."

She was right. He had found love. He loved Sue. Then he'd broken her heart and watched her walk out of his life. "Yes. I suppose I have."

"Why not stay? Why not try once more?" she pleaded. Of course she wanted him to stay, but she had also always supported him in all his life decisions.

He moved away from her, going back to the window. It was easier than looking her in the eyes when he said good-bye. "I can't lose Sue again. And I would rather lose her as I already have, knowing she has a chance at life and happiness, than lose her completely as my wife. I can't watch her live without me. But I can't watch her die with me, either."

He turned and punched the window out at his side, watching his perfect reflection splinter into a thousand pieces at his feet. His aunt gasped as he pushed past her and strode out the door.

Fifteen

"I don't have any man problems," Sue said to Henrietta.

"Don't you, dearest? I've seen you keeping company with my son. You can't hide anything from me, you know."

"It appears not. However, since he's your son, I don't think it wise for us to discuss it. The tea smells lovely. Did you add the berries you spoke of to steep?"

Henrietta clucked her tongue. "You won't get away that easily, dearest."

"I misspoke. Do forgive me. I no longer have any man problems. That is what happens when you no longer have men in your life. No men, no problems." She paused to force a laugh that sounded much like Evangeline's titter.

"Why do we put up with them? Men are such infuriating creatures. They wear horse blinders through life and then still manage to bungle it up in the end. We're better off alone. I've always felt sorry for the horses having to wear those dreadful blinders, forever marching straight ahead, never stopping to look around and enjoy the view. It's sad some horses live entire lives without…"

"My son is not infuriating. My son is perfect. We have a flawless family."

Sue's eyes narrowed on the woman. That day in the garden, Holden had mentioned his mother had murdered his brother. Was that true? At the time, Sue had felt honored to know such pieces of Holden. But now? Had that all been a lie to draw her near enough to kiss? Had she fallen for the tricks of a lothario? She knew him to be a rake, but had everything been a lie to influence her actions?

"Would you like a sandwich, cake?"

"Cake, please."

"Are you certain? It's chocolate. This home is sorely lacking in anything edible, I warn you, but they always serve this chocolate cake. I find it tiresome. The cook clearly needs to find other employment, but she remains…for now."

"I'll try it all the same, if you don't mind." Chocolate cake. He'd compared her artwork to chocolate cake once. Had that story been true? She didn't know anymore. Perhaps it had all been lies with illusions of friendship, caring…love?

Henrietta shrugged and handed Sue the plate.

"You never answered my question about preparing your tea, Henrietta. The flowery scent is delicious in this small dining room."

"I haven't yet added my secret ingredient. This is simply the blend of tea kept in store. I thought we would talk a bit more so I might determine how much of it you need."

"There are dosages? If this tea is medicinal, I shouldn't take it. I don't care for tonics and such. My mother once told me I…"

"You will drink it when you are told!" A vein in Henrietta's forehead pulsed with her words.

"Oh dear. Have I fallen into bad etiquette by refusing the tea? Blast it all, I did it again. Why do I keep making these blunders? And I cursed. Oh drat. Yes. Well. Clearly, I don't have a firm handle on any social situation. Perhaps that's why I'm on the shelf. These things do seem to matter to everyone. Everyone but me. Although Lord Steelings didn't seem to mind. Of course my blunder was asking after you, and now I realize he wasn't grieving your loss at all since he likely had luncheon with you that day."

"Why would he grieve my loss even if we hadn't had luncheon together that day?"

"Because I thought you dead." She gasped and covered her mouth. Why had she blurted that fact? Had she completely lost her mind?

"You are mistaken in several things, Sue Green."

"Obviously, since you're here and we are having tea."

"About that tea. I believe it's time to serve it. If you'll excuse me, I'll retrieve it from my rooms and join you again in a moment." She rose and rounded the table.

"Why not have a maid see to it? Or leave the maids be and let them enjoy the afternoon. I really should be going. I've taken too much of your time already." This was her chance to slip away. She stood and turned toward the door, only to be stopped by Henrietta's tall form blocking the doorway.

"I have plenty of time, dearest." With one last sweeping glance that sent shivers down Sue's spine, she was gone. But it wasn't until a moment later when Sue heard the soft click of a key turning in the lock that she knew real panic. She didn't need to try the door to know she was locked inside. She didn't need to, and yet she did, over and over and over again.

‰∽

Holden leaned farther over Muley's mane, urging him forward. The cobbles of the street raced past as he sped down the street. He needed to be away from this place. The dull ache in his chest would surely subside once he was beyond anything familiar. There would be nothing to remind him of Sue in the next town. He would cease thinking of her and feel whole again, he was certain. Faster! A vendor dove from his path as he rounded a corner near the edge of town. He didn't even spare a glance in the man's direction, only saw cabbages fly through the air and heard the cursing.

There was only one option left to him—leaving London. He would have taken the North Road toward his cottage in Scotland but he'd told Amberstall, the poor chap, that he could stay there until he recovered. Perhaps Wales. He'd never been to Wales. Who would he claim to be this time? A shop owner again? He'd need a name as well. His jaw clenched at the promise of starting over—again.

Why had he thought he could stay this time? Sue. Sue had changed everything. A guttural animal sound escaped from deep within his chest. He knew now. He could never return and he could never have her.

His life was ahead of him—on the road, moving forward, always moving.

Sue's future was ahead of her as well—in London at the next event. That's where she belonged. Having her in his life was only a brief, mad dream. It wasn't where she belonged. Not with him. She would be free with him gone. She would find a husband. Surely her family wouldn't turn her out at the end of the season. At any rate, she'd made her decision clear concerning him.

If it was so clear, why did his mind keep circling it like a bird of prey closing on its kill? Anything that had been between them was already dead and carried off by some other animal. He knew that.

It was over.

The situation couldn't be more final than his leaving town, leaving her to be happy, marry, live her life beside another, bear his children. He closed his eyes for a long blink against the rush of wind. The image of Sue holding a small blond babe sank into his mind—a beautiful sight. He wanted to hold her there, watching her lips curve into a smile.

"Watch it, gov!"

He opened his eyes with a snap and gave a flick of the reins to avoid colliding with a hack. His oath fell behind him on the wind to be washed away with rain and time.

Then he saw it, the Stag and Doe. He'd gone there for a drink with Thornwood a few years ago on one of his visits to town. It was a grimy little tavern, but it somehow managed charm within its crumbling walls and dark windows. Of course, right now he didn't care if it was a dirty hole in the ground, as long as there was whiskey. The stronger, the better. Perhaps it would burn away the ache in his chest—for a while anyway. He pulled back on the reins and was on the ground tying up his horse within the minute.

He flung the door open, breathing in the heavy scent of liquor and dust with a sigh. He hadn't left the city yet, but here he was in another world apart from the one in which he lived. Here he had no name, no family, and no problems. He was only a man in need of a drink.

"A bottle of your best whiskey," he called to the bartender before falling into a chair.

The man behind the bar considered him for a moment before pulling a bottle down from a high shelf. "It isn't the fine stuff I'm sure you're used to, m'lord, but it's the best we've got."

"Is it liquor?" Holden called out across the nearly empty room.

"Yes, m'lord."

"Then it will do just fine."

The man rounded the end of the long bar and set the bottle of dark liquid down on the table. He also offered a small glass cloudy with age and grime, but Holden waved it away. He may need to drink and forget, but he would not be drinking from anything as vile as that. Lifting the bottle to his lips, he let the fire of the drink slide down his throat in a large swallow. Soon his memory of her would fade. Perhaps with another swallow he could forget her. Tossing back more of the whiskey, he paused to see if it was working yet. "No," he mumbled, putting the bottle back to his mouth.

"My lord!"

He turned to see his butler striding in the door.

What happened to no one knowing him here and his plan to be on his way after a drink? "Fezawald, what the devil are you doing here? Is this where you come on your days off? No wonder you require so many naps." He pushed a chair out opposite him with the kick of one booted foot. "As long as you're here, pull up a chair and have a drink."

The old man's face hardened with duty. "I can't do that, my lord."

"Titles and propriety don't exist here, Fezawald." He waved his arm to the side, indicating the dilapidated tavern. "No one cares. Have a seat."

"No, my lord. I followed you here from the Rutledge home. I'm only pleased you slowed your pace so we might speak."

"There's nothing left to say, Fezawald. My word on it from this morning stands. I'm leaving. As always, you will have the run of things while I'm away. Long enough to close up the house and join me, anyway. I'll send for you soon, once I know…Fezawald, what is the matter with you? Stop your infernal finger-tapping on the table and sit."

Fezawald lowered his voice and leaned over the table to say, "There is a young lady in your home being seen to by your mother."

God, no! What had he allowed to happen? His chair slid across the floor with a screech of wood as he stood.

"Do I need to say more, my lord?"

"No, I believe that says it all, Fezawald." He was already tossing money onto the table and striding out the door before his butler could reply.

Sue tried to lift the window sash again with no luck. Henrietta must have known the windows were painted shut and she had no exit. She pushed at the window, only hearing the clinking rattle of the glass against the frame. How long before anyone noticed her missing? Tonight? Tomorrow? She had spent the past day locked in her bedchamber. Would they think her still there? Would they care?

She sank into a chair to survey her surroundings. There must be some way out of this mess. She drummed her fingers on the wooden arm of the chair. Eventually Holden would return home, wouldn't he? Or did he have something to do with all of this? She was trapped in his home after all. Did he put his mother up to this? Did he plan to keep her here until she was well and thoroughly compromised so he might get his way and have her as his mistress? She wouldn't have thought it likely of him, and yet he lied so easily.

His dead mother was alive. That was a rather large falsehood. What else was a lie? When he told her she was beautiful? When he said he cared for her? She didn't know anymore. Perhaps it had all been an illusion. One thing she did know: she did not want to ever see him again. Sitting in this small room, that prospect seemed unavoidable. She needed to escape.

She tapped her finger on the arm of the chair, considering the window again. Then standing, she spun the chair around and lifted it by the back. There was nothing for it but to hold her breath and be done with it. Holden could walk in that door a thousand times over, but he would not find her within the confines of these walls.

She flung the chair, wincing at the crash of the glass as it shattered and fell around her. Pushing the chair into a bush outside, she climbed onto the windowsill.

A breeze blew in through the jagged opening in the glass, greeting her cheeks with the sweet air of freedom. Struggling to balance, she pulled at her skirts where they bound her legs together. "Blast and the devil!" she cried out as she braced her hand on the splintered wood beside her.

"Such a foul mouth, Miss Green. You really should try to be more ladylike when at tea."

Henrietta. Sue's hand tightened on the frame. The impact of glass driving into her hand sent a tremor of pain up her arm.

What had she done?

Heat seared through her palm as the glass pierced farther into her skin. Warm blood trailed down her arm as she was pulled from the windowsill. "No! Let me go! Take your hands off me!"

"And breaking the hostess's windows out of the house is improper on all levels." Henrietta dragged her from the room.

"My hostess should be locked away in an asylum alongside her son!"

"Insulting one's hostess is poor behavior indeed." Henrietta tsked. "I will have to teach you what is proper."

Flailing wildly, Sue tried to get away. She didn't know where she would be taken, and she didn't particularly want to find out. She could see the front door. If only she could reach it. Tugging at the woman's grasp on her waist with her good hand, she tried to wiggle free.

Unfortunately, Henrietta was far taller than Sue and made of steel—or so it seemed. Sue's hand was throbbing with every beat of her heart, leaving small drops of blood across the polished wooden floor.

Her heels slipped as she was pulled into another room and the door was slammed behind her.

"I suppose I'll have to hold you here where I can keep my eye on you."

She was thrown to the floor, her cheek scraping across the thick rug. As much as she didn't want to see Holden again, she scanned the room for him. She blinked tears away, knowing she was alone with Henrietta. Where was Holden?

Sixteen

THE BOTTLE OF WHISKEY IN HIS HAND HAD GROWN HOT in his grasp. He hadn't taken a drink since he'd received the news, but he hadn't set the vice down, either. He may need it later, depending on what he found at his home. He shook his head to throw off the image of Sue in his mother's clutches as he threw open the front gate of Pemberton House.

Glancing up at the stately facade, he took a breath. He would have to face his father and tell him everything. He'd avoided this as long as he could, but he couldn't help her alone, couldn't face this alone and survive it. He knew what he must do, and it began with telling the truth. He rapped the bottle against his father's front door.

When the door was opened, Holden pushed past the butler, calling, "Father."

"My lord, if you would be so kind as to wait in the parlor, I will alert his lordship to your arrival."

"Pardon, but that sounds terribly complicated and time consuming." Holden turned and called again, "Father!"

"Holden?" Thornwood asked from the landing of the stairs. His eyes narrowed on the whiskey bottle in his son's hand as he moved toward the stairs. "You're foxed. And it's not even three in the afternoon."

"Damn it all! It's later than I realized." Holden took an impatient step to the side before turning back to his father.

"When did you begin the festivities, today?" his father asked with a sneer.

"Do I look festive?" Holden countered.

His father reached the bottom of the stairs and gave his butler a quick nod. "Have some sandwiches and coffee brought to the library. It seems my son needs sobering."

"Yes, my lord."

"We don't have time for sandwiches," Holden stated as the butler left the hall. "And I'm not foxed."

His father wrapped his arms across his chest, watching his son. "Why, then, are you carrying a half-empty bottle of whiskey with you?"

Holden frowned at the bottle in his hand in consideration. "Ballast. But that doesn't matter. What matters is Mother."

His father's eyes sharpened. "Have you found her?"

Holden hardened his jaw against the truth and his father's inevitable reaction. "I never lost her."

His father shook his head and studied Holden with a frown. The clock across the hall ticked away what could be the last minutes of Sue's life as he waited for his father's damn assistance. "Explain yourself."

"We don't have time for that now. We must go." He indicated the door at his back.

"Where is she? What have you done?"

"I'll explain on the way."

His father's eyes narrowed into the same disapproving glare Holden had seen on his face all his life. "On the way to where?"

Holden sighed and gripped the bottle tighter in his hand. "To my home, where you will find Mother, as well as an innocent lady I must protect."

⁂

Holden swung open the door of his home. Silence. Where was Sue? If anything had happened to her, if he was too late…

"We will find her, Son. You have my word on it." His father's voice grated in a hushed tone as he clasped Holden on the shoulder.

Holden knew it was only a comforting comment and meant nothing, yet he clung to it. Sue must be all right. He would find her. All would be fine.

Just then, his eyes fell to the droplets of red stretching across the main hall. The trail led into the parlor. Blood. He couldn't breathe. His head whipped to his father in time to see him signal toward the door. Holden nodded, stepping closer to the parlor door with careful steps.

Thoughts of the sight that would soon meet his eyes made his limbs pulse with anger, yet his feet stuck to the floor.

His father gave him a nod of encouragement from the opposite side of the door, his fierce blue eyes narrowing in anticipation.

Every moment he delayed was another moment Sue would suffer at his mother's hand. There was already blood on the floor. Would she even be alive? He reached for the doorknob with one last steadying breath and threw the door open with an exclaimed, "Sue!"

His mother sat at a small table to the side of the room with a teapot raised in the air, ready to pour.

"Sue—where is she?" His eyes scanned the room, seeing no one else within the walls. "What have you done with her?"

"I don't know why you're so upset, dearest boy." His mother dropped a lump of sugar into her teacup.

"*Sue Green! Where is she?*" Holden shouted, with another look around the room.

"Calm yourself, Holden. We were just about to have tea. Won't you join us? And you've brought company, I see." She eyed her husband as he stepped into the room. There was something more menacing than usual in her glare as she said, "Montague."

Holden moved around the high-backed armchair, and that was when he saw it.

A steady drip of red trailing down the side of the chair. He looked up with dread, seeing Sue as he did.

She was curled into the cushions, so small, so frail. Her cheeks were pale under half-closed brown eyes. "*What have you done?*" he yelled at his mother as he bent over Sue.

"Henrietta, stay where you are," his father commanded from just inside the door, moving in to control his wife.

"Sue? Sue, can you hear me?" Holden swept a hand over her forehead before catching her chin in his grasp to look her in the eyes. "I'm here now. She won't hurt you anymore, love. Sue?"

"Holden, I don't feel very well." Her voice was thin.

This couldn't be happening. She had to be all right. He turned her hand over and saw the large shard of glass still lodged in her wrist. With one quick motion, he removed it, which only made her bleed more. His chest tightened. She had to be all right. Tugging out his handkerchief, he wrapped it around her wrist with hasty movements. "You need something to drink. You've bled a great deal."

She nodded, resting her head against the wing of the chair.

He rose to face his mother, moving across the room toward the table in the corner where she was flanked by the columns of closed velvet draperies. His fists clenched at his sides to keep from diving at her to choke the life from her body.

"As I said before, we were about to have a spot of tea when you arrived."

"Tea? You've tried to kill her! You were going to sip tea while she passed from this world?"

"I didn't lay a finger on the girl. I only tried to keep her from further injuring herself. Tea, dearest?"

"You won't be serving anyone tea, Henrietta," his father stated as he loomed over his wife. "You don't belong here."

"You think you can lock me away forever? You can't. I won't go back!" his mother yelled.

Holden slipped past where his father argued with his wife to reach the tea service. "Sue will need to drink something. Then we shall discuss matters." In his mind, matters could be summed up with shipping her straight away to a hospital, but he kept his mouth shut about that detail in the plans, for now. He reached for a cup, only to have it pulled from his grasp.

A smile crept up his mother's face, pulling her skin into harsh lines. "Oh, if it's for *her*, then you must give her the special tea I made just for the occasion."

"It doesn't matter. Just pour something." With Sue's life hanging in the balance, Holden was losing what little patience he had.

His mother poured tea from a second pot on the tray and handed it to Holden. "This should…help her rest. She needs her rest."

His father turned to regard his wife, his face twisting in thought. At least he could keep her cornered until Holden could revive Sue. Once she was safe, then he would deal with the woman.

His father leaned over her chair, staring deep into her eyes as he mused, "I haven't seen you this concerned with someone's care since Samuel."

"Are you accusing me of something, Montague?"

Holden took the cup of tea and returned to Sue's side. Let his parents argue; he needed Sue to be all right. She had to be. Kneeling beside her, he lifted the cup to her lips. "Have some tea, Sue."

"*Don't let her drink that!*" his father bellowed.

Holden pulled the cup away from Sue and looked up. "What is it?"

"Poison," his father stated, allowing the word to hang in the room like the vile substance it was.

Holden stood, his eyes narrowing on his mother across the room. She'd tried to poison Sue after injuring her? She truly was the horrible person his father had always accused her of being. He flung the teacup to the floor and took a step forward in accusation. "You were going to poison her?"

"Don't listen to Montague! He's never understood!"

"Haven't I, Henrietta?" His father's lips twisted in what appeared to be sheer hatred for the woman, and Holden found he couldn't blame him. For the first time in his life, he agreed with his father. "I know what you did all those years ago. I know what you planned here today."

"You know nothing! Nothing, I tell you!"

Holden moved to pour tea for Sue. Hopefully this pot would have a distinct lack of poison within it. How had he allowed this to happen? His carelessness had almost killed Sue. Never again. He would never be manipulated by his mother again. He would never keep secrets that could hurt another again. Never. His hands shook as he poured the tea. He was such a fool.

"You killed our son, and you thought to do the same again today." His father's voice rattled the paintings on the walls.

Holden let him yell. Let the plaster crack in his front parlor and the china rattle in the cupboards. He only wanted Sue to be well and his mother finally gone from his life. His father had been right. Aunt Penelope had been right. And he had been so terribly wrong. He exhaled a fuming breath as he crossed the floor to kneel at Sue's side.

The argument at his back raged on as he lifted the cup to Sue's lips. "Drink this."

She gave him a small nod and grasped the cup with her one well hand.

His mother was still yelling at his back. "I did what

was best for this family—a concept you could never grasp, Montague!"

Holden straightened at her words, turning back to her. "Best for this family?" he cut in. "How are killing my brother and forcing me to be raised without a mother best for the family? I am family, am I not? Do you know I've taken the blame for being the wrong son left behind my entire life? I've spent my whole life running from the mess you made of our family!"

"Samuel was going to hurt you, Holden. You should have seen the look in his eyes." She shook her head. "You were my baby," she whispered, wiping a tear from her eye.

His father's fists balled at his sides. "Killing another child wasn't going to bring back the stillborn, Henrietta."

"My actions protected Holden. You can't deny that," she argued, looking up at her husband. "You locked me away when all I did was help Holden in the same way I couldn't help my perfect little baby."

"Your assistance wasn't needed, Mother," Holden snarled at her.

"Is that your excuse now? Did you think this poor girl would kill Holden so you thought to be rid of her first?" His father lifted an arm to indicate Sue.

"You certainly choose villainous adversaries—a seven-year-old boy and a young lady…" Holden shook his head in disgust. How did he ever think to repair a bond with this woman?

His mother's voice was raised to match his own anger. "This strumpet was going to take you from me. I could see it happening right before my eyes. You're mine, Holden. Mine."

"You almost killed Sue!" he roared.

He heard Sue's intake of breath behind him. At least she was alert enough to listen.

"She already killed Samuel. Why not another? My son, my heir." The words were torn from his father through a clenched jaw.

"I've lost too many children already. I can't lose you, too." His mother dabbed at another tear.

"I believe you lost me long ago, Mother. I simply didn't realize it until this day." He turned back to Sue, casting his gaze over her pale face. She needed a doctor. Unfortunately she only had him at the moment. His brows drew together as he leaned over her, gripping the back of her chair above her head. He took a small amount of comfort in the fact that she was still breathing. She was still alive.

"She's the cause of all of it." Only his father's soft words could have pulled Holden's attention from Sue.

He looked around to see his father taking a step toward him with a frown.

"Sometimes what we see with our eyes within seconds takes our hearts a lifetime to comprehend." He shook his head and stated, "You weren't to blame for Samuel's passing."

"I should have stopped her. You've always said so." Holden cast a concerned glance around at Sue where she rested in the chair before turning back to his father.

"You were a child."

"If I'd been stronger, like Samuel…"

"No. This was all your mother's doing. I was wrong to lay this blame on you."

Holden swallowed any rebuttal he might have made and stared into his father's eyes. It was five and twenty years too late, but that didn't matter, not today.

"Isn't this a lovely tableau of family life," his mother sneered from the corner. "You're going to pull this family apart again, aren't you, Montague? You cannot bear the thought that I love my son as I do. You're jealous! You seek to take my place with him, don't you?"

"You have no place with me, Mother. Not anymore. Not after this. I thought your death long ago was a lie, but now I see it was truer than I could grasp. It seems you are quite buried in my mind, and this time you will remain that way."

"Are you so heartless as to hurt your mother so? I love you, Holden."

"Your *love* nearly killed someone today!" Holden stepped away from the argument, going back to Sue's side. The color was slowly returning to her cheeks, but she was far from well.

His father turned back to confront his mother. "Your words are fraught with the same poison you sought to use this afternoon, and I will not hear them. Holden, we should send for the authorities."

"I think it best for the family name to be discreet about this," he said, thinking of his cousins' plans of marriage.

"I didn't realize you cared for the family name," his father mused as he shot Holden a wondering look.

"I believe there is a great deal you don't realize, Father."

"So it would seem," he replied, his gaze dipping to Sue for a second. "We can send your mother back to

Brooke House, then. They've kept her bed open for me in case I found her."

"She was overly thin and poorly clothed when she arrived here, Father. Even she doesn't deserve such treatment."

"What would you have me do after all she's done to this family? Stand by and allow her to leave? I can't allow that to happen, Holden."

"I won't allow that, either." He'd made that mistake and he wouldn't be that careless again. She couldn't have freedom to wonder the streets, she was too dangerous for that. "There must be a solution. We could have her sent to Australia or the Americas. I have a friend with a shipping business who wouldn't ask questions—well, perhaps not many questions."

"Perhaps," his father replied.

Holden sighed, watching his mother take a long draw from her teacup, draining it to the dregs. She was certainly quiet for someone with rather strong opinions about her future whereabouts. "But it would only be a matter of time before she found her way home—even from such a distance." He wasn't sure how he knew that statement was fact, but it was.

"I will not be traveling anywhere," his mother announced above their hushed chatter.

"You'll be going straight back to Brooke House if I have any say in the matter," his father retorted.

She didn't spare her husband a glance. Her green eyes pled with Holden as her gaze pierced through him. "Dearest son, know that I did it because I love you." She began to choke on the words, her face contorted around a scream. "Love...you." The teacup fell from her grasp as she crumbled to the floor.

Holden watched her fall, knowing he should feel some level of grief, even relief, but he felt nothing. He'd told the truth when he said he'd buried her long ago. She was gone now, by her own hand. It was rather fitting, really, that after causing so much strife, she would drink her own poisoned tea.

"So much loss," his father mused as he peered over the table for a glimpse of her body. A moment later, he went to the door to call for assistance from some footmen lingering in the hall.

Looking weary when he returned, he collapsed into the chair opposite Sue. "You are all I have left, Holden, and you are a grown man. I suppose you'll return to France soon. Continue...your life there."

Holden paused. It must be said. He'd had a lifetime of lies, and he didn't want any more of them. "I haven't told you the entire truth, Father."

"What do you mean?"

He took a breath. "I've never lived in France."

The heat of Sue's gaze warmed him as he stood beside her chair. She was watching him, listening. She would know almost all his secrets now. Ironic that he'd promised they wouldn't have any more secrets earlier this week, with no intention of fulfilling his promise, when now here he was baring all. No more secrets. He turned to glance at her before moving to lean against the edge of a table, face to face with his father.

"That's impossible," his father muttered.

"It's quite possible, believe me." Holden rubbed at

his head to push straight his careening thoughts. He didn't know where to start, and he wasn't entirely confident that Sue would understand once he did so. But she knew of his mother now, she'd witnessed the worst of his lies today, and he couldn't keep these secrets anymore. He took a breath and spoke the truth for the first time in his life.

Seventeen

Sue's head was spinning, whether from exposure to so many lies or from loss of blood was debatable. Had this day truly been real? Unfortunately, it was quite real. She tried to sink further into the armchair. Perhaps with the shock of his mother's death, Holden would forget she was there. But she could never shrink small enough for Holden not to see her. Not anymore.

The last thing she'd wanted when she woke today was to speak to that man again. Yet here she sat, listening to his family reunion while his mother lay slumped on the floor. If she could only stand, she could leave. She would walk away from him and never look back. She shifted her weight and tried to find her feet, but her head was feeling quite detached. Only lasting a second upright, she fell back to the chair and gained Holden's attention in the process. Perfect.

He knelt before her, wrapping his hands around her wrist with a gentleness she didn't know he possessed. How could he think to touch her after all his untruths were brought to light? Without a single apology? He'd spent his life living a lie and had no remorse for it.

She pulled her arm from his grasp, trying not to read the hurt in his eyes at her reaction to his touch.

"You're bleeding, Sue. Quite profusely, if I'm to be honest—which I am making an effort at today." He tried to grin, but his brows were drawn together in concern.

"Very well, then." With a sigh, she lifted her injured hand to him.

He removed the handkerchief from her hand and tossed it aside. "How did it happen?"

"It was a failed attempt at leaving your home." She wanted to leave his home right now.

"Through the convenient door made of knives I have? Sue, these cuts are rather deep."

She shrugged. He wasn't there; he would have done the same. "Your dining room windows were painted closed."

"Ah. That room needed redecoration anyway. I'll bandage it the best I can for now."

She nodded, watching as he pulled at the knot of his cravat, ripping it from his neck. Wrapping the fabric around her hand and wrist, he bandaged her wounds until all she could see was white. The fabric was still warm from his body, blast him. And it most likely smelled of him, too, but she would not be sniffing it—ever. She would thank him, return home, and promptly remove this bandage

"I never wanted you to be pulled into any of this," he offered without looking up from his work. "My apologies for any pain she inflicted upon you."

A halfhearted apology—for her near death and not for his lies. Her jaw tightened around her reply. "You mean the mother you told me was deceased? Is that to whom you're referring?"

"Yes. Her."

"I'm quite fine, thank you for inquiring." She tried to tug her hand from his grasp, but he held the fabric of her bandage tight in his hands.

"Sue." His eyes met hers for a second as he seemed to consider his words before looking back down at the knot he was tying across her hand. "I'm not what I seem."

"I've noticed. Nothing around here is what it seems."

"Can I tell you a secret?"

"Aren't you out of those?"

He lifted his face to hers. He was too close. "I've never so much as visited France. I would like nothing more than to go there someday, though."

"You've never even been there?" Were his lies endless? Did she know this man at all? She'd been so sure only a few days ago. "Where did you live? You've been away years, have you not?"

"I was a fisherman in Iceland for a few years. It's more lucrative than you would believe, but quite smelly work. Once I'd saved enough funds, I went to Belgium. I had a shop on the square in Brussels. I lived upstairs, ate far too many chocolates from the shop next door, and sold antiquities."

"Fish and antiquities. Do I know anything true of you?"

At his hard stare and silence, she guessed at his answer.

Did she want to know more? Her hand be damned; she needed to leave. "Well, then. If we're finished here, I need to return home."

"I came most recently from Scotland where I have a cottage."

"Not France," she clarified.

"No." His eyes searched hers, looking for something she didn't know if she possessed any longer.

Had everything been a lie? His stories, all creations he invented? Every word of who he was, a fabrication? "Was any of it true?"

"Pieces. The bits that were me were true."

"How can I possibly find those pieces in this pile of falsehoods, Holden?"

"Trust what you know of me."

"What do I know of you, Holden? What could I possibly know?"

"I wanted to tell you. I wanted to be honest."

"Then why weren't you? It was all a grand deception, wasn't it? Oh, you always have your reasons, but it's deceit."

"I had reasons. Sue, you have to understand."

"Why?" She tried to pull her hand from him once more, but he held the ends of the fabric, tying her to him.

"Because I need you to understand."

"It doesn't change anything. Even if I did understand, I wouldn't accept your offer from last night."

"But it does change things. I never meant to hurt you, Sue."

"You lied to me. Your entire life is a fairy tale you thought would sound dashing to those around you. How do I know what's real?" She had to ask him. She needed to know, even if she couldn't trust the answers. She lowered her voice to a whisper. "When you said you cared for me? When you said I was beautiful?"

"Always, Sue. Always."

"I want to believe you."

"But you don't."

"How can I believe anything you say to me?" One tear threatened to slip down her cheek, but she blinked it away with a sniff.

"You know me."

"No." She tore her hand free of his and stood. "I don't." She moved away from him, pausing as she reached the door. Turning back to him, she swallowed back every fiber of longing in her body and said, "Please send for a carriage. I'd like to return to my home."

∽

"I could have taken your carriage without your company, you know," Sue stated as she clung to the seat of the phaeton with one hand.

"After what you've endured today? It was either this or I could carry you with me on horseback." He tossed a grin in her direction, but her eyes were focused on the street ahead. "I thought you would prefer this."

"I should have taken a hack," she grumbled.

As if he would allow her to climb into the confines of a hired hack after having her life threatened. He would carry her home on his own back before he would allow such a thing. Not to mention that he wanted a few more minutes with her. Could he make her see? Was forgiveness on any level out of the question? "Sue..." he began.

"I would prefer Miss Green, if you please."

"Would you? Sue, I know things between us have become strained..."

"Is that what you call this? Strained?"

A silence fell between them that threatened to suffocate him. This morning he'd thought to ride away and never see her again. Why couldn't he allow her to leave now? She clearly wanted nothing further to do with him, yet he couldn't oblige her wishes. He needed her. He glanced to the side. She was turned away from him as far as the bench seat would allow, an escaped lock of her burnished gold hair pressed to her neck by the breeze. He couldn't imagine never touching her again or, even worse, never laughing with her again.

She must see reason. He couldn't go on without mending things with her. He couldn't. He loved her and he would never stop trying to win back her heart. "Where I've lived and my life circumstances don't change who I am, Sue."

"You're right. You lied to me from the beginning. Should that fact make me reconsider being your mistress? Isn't that why you care what I think of you? Because you want me to reconsider your proposition? I won't."

He nodded, his eyes trained on the street ahead of him. He was such a blasted idiot. He shouldn't have propositioned her in such a manner. Of course her worth was greater than that of a mistress. He should have known that. Somehow he would find a way to make it right, but that day was clearly not today. "I believe we're at your home." He drew the phaeton to a stop and jumped down. Coming around the conveyance, he lifted her to the ground.

She slid from his grasp and began making her way up the steps. "You don't have to see me inside."

"I will, all the same."

The door was opened by an aging butler whose eyes flared at Sue's appearance for a moment before he stepped from view as the door opened wider. Holden shouldn't go inside, but he didn't want to leave, either. He stepped over the threshold, pretending not to notice Sue's glare in his direction.

Her mother paused on the bottom step of a large staircase when she saw them in the doorway. "Sue! What has happened to you?"

She removed her hat and tossed it onto a table as if nothing important had happened today. "I...fell in the park. Lord Steelings was kind enough to come to my rescue and bring me home. He was just leaving."

"Nonsense. He must come in for tea." Her mother smiled in his direction, leaving him feeling like a mouse invited to dine with a cat.

"I can't stay, my lady. I only wanted to see Miss Green inside safely."

"Indeed. We wouldn't want her to fall again. Someone might see her." She glanced at Sue, disgust written across her face as clearly as if it were painted on her cheeks. "She doesn't have the natural grace my other daughter possesses."

"My lady, with all due respect, you wouldn't know natural grace if it bit you on the arse." He paused at her gasp, allowing his words to sink in. "Do you even realize the talent your daughter has for painting? The beautiful way in which she sees the world? And you treat her with disdain. You should be ashamed of yourself, Lady Rightworth, for attempting to hide such a treasure away and denying the world a view of such splendor."

"*I never!*" she bellowed before turning on Sue. "Did you put him up to this, you despicable little…"

"My opinions are my own, my lady. Now, if you'll excuse me, I'm sure my presence is needed at home by now." He offered Sue a tip of his hat and a smile that he prayed she would find endearing. "Good day, Miss Green."

As he turned to leave, he heard her murmur a small, "Good day."

In that tiny phrase, he found hope.

❧

They stood frozen in silence until the front door closed and the butler left the room. As soon as they were alone, her mother turned to her. "A gentleman's opinions are never his own. What have you said to turn his view of our family so?"

Holden was right. Her mother should be ashamed of her actions. Sue didn't have to stand here and be bashed about the head with insults. She'd survived an attempt on her life today, and she would survive this. "I believe you turned his view of our family all by yourself, Mother."

"Won't it be a shock to him when you're packed away to Scotland and he is forced to interact with this family without your influence. What will he think of our family then?"

"Very little, I'm sure."

"I never!" she exclaimed, drawing back away from Sue.

"You really should work on your conversational skills, Mother. Society expects you to say more than two words in a discussion. I'm fairly certain that's one of *your* rules."

"Sue Green, you will soon be gone from this house, and I, for one, look forward to the day with great anticipation."

"That reminds me, Mother. I should inform you that I won't be going to live with Great-Aunt Mildred at the end of the season. I plan to go to Paris, sell my paintings on the streets, and tell everyone I speak with that you, Lady Rightworth of Rightworth House, are my mother. That is how proud I am of you and your treatment of me."

She tilted her head and gave her mother a wide smile. "Now, if you will excuse me, I've had a trying afternoon, and I would like a bath and a tea cake—perhaps not in that order."

She left her mother gaping at her in the hall as she climbed the stairs. That woman would never control her actions again. She would flee to France before she would continue to live under her mother's rule after the season.

≈

Sue had finished one painting and moved on to sketching bits of life outside her bedchamber window. If she kept her hands moving, creating, she wouldn't have time to think about all that had happened yesterday. This was her plan. She sighed as she darkened a line on the paper. Her plan was admittedly not working, as she couldn't keep her mind from returning to Holden again and again.

A light knock sounded at her bedchamber door. "Sue?"

"Come in," she called out to Evangeline as she looked up from her sketch.

Her sister stepped into the room carrying a box and closed the door at her back, a mischievous grin covering her face.

"What is that?"

"It came for you." Evangeline's eyes flashed with glee as she set the box down on the small table where Sue's tea from the morning sat abandoned. "With the mood Mother is in, I feared she would smash it before she would give it to you."

Sue set her sketch pad down and crossed the room, her heart pounding. She couldn't handle any more surprises, not after yesterday afternoon. Opening the lid on the box, she held her breath as she peered inside. Dark swirls of frosting dusted with white sugar sat inside a perfect ring of tiny candy flowers.

Chocolate cake. Damn him. She blinked away the tears in her eyes and inhaled the chocolate-scented air.

"There was no note, only instructions to deliver it to you. Who would send you such a gift?" Evangeline asked as she looked over Sue's shoulder.

Sue smiled up at her sister before returning her gaze to the cake. "Someone who loves chocolate cake." There was a small grain of truth. He loved cake. She frowned and shook her head. Somehow that truth mattered more than his mother's existence or where he'd lived for the past eleven years.

Her hand gripped the edge of the table beside the box as she stumbled on her thoughts. He'd lived in so many places, always running... Freedom. Was that what he was searching for? Holden had fled the country to be free of his past. He wanted to live just as she did. And she'd berated him for it. She recoiled at the pang of guilt that surged through her at the thought.

His mother had clearly been unstable. She'd killed his brother and tried to kill her. Of course he'd lied. He'd lied to protect his family from scandal. He'd lied...to protect her? Did he care for her?

Did he...love her?

I can't marry you. His words flooded back into her mind with the force of a raging river. He hadn't said, "I don't wish to." He'd said, "I can't." Perhaps he was only attempting to shield her from his past, from his life. He hadn't propositioned her to be his mistress because he didn't see her worth, he'd offered all he could given his circumstances. But, his circumstances had changed yesterday afternoon hadn't they? If he'd only been protecting her from the secret of his ill mother, then perhaps... She didn't realize she was crying until she felt her wet cheeks. "Chocolate cake," she whispered to herself.

She did know him. She knew his heart. All the meaningless words in the world couldn't cover up the truth of his heart.

"Evie, I believe I've made a terrible mistake." She brushed her tears aside with the back of her hand.

Evangeline wrapped an arm around her shoulders. "Terrible mistakes can sometimes lead to happiness, can't they?"

"I hope so," she muttered, leaning her head against her sister's shoulder.

He had wanted to marry her that night on the

terrace; she was sure of it. Did he still? After everything that happened yesterday? Perhaps there was the
small chance that, through it all, he cared for her.

❧

Holden stepped into Thornwood's parlor, the room
was decorated in an abundance of flowers in celebra-
tion of the duke's recent elopement. He was here to
congratulate his friend on his recently acquired leg
shackle, yet his eyes were already sweeping the room
for Sue. It had been weeks since he'd left her angry,
injured, and rumpled in the main hall of her home.
He'd kept himself busy becoming reacquainted with
his father, making arrangements to visit Pemberton
Hall, and visiting with his cousins, yet his mind was
never far from Sue.

He heard she'd attended what was to be Miss
Phillips' betrothal ball, but he hadn't seen her there.
Granted, he'd had his hands rather full that night,
pummeling Miss Phillips' brother and restraining
her betrothed while Thornwood stepped into the
man's place. Thornwood was married. It was hard
to believe, but made perfect sense all the same. His
friend was across the room just now, chatting with his
mother, yet his eyes barely strayed from his new bride.
Marriage. For as much as gentlemen ran from it, it
didn't seem so terrible from this angle.

Stepping around a gentleman lingering in conversation by the door, he saw her. Her head was
thrown back in laughter as she reached for a cake
from the buffet against the wall. She turned back to
Thornwood's younger sister, Roselyn, as she replied.

He couldn't hear her words, yet they made him smile all the same. She glowed in a golden gown almost the color of her hair. When she saw him, would she cease smiling? He held back for a moment, memorizing the joy in her eyes in case his presence shattered it.

His gaze must have alerted her to his arrival, for she turned a second later. Then, as he'd feared, the smile slipped from her face.

Crossing the room, he neared her. What would he say? He'd stayed away all this time to allow her anger with him to settle, but perhaps that had been the wrong approach. He'd practiced words in the mirror only this morning, yet the carefully honed apology evaporated in her presence like yesterday's rain on a warm afternoon.

He needed to talk to her, to try once more to explain things. There was nothing for it but to begin. "I need to speak with you."

"That sounds rather ominous."

"It's not so much ominous as remorseful."

Her breasts rose and fell on shallow breaths as she looked up at him. "Remorseful. For this?" She raised her recently injured hand. "It's mended now, so there's no need…"

"No, in the past." He led her farther from the gathering of people so they could speak. "I offended you, Sue. Although it was never my intention."

"On which occasion?"

"Perhaps all of them." He chuckled at her nod of agreement. "I see you aren't going to play the coy 'Oh, your actions are perfect, my lord' bit."

"I wasn't planning on it. If I'm to be honest, I'm

rather enjoying your discomfort." She smiled up at him. "You aren't remorseful often, are you? You seem out of practice."

He shook his head and glanced away before returning his gaze to hers. "This may be the first time I've ever expressed true remorse, now that I consider it."

"I can tell. You really should begin with an explanation of your improper action."

"That's where it gets difficult. Sue, I never meant to mislead you. I've lived shielded by lies most of my life. When I met you…" How was he to explain this? Perhaps there was no way in which to explain it. He sighed. "I'm sorry. I should have been honest with you from the beginning, or at least from the middle."

"I'll take honesty in the end."

"Will you?" His chest tightened at her slight shrug. Did that mean she was willing to forgive him?

"Sue, you deserve more than my offer to be my mistress. I would provide a comfortable life for you, but there is more to life than comfort. I've been comfortable for years without truly living. I see that now. You helped me see that. All I could provide you then was my protection, such as it was."

"And now?" Her jaw tightened around the words.

"My circumstances have changed."

"As have mine."

"Have they?" His heart stopped. Was she spoken for? Was he too late?

"Yes. I'm leaving next week for Paris. I'm going to make a fresh start of it, be an artist. I don't want to hide behind initials any longer. You helped me see that."

He nodded and cast his eyes toward the nearby

window. He couldn't lose her again. Turning back to her, he asked, "Would you mind having a friend's company on your journey?"

"I believe I would like that very much. Do you know of such a friend?" A blush crept up her neck, turning her cheeks pink.

"Perhaps 'friend' is the wrong word, though. I've felt so for some time."

"Yes. But what word would you use?"

Husband. The word flew into his mind with a ferocity that made him blink. Would she have him? He had to try. If he didn't, he would always wonder and regret. "That remains to be seen. There are things to be determined first."

"What sort of things?"

"If you're willing to marry me, for one."

She froze for a moment before her lips parted on careful words. "Will you always tell me the truth? Even when I look hideous in a gown?"

"That would never happen. You're just as beautiful in gowns tied up with ribbons as you are covered in paint. Actually, I believe I would prefer you covered in paint—wet, slick paint all over your skin as you slide…"

"Holden!" she exclaimed in a loud whisper as she shoved him.

A grin he couldn't conceal covered his face. "Is that a yes?"

"Yes." She smiled up at him.

He tugged her hand into his grasp. *Yes. She said yes.* "Let's go now."

"Now?"

"Sue, I've followed you across England, through ballrooms, around gardens, and I will happily follow you to Paris. I want you in my life. But I want you to be my wife—now."

"What of the banns? My family? Your family?"

"We've lived enough of our lives with our families in mind. Do you really want to continue to do so for another three weeks while banns are posted?"

Her brow creased in a line he wanted to kiss away. "No, but…"

"Come with me, Sue. Be my wife."

"Gretna Green, just as our friends did?"

"Calais, on our way to Paris. With a stop-off at home first."

"Why do we need to stop at your home?"

"Our home. It will be your home, too, now. And we can't very well begin our journey together, let alone our life, without first packing a lunch for our trip, or perhaps simply a large basket of sweets." He laced her hand around his arm. She was finally where she belonged—at his side where he would never lose her again.

He looked down at her with only one question left lingering in his mind. Oddly, it was a more difficult subject to broach than marriage. He let a relaxed smile he did not feel cover his face. Soon he would tell her the extent of his feelings for her. And soon he would know if she felt the same.

❧

They crashed through the bedchamber door to the sound of her gown ripping and the knowledge that she didn't care one whit. The purpose behind their stop at home had shifted once they were in the carriage together—alone. She laughed against his lips at his attempts to kick the door closed while she tugged on his bottom lip with her teeth. Pulling at the knot of his cravat until it hung loose in her fingers, she splayed her fingers across the warm skin of his neck. Rough male skin with a hint of stubble abraded her palm. She breathed in the spicy scent of his shaving soap as his lips met hers once more.

Cool air caressed her skin as he ripped her gown further and it fell to the floor around her in a discarded heap of silk. He glanced down with a chuckle that rippled through her bones. "I'll buy you another."

"Or we could stay nude for the duration of our marriage." She pushed his coat from his shoulders with a grin.

"That could be arranged." He lifted her off the ground, cupping his hands on her bottom to bring her closer to him.

Her legs twisted around his waist as her hands sank into his hair. Her eyes met his for a moment. In that moment, they both froze. She couldn't believe this was real. Was he thinking the same? The thought vanished as his lips slashed across hers with a hunger she felt as well. His mouth trailed down the column of her neck, and her head fell back on a whimper as her fingers tightened in his hair.

Carrying her across the room to the bed, he set her on the edge and ripped his shirt off over his head, his untied cravat still hanging about his neck. The line of white fabric rested on the thick muscles of his chest and drew her eyes down to another line—the small trail of golden hair disappearing into his breeches. Without pause, she wrapped her fingers around the ends of the fabric and pulled him down to her.

His lips met hers in a hungry kiss, demanding she match his every move. A moment later, her breasts were freed as he had unfastened her stays without her notice. He broke the kiss to kneel on the bed over her, gazing down at her. "Lovely, absolutely lovely," he mused.

When she tried to pull him down by the tails of his cravat again, he stopped her with the touch of his hand and a wicked gleam in his eyes. Grabbing the length of fabric, he unwound it from about his neck and laid it across her stomach.

"What are you doing?"

"You began this game."

"I fear your games. They always end with me in a compromising position."

"Exactly," he offered around a grin. "Do you trust me?"

"Yes. Completely." She blinked up into his face, knowing it was the truth.

"Then give me your hands."

When she complied, he gave her fingers a brief squeeze. Flipping her hands over, he saw the red scars of her injury scrawled across her palm and leading in a jagged line up her wrist. Leaning down, he brushed his lips against her barely healed skin. His gentle kiss held an unspoken promise that it would never happen again. He didn't need to say the words; she knew it was the truth. He straightened, pressing her wrists together and binding them with his cravat. Moving over her, he braced a knee at her side and lifted her until she lay diagonally across his large bed.

Her heart pounded in her ears. What was he doing? Was this sort of activity what happened behind closed bedchamber doors across London? All these years and she hadn't had a clue...

His hands swept down her arms, coming to rest on her hands. His eyes met hers for a moment as she gave him a hint of a nod. Apparently that was what he was waiting for because the next she knew, her arms were above her head being tied to one of the tall posts. When she arched her head back to see, the fabric pulled at her wrists, pinning her to the bed.

The scruff of his chin tickled her skin as he made a path down the inside of one arm with his mouth. He slid over her shoulder, pausing to pull at the lobe of her ear with his lips. Her body arched into him, and she was maddened with the need to touch his skin, feel him, hold on to him. He moved down her body, lavishing kisses on every inch of her skin until a sound of complaint escaped her throat.

He didn't change his pace, only drove her further over the edge of insanity when he tugged the tip of her breast into his mouth, drawing circles there with his tongue. His teeth grazed the hardened peak, and he flashed a grin at her before moving farther down her body. He was driving her mad on purpose—the annoying man. She tugged at her bindings once more but the knot didn't budge. "I need to touch you."

"Shhh, you only need to feel. Trust me." He kicked off his breeches and boots and knelt before her like a devious Greek god looking down on the world and wondering where he would next wreak havoc.

She flinched under his gaze, bared to him, exposed. She licked her lips, her mouth suddenly dry. But with a touch of his hand to her hip, she stilled. He spread her legs with a nudge of his thigh and ran his hand in a lazy path up and down her side until she relaxed.

She wanted his hands on her. She wanted to be touched everywhere. She wanted him. "Holden." The whispered plea hung in the air between them as she gazed up at him.

He leaned over her, kissing her as he slipped a finger into her core. She arched into him, her breasts grazing against hardened muscle. He strummed his hand against her once more and she curled into his touch, her knees rising to brush against his sides. He pulled away from their kiss a moment later but didn't go far as he braced himself on his elbow to look down at her. The length of him poised at her entrance.

"This might hurt a bit, but I promise it will never hurt again." He was shaking with need as his hot skin covered hers.

At her nod, he angled her hips and drove into her with one long stroke. He claimed her cry with his mouth as he stilled, allowing her to relax around him. She felt full, deliciously full, with Holden's weight pressing down upon her. Then he moved. Her breath caught as he withdrew and slid into her once more. This time there was no pain, only a building, agonizing need for something she knew only he could provide. His hands roamed her body as he pounded into her. Pulling her knees up, he slid into her again, driving deeper.

Her eyes closed as she began climbing toward a release unlike anything she'd experienced before in his arms. His hands tightened on her as the speed of the moment increased. *More, more*, her body chanted until she cried out, her eyes opening to see Holden as she spiraled out of control and came to land back in his bed. His body flexed above hers as he drove into her one last time.

He withdrew from her and reached up to untie her hands from the bedpost before collapsing beside her. She shook the binding from her wrists and curled into his side, laying her head on his chest as she traced the lines of his muscles with her fingernails. Finally she was free to touch him. He wrapped his arms around her, rubbing her back in gentle strokes.

After a few minutes of silence she asked, "Holden, will you really take me to Paris?"

"We can leave first thing in the morning. Well, perhaps not first thing. That sounds rather early for the evening we have ahead of us."

"More? But it's still afternoon."

He lifted his head. "Are you complaining of my attention?"

"Never. I want to spend all of my evenings this way, wrapped in your arms."

"Sue?" He pulled her onto his chest so they could see one another. His brows were drawn into a deep vee with concern. "I have to confess, I do have one last secret."

Her heart pounded. She almost didn't want to know—almost. "What is it?"

He brushed the fallen hair from her face. She could

read the tension in his eyes, the fear. "I love you." He took a breath, his gaze softening on her. "I've loved you since the night you kicked me in the nose, and I will love you until the end of my days."

He loved her? Her eyes burned as she sniffed away tears and smiled down at him. "In the vein of honesty between us, I have a similar secret. I love you, Holden."

He sighed in relief and smiled up at her, pulling her closer in the process.

She placed a hand over his heart to feel it hammering beneath her palm. "No more secrets. I don't want any untruth to come between us again."

"My lady, I don't want anything between us at all." With that, he rolled with her across the bed and proceeded to show her exactly what he had planned for the remainder of that evening and every evening following until the end of time.

Enjoy a sneak peek at Elizabeth Michels'
next Regency romp

How to Lose a Lord in 10 Days or Less

ANDREW HAD NEVER SEEN ANYONE SO VISIBLY UNCOM-
fortable in a dress. He smiled up at her as he helped
her down from the open carriage. Although he didn't
want her to be in such discomfort, in some dark
corner of his mind, he was happy to not be alone
in his distress. He sat her down on the ground and
retrieved her walking stick before turning back to her
with a grin.

"What's so amusing? It's my gown, isn't it?" She
pulled at the lace trimmed neck and tugged on the
skirt where it fell over her hip. "I look ridiculous. I
knew I would."

"Katie." He stilled her hands within his own.
"You're beautiful." The statement seemed to shock
her as much as it did him, yet it was true. She was
radiant in the light green gown. Her pale eyes shown
in the fading light of the afternoon. Her hair was even
half bound, with only a few fiery curls falling over
one shoulder. He left his hands covering hers for one
second longer than was appropriate before pulling back
to offer her escort into Thornwood Manor.

"Beautiful in this? Not likely," she muttered, laying a hand on his arm.

"I assure you it is quite likely." He nodded toward the front door where a butler awaited their entry. "Let's be done with this evening, shall we?" He sighed as he looked up at the dark stone structure looming over them in overbearing arrogance, just as its owner was prone to do.

She leaned close to him to whisper, "I believe you are as thrilled about this evening as I am about wearing a blasted gown."

He quirked a brow at her. "Do you know you are the only lady of my acquaintance who doesn't enjoy getting dressed?"

"You make it seem as if I go about naked." She crinkled her nose, making her freckles dance.

"You might as well. Those breeches don't hide anything at all."

"Really?" She slowed her pace. "I hadn't noticed. Perhaps I should wear skirts."

"No!" He cleared his throat and turned his attention back to the butler awaiting them at the door. "I wouldn't want you to change into clothing that doesn't suit you."

"Gowns, weighty jewels, and itchy laces don't suit me, that much is true."

Andrew glanced down at her bare neck. She wasn't wearing any jewelry except for the small ovals of black jet on each ear. She was so different.

His mother had come close to sending his father to debtor's prison with her taste for finery when he was a boy. Her greed had forced Andrew into his role as a horse breeder at age ten, all to pay for her shopping habits. The strain of it had killed his father, months too soon to see Andrew's ideas and hard work see the first hint of success. Even if his father hadn't passed away in debtor's prison, his mother had ended his life and ripped him from Andrew's in the process.

It was rather refreshing to find a lady who didn't desire to spend all her money on frivolous matters.

His eyes narrowed on her. Katie must have different interests on which to spend all her father's funds. Her cottage was full to the rafters with such things after all. But…surely her paints, books, and musical instruments didn't cost that much. Having interests wasn't such a crime.

He led her into Thornwood Manor. The butler left after taking their hats and such and went in search of their hosts for the evening. Andrew turned back to Katie. No matter how much he discovered about her, he still wanted to know more. He ran a hand through his hair, pushing it back from his face.

Everything in life should sort easily into categories to be filed away in an orderly fashion. Katie was a lady, but she defied every rule of the female persuasion and refused to be filed away anywhere. Therefore she remained sitting on the desk in his mind, unfiled, uncategorized. This was what he'd decided last night when he lay awake, at any rate. It would explain why he kept thinking of her—she was unfinished work, a project from the day left to complete.

"Why are you looking at me like that?"

"I wasn't aware I was looking at you in any particular fashion."

"You're scowling."

"Was I?"

"Indeed."

"It must be the atmosphere here," he grumbled, pulling his gaze from her.

"I've always thought of Thornwood Manor as misunderstood." She smiled as she trailed a finger over the carving on the dark wood staircase leading to the upper floors. "It seems a dreary place, but there's an understated pleasantness."

"Quite understated," he muttered as he glanced around at the portraits of angry-looking Thornwood ancestors lining the walls.

Moving farther into the main hall, he was squinting up at the heavy timbered ceiling when he heard laughter coming from a room down the hall as a door was thrown open. Lillian Phillips—or Her Grace now, he supposed—came to greet them. She didn't look like he remembered her, yet he knew her all the same. Her hair wasn't bound so tight as to look painful anymore. She had an ease to her smile now that she hadn't possessed before. Could she be happy with Thornwood? He must have greatly misjudged her a year ago if that were true. He shook his head and offered her a nod.

"Lord Amberstall, we were so pleased to hear you were in the neighborhood," she greeted as she moved closer.

The last time he'd seen her had been the day of the blasted exhibition. She'd been under consideration for his wife. To the victor go the spoils, it seemed. It was just as well; he had no true desire to wed beyond duty to his title, and there was no rush on that score.

"Your Grace." Andrew bowed over her hand.

"Do come in." With a smile, she motioned to an open door behind her. "Everyone has gathered in the parlor."

"What wonderful news," he muttered, as Katie wound her hand further around his arm and gave it a slight squeeze.

⤸⤸

This had been a terrible idea. Andy moved beside her like one of the tiny soldiers her brothers played with when they were children—made of wood with a painted-on smile. Thornwood would most likely be equally uncomfortable, and his poor guests, Lord and Lady Steelings, would have to witness the entire event. Worst of all, the damned lace trim on her dress was itchy. She wiggled in an attempt to not touch her skin to it, which was completely hopeless as it lined the neck and capped the short sleeves.

"Katie? Katie Moore?" a lady asked as she crossed the room.

Did they know one another? She had brown hair and was not beautiful in the typical sense of the word, but lovely in a different sort of way. Katie couldn't place her, yet she knew she'd seen the small lady before.

"We met in London at a garden party," she supplied with a smile. "Sue Green, although I became Lady Steelings not too long after that day. You can call me Sue, though."

"Oh, yes! You assisted me back into my dress."

"Why were you out of your dress? Or perhaps I shouldn't even ask," Andy said.

"It was hot," she explained with a shrug. She glanced between Andy and Sue for a second. Was she supposed to offer introductions? Details like this always left her feeling befuddled. She'd had only the most basic of training in society, but as it didn't interest her terribly she'd promptly forgotten every word of it as she rode away from London. Was Andy supposed to do the introductions because he was a man? Perhaps it was Sue as she was the highest ranking lady in the conversation…"You do know one another, don't you?" she finally blurted out.

Sue smiled and dipped in a slight curtsy. "Lord Amberstall, we were surprised to hear you were in the neighborhood."

"It certainly wasn't a planned stop on my journey, but Miss Moore has been a perfect hostess."

"Have I?" She raised an eyebrow in his direction. He complained a great deal for someone who thought her perfect in any regard.

His smile turned genuine for a second before he glanced across the room and it slipped from his face. "If you'll excuse me, I need to go greet our host. Lady Steelings," he offered with a nod.

"It's Sue. I said that only a moment ago, didn't I? I've never understood why we can't speak more openly among friends. It is true I've always been a proponent of chatter, some even think I speak too much, but I've always thought…" She continued to talk about talking, but Katie's thoughts were with the gentleman who had just left her side.

Katie watched Andy go. He would either make amends with Thornwood or the rug in this parlor could forever be stained with their blood—only time would tell.

"He seems well," Sue mused, gaining Katie's attention once more.

"Do you think so?" She glanced back toward Andy in concern. "He looks rather pale to me."

"So does Thornwood," she whispered.

Katie smiled at her. "I suppose you're right."

"I'm so pleased to see you again. I knew when I met you, we could be friends. I told my husband that very day; well, he wasn't my husband at the time, but he is now…"

Katie looked past Sue to where the men were gathered near the fireplace. Thornwood did look a bit pale this evening. She wished she could read lips and know what was being said. She would have to work on that. Surely she could teach herself to read lips just as she taught herself to throw pots, play most musical instruments, and paint murals. Of course, once they went into the dining room she wouldn't be as far from Andy and would be able to hear what was said between the two men.

When she saw Lily return to the room, Katie grabbed her chance. "I'm famished! Aren't you simply starved?" Katie pronounced rather loudly to Sue, causing all conversation in the room to cease for a second as everyone turned to stare.

"I couldn't agree more," Thornwood chimed in. "Enough of these dreadful pleasantries. Let's move to the dining room."

Lily covered her surprise at the abrupt change with a small nod. "Yes, I believe everything is ready. Only, have you seen…"

"Without me? Thornwood dear, where are your manners?" The dowager duchess swept into the room, scowling at her son.

"My manners became hungry while you took an hour to repair your hair…and it still looks the same to me. Lily, has my mother's hair changed from this afternoon? Not a single strand has moved."

Lily shot her husband a narrow-eyed glare in response while the dowager duchess turned her back on her son to greet their newest guest. "Lord Amberstall, how lovely it is to see you again. Your mother will be ever so envious that I was able to dine with you this evening."

"Your Grace." He bowed over her hand. "The invitation was very kind of you."

"Now, may we dine?" Thornwood asked, clearly annoyed at the delay.

"Certainly, dear. Lead the way," the older woman offered with a wave of her arm.

Andy fell into step behind Steelings and Sue. Katie stood watching the commotion for a moment before noticing Andy had his arm extended to escort her.

"I can walk to the dining room. I do have my walking stick and it's not that far," Katie complained.

"I meant no offense to your abilities," he leaned close to whisper. "I'm supposed to escort you to the dining room."

"Why?"

"Because that is the way of things. It's what you do."

"Perhaps it's what *you* do," she mumbled under her breath.

"Along with the rest of gently bred society." He

wrapped his fingers around hers and placed them on his arm.

"It seems silly when I can find the dining room just fine on my own. I *have* been there before, you know."

"Then you can assist me." He grinned down at her and gave her hand a brief pat.

With a roll of her eyes, she began moving down the hallway after the others. Seeing that it was pointless to carry it, she left her walking stick leaning against a door frame in the hall and wound her other hand around Andy's arm as well.

"You're practically hanging on my arm, you know. I thought you could walk on your own."

"I thought you were strong, but here you are complaining of a lady's weight on your arm," she retorted.

"I'm not complaining." He looked down at both of her hands before sliding his eyes back up to her face in a way that made her blush. "It just isn't proper."

She tightened her hands on him, drawing him closer to her side as they walked toward the dining room door. "I'm not proper."

"I've noticed," his deep voice rumbled near her ear.

She glanced up, expecting to see a scowl on his face, but was met with a warm grin that lit his golden eyes. Her breath caught in her throat and she wasn't sure why. She stopped for a moment in the doorway to the dining room, unable to look away from his gaze. The rest of their party moved ahead and were reaching their seats when she finally unwound her hands from his arm and fled to the other side of the table.

What sort of spell was he casting on her with his heated looks and teasing grins? She found her seat next to Sue and flopped into it with her pulse still racing. She studied her empty plate for a few minutes, not trusting what she would find in Andy's eyes if she looked up.

"Lord Amberstall, did I hear rightly that you've been in Scotland all this time?" the dowager duchess asked from farther down the table.

"Yes, Your Grace. Steelings was kind enough to lend me his cottage there."

"You've been living in a cottage? Really, Amberstall." The dismay written on the dowager duchess' face was akin to discovering he'd been living with a family of wild jungle cats.

"What's so terrible about living in a cottage?" Katie asked as she attempted to adjust her gown so that the lace didn't touch her as she leaned forward in her seat.

The dowager duchess sent her a stern look over the rim of her wine glass. "You know my thoughts on that matter, dear."

"Perhaps the word *cottage* is deceiving in this case. Steelings has a livable home with two servants there." Andy sent a knowing glance at Katie from across the table.

Her soup spoon clattered to the table. She usually had such nimble fingers. What was wrong with her this evening? She shook her head and retrieved her spoon before anyone could comment on her clumsiness.

"Oh, perhaps we should visit, while we're traveling," Sue suggested from Katie's side. "I would like to see my husband's lands. And I've never been to Scotland."

"Anything you wish, my lady." Steelings grinned at his wife.

"Oh, Sue, you can't possibly wish to go to such a damp and hostile environment," the dowager duchess argued. "No offense, Steelings."

"None taken, Your Grace."

"I think it would be lovely. Sometimes the harshest environments inspire us, if only to simply enjoy the warmth of a fire. Don't you think so?"

"But there's nothing there, dear. Lord Amberstall, tell her the truth of Scotland. However did you fill your days? A year in such a place, I can't imagine."

"The rest was needed," Andy answered as he stared into the depths of his soup.

"How much rest can one stand?"

"Mother," Thornwood warned, causing a distinct silence around the table.

"I trust all was in order in Scotland, Amberstall?" Steelings asked, finally redirecting the conversation. "Were the sheep where I left them?"

Andy lifted his gaze to Steelings with a thoughtful frown. "There are a few more of them now."

"Are there?"

"I'm sure your man of business will inform you of the details soon. I made quite a few improvements, offset by the increase in the numbers of your sheep, of course."

"You grew that weary of the sights? You do know there's a little inn nearby with decent lager and a brunette bar maid who will…" Steelings broke off with a sheepish look at his wife.

"Oh, don't stop on my account. Please, continue your story."

"She brings lager to your table and sings songs

about the sanctity of marriage," Steelings concluded with a smile.

"I don't think you're being entirely truthful, darling."

"You're right." Steelings laughed, taking a sip of his wine.

"Really, Steelings," the dowager duchess admonished as Thornwood chuckled from the head of the table.

At the older woman's continued scowl, Katie thought a change of subject matter was in order. "Amberstall is quite good at overseeing improvements. He has already seen to several repairs at my stables."

"That was nothing." He shook his head. "You're seeing to my horse. It's the least I can do."

"We heard of the difficulties you've had with your horse, Amberstall," Lily said, looking down the table with a sympathetic smile.

"Yes, Shadow's Light took quite the fall."

Thornwood leaned forward, meeting Andy's gaze. "If you need to continue your journey faster than Shadow's Light can heal, you can use one from our stables."

"No!" Katie and Andy said at the same time. They shared a guilt-ridden glance, then both turned their attention back to their food.

"That won't be necessary," Andy added after a moment. "Thank you for the offer though."

Katie glanced up the table to where Thornwood sat looking terribly amused over something.

"Amberstall, now that you've returned to the country, will we see you in London?" the dowager duchess asked with a joyful gleam in her eye that Katie didn't quite trust.

"Yes, I should have things sorted on my estate in time for the season." He attempted a smile, but it didn't reach his eyes. He must be focused on management of his estate, not London life. She felt quite the same about London, which was a bit ironic.

"Perfect! And Katie, I assume you will be returning to town as well?" the dowager duchess asked.

The question caught her off guard. Was anyone expecting her to make another trip to London? Surely not now. Her place was on Ormesby lands, within her cottage. She had a limp. That was supposed to keep her safe from such things. "I hadn't planned on it, Your Grace."

"Don't be silly, of course you're coming to London. If your father doesn't plan to attend, you can come with us. Roslyn will be home by then and I'm sure she will want to visit town."

"I don't think I should…"

"Of course you should, dear. And I'm sure Amberstall here will want to renew his acquaintance with you. Won't you, Amberstall?"

"Of course."

"Will you continue the tradition of the party at Amber Hollow?" Sue asked.

"I'm not sure I should, under the circumstances," Andy hedged.

Lily coughed, choking on the sip of soup she'd just taken.

"What a shame. Lord Steelings and I have fond memories of the last gathering there."

"Oh, come now, Lord Amberstall, the party always proves entertaining," the dowager duchess said, glancing over to Lily, who was still trying to recover from the soup. "And clearly Her Grace agrees with me."

"Oh, indeed," Lily managed to say.

"The degree of entertainment is what concerns me."

"I found it quite entertaining," Sue mused, clearly misunderstanding Andy's meaning.

Andy's grip on his wine glass threatened to shatter the crystal, but when he glanced up it was with a pleasant smile. "Are you expecting a harsh winter here on the moors?"

The dowager duchess pursed her lips and studied Andy over the rim of her wine glass as she took a drink. She may allow the subject of the party to die for now, but it was far from over. Katie'd seen that look in the woman's eyes before and it never boded well for the recipient.

"I do hope not," Lily replied. "I'm already looking forward to working in the rose gardens when the weather warms."

As the footmen came around to retrieve the soup course, Katie leaned back to give him room to lift her bowl from the table. But when she moved, the lace trim across the back of her neck scratched across her skin, making her squirm within her gown. This would be the last time she would ever let Mrs. Happstings choose a dinner dress for her. She arched her back in an attempt to find comfort within her clothing, bumping the footman's arm with her head in the process.

She gasped and looked up, hoping the dregs of her soup would not find their way into her hair. The young man was fumbling to regain control of the silver platter. But, just as he did, offering her a small nod, her spoon slipped from the edge of the platter.

There was a clatter of china on silver as the footman tried to grab the utensil before it fell. Her eyes closed in silent anguish as the pea soup covered spoon slid down her spine, trapped within her itchy dress.

The footman gasped and made to reach for it. His fingers were a breath away from reaching into the back of her dress when he must have thought better of it and pulled away.

"Is everything alright?" Lily asked from down the table.

"It's fine." Katie turned to look up at the footman. "It's fine," she repeated.

His face was bright red as he paused beside her, clearly not wanting to leave her side when she had a dirty spoon in her dress.

Her eyes flared on him in a silent plea that he leave before he finally fled the room with the platter in his hands.

Had anyone seen what had happened? Her gaze slid around the table. Only Andy was staring at her in wide-eyed horror. Of course. He would have to be the one to know she now sat with a dirty spoon down the back of her dress. She bit her lip and looked down at the table. She had done the proper thing, hadn't she? She couldn't very well strip down to remove a spoon from her dress in the middle of the Thornwood dining room.

The next course was served just as Sue leaned close to whisper, "You know you have a soup spoon in your dress, don't you?"

"Do I?" Katie tossed an innocent smile at her.

"At least soup is warm," she whispered. "I once spilled elderflower ice down my dress. I don't recommend it—quite cold, you know."

"Ice does tend to be cold." Katie was having difficulty making idle chatter under the circumstances

"Perhaps I can help," Sue offered.

"I know I loosened my dress in public before, but I'd really rather not…"

"Did you know," Sue announced, gaining everyone's attention, "that it is customary in France to stretch one's legs between courses of a meal?"

"No it isn't," Thornwood argued.

"Oh yes, it is indeed. Steelings, tell them, darling." She looked at her husband with an expectant smile.

Steelings studied his wife for a moment before saying, "The French stand between courses, just as my wife proclaims."

"What?" Thornwood narrowed his eyes at his friend.

Sue cleared her throat and stood. "So, in honor of our recent return from France, I think we should all stand. I feel refreshed and ready for the next course already."

With a screech of chairs sliding away from the table, everyone stood. Only the spoon was still lodged in Katie's stays against her back.

"The French have such interesting ideas." The dowager duchess chuckled as she stood, looking up and down the table at everyone. "Standing…it's so foreign!"

"Where did you eat in France where they did this?" Thornwood asked Steelings, finally rising to his feet.

"The question is where did you eat where they did

not?" Steelings shot a questioning glance at his wife, but supported her lie all the same.

"It's not working," Katie whispered to Sue with an extra wiggle.

Sue pursed her lips for a moment before announcing, "In France, when having a truly abundant feast with beloved friends, they also hop...to show their gratitude for the hospitality. I'm grateful for the company this evening." She bounced on her feet. "Aren't you pleased with the food tonight?" She looked at Katie.

Katie hopped on her feet, trying to dislodge the spoon. "I'm quite grateful for the hospitality, as you can see." Her eyes flared as she looked across the table to Andy for support.

He gave her a tiny shake of his head before finally rolling his eyes and bouncing once on his toes. "I too am pleased to be here."

"And I'm the one they call mad..." Thornwood mused from the head of the table. "The French do not bounce, hop, or in any way jump between courses."

Lily leaned toward her husband. "If our guests say this is French custom, then so it is."

"If Steelings told you the sea spilled into a great teacup on the horizon, would you believe him?" Thornwood grumbled in response.

"It doesn't, just so you know," Steelings cut in. "That teacup business was nonsense, but bouncing in France is fact."

"Thank you for your honesty," Lily replied with her eyes narrowed on her husband.

Katie was still bouncing and squirming at her place

at the table. The damned spoon! With a final shake of her bodice while arching back over her chair, the spoon fell to the floor with a loud clatter. She smiled at Sue. "I believe we can sit now."

"Yes, let's sit. We wouldn't want our food to get cold."

"Oh, that was fun. I should to travel to France—such a festive people," the dowager duchess said with a smile as she sat down.

Andy was studying the food on his plate, refusing to meet Katie's eyes, although his shoulders shook with silent laughter. Well, at least her discomfort was serving some purpose this evening. She sighed and took a bite of her food.

"I'm so pleased we met again," Sue offered with a chuckle.

"I still find it hard to believe that you remember me."

"Some people are unforgettable."

"I agree," Andy added with a smile.

Steelings lifted his glass to his lips with a frown as he looked down the table at her. "I believe we met once in London as well. Your family's home in town is across the street from Rutledge House, is it not?"

"It is." Katie tilted her head, studying Steeling's face. He did look vaguely familiar—tall, thin, but not overly so, with dark green eyes. She had seen him somewhere before. "Did we meet there?"

"You actually beat me soundly in an impromptu horse race down the street."

Thornwood let out a great round of laughter from down the table.

"She what?" Andy asked, leveling her with a glare across the table. "You raced through the streets of London?"

"Yes." She looked down at her plate. "That was before…"

"She beat you, Steelings?" Thornwood was still laughing.

"Go on and laugh. Miss Moore is a talented rider."

"Was," she corrected, lifting the glass of wine to her lips with a shaking hand.

"And will be again one day," Andy added. He was watching her in that intense manner he had that made her squirm more than any itchy lace could accomplish.

She didn't know what to say. She couldn't argue with him with this many neighbors and guests watching them. She could feel heat rising in her cheeks, and everyone's eyes on her, assessing her injury, assessing her. She looked down at the food on her plate and did the only thing she could think to do. Taking a large bite of beef covered in a rich butter sauce, she exclaimed, "Mmm…this is delicious!"

"It's my favorite as well," Lily replied with a smile.

"I could help you ride again, you know, if you wish," Andy stated, clearly not deterred by her change of subject.

"I don't wish." She met his gaze across the table in silent challenge. Her heart was racing. There seemed to be something akin to hope in his gaze, but she'd given up on such fruitless emotions long ago.

His jaw tightened as he said, "The food is quite good, Thornwood. I'm glad I was able to attend this evening. Perhaps there is reason to our paths in life, a reason why Shadow's Light was injured here of all places." He raised an eyebrow at her.

Was he implying that he was here to teach her to once again ride a horse? What arrogant rubbish! "Or perhaps your visit is pure coincidence. You could have just as easily been tossed from Shadow's back at the next town over where you would be dining with the local gentry there." Katie raised her glass to him and drained the last of her wine.

"Either way, we are glad to have you in the neighborhood for a time. Although, I think you're better off here than with the Dunley family down the road a stretch—insufferable people," Thornwood said without his usual irreverent tone.

Andy nodded to Thornwood with a grim smile before turning back to Katie. He seemed to be daring her to make a move, as if this was a game of chess.

Damn, that was something else she would have to put on her list to learn—chess. Not that it would help in this circumstance. Still, there had to be something she could do. Lifting her knife to her lips, she stuck out her tongue and took a giant lick. "Delicious," she stated, licking the buttery sauce from the corner of her mouth.

With a satisfied smile, she watched Andy's face contort in shock mixed with some other emotion she didn't recognize. All she knew was that look in his eyes seeped heat through her body and into her bones. Just when she was sure she'd won, she had the oddest notion that in truth, she'd lost.

Acknowledgments

I would like to thank my family for supporting me in my dream to be an author, my friends for enduring my neglect while I write, and the amazing industry professionals with whom I've been fortunate enough to work. A special thanks to Michelle Grajkowski, my fabulous agent; Leah Hultenschmidt, my awesome editor; and the entire Sourcebooks team. Thank you for believing in me and my stories. Thanks to my critique partners, blog partners, sisters, and friends: Heather McGovern, Jenna Patrick, Lori Waters, Jeanette Grey, and Sydney Carroll.

To Carolina Romance Writers and Romance Writers of America, I appreciate all that you've done and continue to do to help me grow as a writer. And a huge thank you to Mike, Sylvia, John, Webb, and my Dad for all that you do to keep my world spinning around. I couldn't have done this without you! Thank you!

~E. Michels

About the Author

Elizabeth Michels blends life and laughter with a touch of sass into the Regency era. This flirty debut author turns ballrooms upside down, and challenges what lords and ladies are willing to do to get what they most desire. She lives in a small lake-side town in North Carolina with her husband, "Mr. Alpha Male," and her son, "The Little Monkey." Elizabeth is furiously typing away at her next novel while dinner burns in the kitchen. She loves to hear from her readers. Please visit her website at www.elizabethmichels.com.

Must Love Dukes

Tricks of the Ton

by Elizabeth Michels

She can't resist a dare

Lillian Phillips could not imagine how her quiet, simple life had come to this. Blackmailed by the Mad Duke of Thornwood into accepting one wild dare after another...all because of a pocket watch. Desperate to recover her beloved father's pawned timepiece, Lily did something reckless and dangerous and delicious—something that led to a night she'd never forget.

He has a reputation for scandal

When Devon Grey, Duke of Thornwood, runs into the mesmerizing, intoxicating, thieving woman who literally stole from his bedchamber—with his new pocket watch—Devon plots his revenge. If the daring wench likes to play games, he's happy to oblige. After all, what's the use of being the Mad Duke if you can't have some fun? But the last laugh just might be on him...

For more Elizabeth Michels, visit:

www.sourcebooks.com

How to Lose a Lord in 10 Days or Less

Tricks of the Ton

by Elizabeth Michels

❦

Their love sparks in the stables

After years away from home, Andrew Clifton, Lord of Amberstall, is attacked by a hired hit man on his way back to London. But with an injured horse and no shelter, Andrew becomes the unintentional houseguest of the Moore family.

But it's bound to be a bumpy ride

Katie Moore could always be found at the stables—until her riding accident. Now she locks herself away from Society—embarrassed by her injuries. While Katie tends to Andrew's horse, the two are at odds about everything, except their feelings for one another and the danger that they're about to discover on the road ahead...

❦

Praise for *Must Love Dukes*:

"Michels's fast-paced debut is sweet and...accurately depicts the difficulties faced by nineteenth-century aristocratic women." —*Publishers Weekly*

For more Elizabeth Michels, visit:

www.sourcebooks.com

Much Ado About Jack
by Christy English

How to become London's most notorious widow:

1. Vow to NEVER re-marry

2. Own your own ship and become fabulously wealthy

3. Wear the latest risqué fashions in your signature color

4. Do NOT have a liaison at the Prince Regent's palace with a naval captain whose broad shoulders and green eyes make you forget Rule #1

Angelique Beauchamp, the widowed Countess of Devereaux, has been twice burned by love, and she is certain that no man will ever touch her heart again. But that doesn't mean she can't indulge a little—and it would be hard to find a more perfect dalliance than the dashing Captain James Montgomery.

After a brief but torrid affair, James tries to forget Angelique and his undeniable thirst for more. The luscious lady was quite clear that their liaison was temporary. But for the first time, the lure of the sea isn't powerful enough to keep him away…

Praise for *How to Tame a Willful Wife*:

"Refreshingly honest and passionate."—*Publishers Weekly*

For more Christy English, visit:

www.sourcebooks.com

WITHDRAWN